Dedication: To my Phoobs, through our ups and downs, through good times and bad, you're the person I want by my side. Love you.

pretty little THING

LK FARLOW

"ATF, GET YOUR WALLETS READY!" The DJ's voice booms through the club, letting me know I better get my ass out there. "Because up next is your *all-time favorite*, Birdie!"

Even backstage, the whoops and hollers drown out all other sounds as men pull out fresh stacks of cash.

This job is literally the definition of *same shit, different day*. But the money I make is more than worth the monotony of shaking my ass for horny old men. Plus, it's not like they can actually touch me—security would toss them so fast they probably wouldn't even make contact.

I check my mask and pasties one last time and then strut out onto the stage, swaying my hips in a way that's much sexier than my accompanying music calls for, but still, the crowd eats it up.

My eyes scan the audience as I dance, alternating between working the pole and the floor.

I'm halfway through my routine when a guy I've never seen before bolts out of his seat. The intensity of his gaze is alarming. With his tanned skin, dark hair, and rippling muscles, he's easily the most attractive man I've ever seen.

For a split second, I think he's about to rush the stage, but then he turns and heads for the bar. I'm as disappointed as I am relieved, and I'm not sure what that says about me.

The rest of my routine goes off without a hitch, and I quickly gather the cash littering the stage, making a big show of fanning myself with the bills before blowing a kiss out to the crowd and then retreating back behind the relative safety of the curtain.

"Good set," Walter says, keeping his eyes squarely focused on mine. Being that he's built like a brick shithouse with the temperament of a grandpa—until messed with—and totally into dick, he's easily the best part about working here. He watches out for his girls and only hires staff who share his ideals of *look but don't touch* and *fuck around and find out*.

"Thanks, Walt. Want me on the floor?"

He shakes his head. "You got a VIP."

"Oh." My heart thumps a little harder in my chest. Being one of the newer girls on the roster, Walter hasn't put me on the list for private shows... until now. "Okay."

"You're ready, kid." He steps aside, inclining his head toward the door down the hall. "He wanted a bed, but Ronnie talked him down to a couch. Still shelled out the big bucks for a private room, though."

"Okay," I say again, feeling more confident. Walt wouldn't have put my name on the list if he didn't think I was ready. He's about people over profit and takes the comfort of his girls very seriously.

"Marcus will be outside of the door the entire time. If he tries anything, hit the panic button. Got it?"

I nod. "Got it."

Walter grins. "Atta girl. Now go shake that ass like you're getting paid to do it."

My confidence grows as I head toward the VIP room. I know from hearing the other girls talk that this is where the big bucks are made. And seeing as I'm already bringing home enough to cover my rent and childcare, anything I make back here will go straight into a savings account for my son.

I nod to Marcus as he opens the door, letting me into the room. "Hey there, hand..." My words trail off as I take in the hottie I noticed during my set, sprawled out on the couch like he doesn't have a worry in the world.

Quickly, I regain my composure. "Hey there, handsome."

He rakes his teeth over his lower lip as he slowly takes me in, dragging his eyes over every inch of my body.

My breathing accelerates under his appraisal. His gaze feels hot and heavy, almost like a physical caress against my exposed skin. And I can't help but wonder if him looking at me feels this good, how much better would his actual touch be?

The man is gorgeous, like out of this world attractive, and he's here... with me. *He's literally paying money to be here with me.*

"You seem nervous." It's a statement, not a question.

My hottie's voice is unlike anything I've ever heard before. Deep and rich, like syrup.

"Maybe a little," I whisper, rubbing my fingertips over my thighs.

"Would it make you feel better if I told you this was my first time?" His lips tip up in what has to be the sexiest smirk I've ever seen.

"You'd be lying." *Right? Surely a man like him knows his way around a strip club.*

"Cross my heart." He draws an 'X' over his chest, and

maybe it makes me an idiot, but for some reason, I believe him.

The thought of this being both of our first times in the VIP room sends a whole new rush of nerves—and maybe a little desire—rushing through me.

His lips tip up in a grin as his eyes zero in on my anxious fidgeting. "No need to be shy with me, Bluebird."

"What?" I feel my brows furrow beneath my mask.

Hottie shrugs. "They call you Birdie, and you have the bluest eyes I've ever seen. Seems fitting."

It's been so long since a man has complimented me one-on-one—obviously they yell all sorts of things from the tip rail, but *smother me with your tits baby* isn't really a compliment—that him simply noting my eye color has my brain going a little haywire.

"Well." I run my fingers over my thighs again. "I guess we should get started. Wanna make sure you're getting what you paid for, and all that."

He jolts forward, as if he wants to say something but can't find words. His mouth opens and closes, as he wages some kind of internal war, before finally he settles back against the couch and nods for me to continue.

A new song starts, and I move to the center of the room, swaying my hips to the beat. This music is different from what I dance to on stage, and I find myself slightly off count.

Though, judging from the way Hottie's eyes are eating me up, it's safe to say he either doesn't notice or doesn't care.

My confidence grows with every second, and when he pats his thigh and beckons me closer, I find myself willingly straddling his leg as I dip, roll, and sway my body.

The crotch of my leather shorties brushes against his thick thigh as I drop down to grind on him, and while I'll never in a million years admit it out loud, the heat of his leg between mine nearly makes me moan.

I guess not having sex in over four years will do that to you.

"Fuck, Bluebird," Hottie groans when I thrust my tits into his face.

He wants to touch me—his heavy breathing, clenched fists, and massive erection are dead giveaways. But not once does he ever try. Despite being turned on and hard as steel, my sexy stranger remains the picture of respect.

A fact that only makes him hotter.

A fact that makes me want to reward him.

I shimmy away from him, moving so that I'm standing between his legs with my back to him.

His sharp intake of breath when I arch my back and roll my hips only spurs me on.

Gathering my hair in one hand, I lift it off my neck as I wind my body down until my ass is rubbing against his thick erection.

"Fuck, Bluebird," he groans, his hips thrusting forward ever so slightly. "You're killing me."

I lean forward and wrap my hands around my ankles, making sure he has a good view of my leather-clad pussy before rubbing against him again. "Do you want me to stop?"

I've never once been this bold with an ATF patron. Even with men at the tip rail shoving money down my shorts, I've always remained a little bit aloof.

But with my sexy stranger, I find myself wanting to throw caution to the wind. I want to touch and tease and play.

Maybe because he's the kind of guy I'd be interested in outside of these four walls?

"God, no," is his sharp reply. "Never."

His voice sounds like pure sin, and it sends an anticipatory shiver down my spine.

"Good." I lower myself fully, leaning back against his chest and laying my head on his shoulder. His body is rigid beneath mine, like it's taking every bit of his willpower not to snap.

I roll my head to face him, nuzzling my face into the crook of his neck. "You... you can touch me." I swallow and lick my lips, my tongue accidentally grazing his warm skin. "If you want."

He doesn't hesitate in wrapping his strong hands around my hips. "Here?"

I nod and then place my hands over his, guiding them up to my breasts. "Or here."

His fingers flex as I continue to rock my hips.

"You're perfect." He rubs his thumbs over my pastie-covered nipples. "What's your name?"

Drunk on his touch, I almost tell him. Luckily, Marcus bangs on the door, signaling the end of our time together.

I slide from his lap on shaking legs, wondering what in the hell came over me. How did I go from VIP room novice to practically dry-humping a stranger?

Shame coats me from the inside out, and I rush from the room without saying a single word.

Tears sting my eyes and worry turns my stomach. This isn't who I am. Yes, I'm a young, single mom, but I'm not easy. Hell, my baby daddy is the only person I've ever slept with—and clearly that turned out well.

Yet, Hottie had me ready to spread my legs and bounce on his dick all night long, and I don't even know his name.

"How'd it go?" Walt asks, as I step into the locker room. "He hurt you?"

I shake my head. "No. I just...it was...intense."

He nods like he understands. "It can be that way. Take the rest of the night off."

"I can't. I need—"

Walter wraps his meaty paw around my elbow and walks me to my locker. "Your VIP stint more than covers the rest of the night. Go home and snuggle that son of yours, and I'll see you tomorrow."

"Are you sure?"

He smiles down at me, like a doting father would at his daughter. "Positive. Now, scram."

I thank him again, pull on my leggings and hoodie, grab my bag, and dart out of the back door.

Walt's right—spending the rest of the night snuggled up with my son is exactly what I need to get my head on straight. I don't strip for fun, and I certainly don't do it to meet men.

Everything I do is for my son, and I'm not about to let some TDH—tall, dark, and handsome—stranger get in the way of doing what's best for him. No matter how freaking hot he is.

"ARE YOU DOING OKAY?" my brother asks, sighing into the phone. "Are you sure I can't send you any—"

"I don't want your damn money, Phoenix," I growl, clenching the phone between my fingers. We go through this same song and dance every time we talk. And while I know he means well, it grates.

"I'm not like Mom and Dad—there's no strings attached here, Frank."

My grip loosens, and a soft puff of air escapes me. "I know you aren't, but I want to make it on my own—I *need* to..." *To prove to them I can,* I add silently.

My relationship with my parents has always been strained—probably because I look exactly like the guy my mom cheated on her husband with when she conceived me. Oops. Not like it's my fault she slept around, yet for some reason, I've always been the one to pay the price.

So, it's no surprise that telling my lovely parents that I was pregnant at seventeen went over like a lead balloon. Honestly, I was prepared for their anger, and even their disappointment. What I wasn't expecting was their complete and utter dismissal.

Who knew all it took to ruin our relationship once and for all was a seven-pound-ten-ounce bundle of joy?

I should have known. Because just like with Mom's affair, anything that doesn't fit into Franklin and Winnie Davenport's picture of perfection gets tucked away to the very back of the closet.

In my case, the closet was an adoption agency, and when I *vehemently* told my parents I wanted to keep my baby, they did what every well-off family does with things they no longer have need for—they threw me out.

And yes, my mom had the audacity to name me after her husband, despite him not being my father. She was almost able to pass me off as his, until my features really sharpened at around two and he realized I looked just like his *former* business partner.

"I get it." He pauses. "But sometimes asking for help—"

"So, help me God, I will end this call." There's no heat behind my words, because in actuality, aside from my son, my brother is all I have in this world.

The fact that he's a rockstar is a moot point for me, because I refuse to accept handouts. From anyone. Ever. Even him...*especially him.*

"Fine, fine. Stubborn ass." I can practically see Phoenix's eye roll as his raspy laugh filters through the line, instantly erasing my frustration with him. "How's little man?"

"Maverick's good. Growing like crazy. You won't believe how tall he is when you see him."

Phoenix sighs again. For as much as he loves performing, I know he's worn down from years of constant touring. "I need to make some time to come visit."

"We both miss you."

"Say the word, and I'll fly y'all—"

"Phin." I inject steel into my tone.

"Frankie."

I know he thinks I'm being stubborn—and sure, part of me is—but I have obligations. I can't just pick up and hop on a plane to visit him in whatever city he's in. That's not how the real world works.

"I have a job and classes, and Mav has his routine." A sniffle breaks free. I *really* miss my big brother. "But we definitely want to see you."

"If you really wanted to see me—"

The alarm on my phone blares to life, conveniently blocking out Phoenix's pleading—in the nick of time, too, because while he doesn't know it, I was dangerously close to giving in. It really would be easier for me to go to him, since he's on tour and all. But I've seen firsthand exactly how money and the power imbalance between the haves and the have-nots can destroy relationships.

I'd rather die than let something like that ruin my relationship with Phoenix. Aside from Maverick, my older brother's the only good thing in my life.

"I'm going to be late for my next class; I gotta go. Love you!" I end the call before he can reply, shoving the phone back into my bag so I can haul ass across campus toward the arts building.

My phone trills again, telling me I'm really out of time right as the building comes into view.

It's a tall and modern thing, made of mostly glass. It really sticks out, since the rest of the buildings at CVU have an almost cabin-slash-lodge-like quality to them.

"Watch it!" a random guy yells as I nearly bowl him over as I race down the cobblestone path.

"Sorry!" I shout without stopping. As much as I hate being rude, I hate the thought of being late even more. Mostly because of the attention that comes with it. A full-body shiver rolls over me at the thought of all of those eyes on me.

It's an easy assumption that since I take my clothes off for money, I must love attention, but that couldn't be farther from the truth.

Stripping is a means to an end, a way to make sure I'm able to give my son the life he deserves.

When I'm dancing, it's almost like I disassociate. From the second I slip my mask over my eyes, I'm nothing more than a set of tits in heels. The anonymity of being Birdie creates a sense of safety, and whether it's real or perceived, I cling to it.

I fly into the classroom with only moments to spare, and settle into the first empty seat I see. My heart is still racing —I'm talking pounding so hard it feels like it might jump right out of my chest—but I made it, and that's all that matters.

"One of those days, huh?" a soft voice asks from my right.

"Um." I slide the strap of my bag from my shoulder and secure it over the back of my chair before giving my attention to the person beside me. My tablemate is breathtaking, with bronzed skin, the bluest eyes, and long blonde locks. "Yeah. You could say that."

She grins and flips her hair in that way only pretty girls do. "I'm Stella."

"Okay," I draw the word out, trying to figure out why she's talking to me. Bright and bubbly girls who ooze optimism don't typically befriend dark and moody single moms. At least not without ulterior motives.

"What's your name?" she asks, completely unperturbed by my lack of enthusiasm.

"Frankie."

"Ooh." Stella bats her lashes. They're so long and sooty, I can't help but wonder if they're fake. "That's pretty."

I nod my head, praying for this conversation to end.

"What are you majoring in?"

"Business."

She wrinkles her nose. "I'm majoring in early childhood education." A sigh escapes her perfectly glossed lips. "All of the women in my family are teachers."

"That's nice."

"I know, right?" She turns in her chair so that she's facing me. "A lot of people think I feel pressured to do it since it's like a generational thing, but really, I just love kids and feel like I can make a difference in their lives, you know? What about you? Do you like kids?"

Did she even stop to breathe?

I give a noncommittal shrug, not wanting to discuss my son with a stranger.

"I bet you'd make really pretty babies." She sighs again, and her entire body melts into the chair as she exhales. She kind of reminds me of a Disney princess, all prim and soft and dainty.

"Um." All I can do is blink at her. Because, seriously, who says that to a stranger?

"Good morning," a booming voice calls, and I snap to attention. "I apologize for the delay, but let's jump right into things."

Twisting around in my seat, I grab a notebook and pen from my bag. Most people type or dictate nowadays , but in my opinion, nothing is as good as old handwritten notes.

"I'm Professor Clayton, and I've been teaching Intro to

Art for six years. Prior to accepting this position, I worked as both a freelance artist and a curator at Xavier Neill Gallery." I'm sure her credentials are meant to be impressive, but my knowledge of the art world is limited. I just like doodling and needed an extracurricular.

I listen intently as she covers the bullet points in the syllabus, from grading to office hours, making little notes here and there.

"This week, we will cover the basics of drawing, from sketches to lines and contouring to blending. You will need your sketchbook, pencils, viewfinder, and black markers this week. If you don't have the required items, I have a few on hand for you to borrow." She pauses, checks the time on her watch, and then reminds us of the assigned reading before effectively dismissing the class.

"Crap!" Stella mutters, drawing my attention. "What pages did she say to read?"

I nod pointedly toward her phone as I slide my notebook back into my bag. If she'd have been paying attention instead of texting, she would know.

My judgment must be written clearly on my face, because her cheeks bloom pink as her shoulders curl. "I know." She tucks her phone into her back pocket. "I should have been listening, but my best friend... and I just wanted to make sure she was okay."

Ugh. Her concern for her friend tugs on my heartstrings. *Stupid heartstrings.* Maybe it's because I don't have anyone who looks after me like that, but I find myself softening toward her—but only a little.

Standing, I grab my bag and heft it onto my shoulder. "Two-thirty-eight through three-sixteen."

"Ah!" she squeals as she flings herself from her seat and

into my personal space. My entire body freezes as she wraps me in a hug. "Thank you so much!"

I shake off her hold and take a step back. Clearly this chick has no sense of boundaries. "Don't make it a habit."

"You're kind of prickly. Like a cactus. But one of those ones that flower. Has anyone ever told you that?"

"Nope." I take a backward step, putting a little distance between us. "Just you."

She beams, like I just told her she won free coffee for life. "Oh, I'm the first. Yay!"

"Right." I move closer to the door. "I'm gonna—"

The little blonde ball of sunshine cuts me off before I can make my escape. "Do you want to get coffee?"

A small, teensy-tiny part of me wants to say yes, if only to have a friend. Instead, I shake my head and mumble out some lame excuse before turning and leaving.

My eyes burn with unshed tears as I tear down the hallway. But I know it's better this way. If I never invite anyone into my life, my heart can't get broken when they inevitably leave.

"I'M HAPPY FOR YOU, MAN," I say, clasping my roommate's hand as I pull him into a one-armed hug. "You and Macy are the real deal."

Ben nods as a smile curls his lips. "Thanks, man. I appreciate it."

"Y'all set a date yet?" He's been talking about proposing to her for so long that it wouldn't surprise me at all if they fast-tracked the wedding.

"I actually wanted to talk to you about that before the party starts." He swallows roughly and tugs at his collar.

"Okay," I drawl, leaning back against the kitchen island. "What's up?"

Ben lowers his gaze and rubs at the back of his neck. "It's just that...Macy and I...we think..."

Dread and disbelief pool in my gut. Even though I know what he's going to say, I ask, "You and Macy think *what*?"

He straightens to his full height, squares his shoulders, and looks me in the eye, delivering the news like a man. "We think it would be best for you to move out before the wedding."

I nod, frustrated but not truly mad with my business partner. I always knew our living arrangement was temporary, but from the minute he decided to pop the question to his longtime girlfriend, he assured me I'd have until the wedding to figure things out. "How long?"

A look of guilt flashes over his features as his gaze settles on something over my left shoulder. "Mace wants to start moving in tomorrow."

"Tomorrow?" My disbelief gives way to anger. I totally understand the two lovebirds not wanting me to live with them—hell, I would feel the same if the roles were reversed. What I wouldn't do is kick one of my best friends and business partner out of the house he poured his blood, sweat, and tears into renovating, with less than twenty-four hours notice.

I clench my fists and my jaw to keep from lashing out. "I see."

"Do you?" he asks hopefully.

I'm torn between brushing this off and giving him a piece of my mind. I weigh the pros and cons as I stare him down, not entirely hating seeing him sweat. The jackass knows he's wrong. And for the sake of our business, I'm going for honesty, because the last thing I want is for this to blow up later.

"Truthfully? No." Ben starts trying to explain himself, but I don't give him a chance to speak. "I get you and Macy wanting the house to yourselves, really, I do. No hard feelings there. But asking me to move out without any kind of notice is bullshit."

He curses under his breath. "I know, man. I tried telling her—but her lease is up, and if she re-signs it—"

"Save it, man." I shake my head. "For the sake of our

business, I'll let it go, but you and I both know what you're doing is shitty."

"Orion, please—"

"There's nothing you can say, man. I love you like a brother and would do anything for you. It's just a shame you couldn't have even an ounce of consideration for me." *So much for letting it go.*

Ben sighs. "I'm sorry. You have to know I—"

The sound of the doorbell cuts him off, giving me a chance to escape.

"I'll be out by dinner time tomorrow." I push off the island and look him in the eye as the bell chimes again. "Wouldn't want to keep your guests waiting."

I stalk up the stairs to my bedroom, knowing I'm not in the right frame of mind to mingle and celebrate the happy couple's engagement.

Instead, I decide to get started on packing. The only upside of my current living arrangement is all of my shit is confined to my bedroom and en suite bathroom. The furniture and everything else belong to Ben.

Then again, maybe that's not such an upside, because now on top of finding somewhere to live, I'll have to furnish it. *Fucking lovely.*

I'm emptying my fourth and final drawer into my duffel bag when someone knocks on my bedroom door. "What?"

"Grumpy, grumpy," my sister murmurs as she steps into my space. "Whoa! What's going on?"

I slide the drawer back onto the track. "Packing."

"Why?" Stella's nose crinkles as she looks between me and the hulking blond man behind her—also known as Samson, my lifelong best friend and her boyfriend.

"Because." I toss my bag onto my bed and tug the zipper closed. "Ben and Macy want me to move out."

"Um..." Stella moves around me and perches herself on the foot of my bed. "When?"

"Tomorrow."

"What the fuck?" Samson barks. "That's..."

"Fucked up?"

"Yeah, that."

"What are you going to do?" Stella asks, worrying the ends of her long hair between her fingers.

"Move out," I say with a deadpan expression.

The worried look on her face hits me like a punch to the gut. It's my job to worry about her, not the other way around. "Where to?"

"Hell, if I know, Smalls." I shrug.

I stand from the bed and start pulling things out of my closet, discreetly watching the weird looks Samson and my sister keep exchanging in the mirror hanging on the back of the door.

I swear, if the two of them weren't so fucking perfect for one another, I'd be repulsed by how in sync they are.

Samson shakes his head at whatever Stella is silently saying with her wide eyes and pinched lips. He winces. She nods. And then my best friend nods as well—albeit reluctantly.

"You could crash with me for a few days," Samson murmurs. I catch his gaze in the mirror, and can see he means what he says. I'm half-tempted to take him up on the offer, but I know Stella sleeps over more often than not, and the thought of hearing them fuck is almost enough to make me want to shove nails into my ears.

"Nah, man. I don't want to impose."

Stella widens her eyes again, shooting daggers his way.

"Chill, Smalls," I say, turning to face them. "I don't

want to be y'all's third wheel. I'll just crash with Mom and Dad until I find my own place."

"Are you sure?" Stella asks.

I suck in a deep breath and then slowly blow it out. I swore when I moved out that I'd never move back. I love my parents, but they are grade-A meddlers. But I'll take my mom's interference over hearing my sister's sex sounds any damn day.

"Yeah. I'm sure."

They exchange knowing looks once more, and then Stella stands, crossing the room toward Samson. "Okay, then. Do you want to go down and join the party?"

I snort. "Uh, no." There's only one place I want to be right now, and it's not downstairs celebrating the happy couple.

No. I need to see my little Bluebird.

"Okay." Stella draws out the word as she opens the door and steps out into the hall.

Party noises trickle up the stairs; from the sound of it, they're toasting Ben and Macy.

Samson shoots me a knowing look. "You heading out to—"

"Yeah," I cut him off before he can say the name of the club and spark a conversation with my sister that definitely does not need to be had. He knows me well enough to know I'm obsessed with a certain dancer there.

"All right, man. Be safe."

I nod and follow them down the stairs, already anticipating the sweet relief that only my Bluebird can bring.

"GOING HOME to that boy of yours?"

"You know it, Walter." Even though Maverick's been asleep for hours, all I can think about is snuggling up to my little man until the sun rises. He's at that fun age where he still wants his mama but is also fiercely independent.

"Let me call someone to walk you to your car."

My lips tip up into a small smile at Walter's protective nature. It doesn't matter if it's broad daylight and you're parked at the door, he never lets his girls walk out alone.

I nod as I stifle a yawn. Even with my hottie stopping by, tonight seemed to drag, almost like it was slow-mo.

My feet hurt, my head is pounding, I'm hungry, I need to catch up on my world history reading, and the only thing keeping me going at this point is knowing I'm providing for my son—oh, and coffee. That helps, too.

"Ready?" Kasey asks, tipping his head toward the door.

I nod and follow behind him.

"Where are you parked?" He scans the lot like he'll magically know which car is mine.

"The silver Taurus."

He glances back at me, his brows furrowed. "Huh."

"What?" I lengthen my stride so that I'm walking next to him.

"Just not what I pegged you for."

"Right, well." We stop at the bumper, and he waits while I slide my key into the door to unlock it. "Thanks."

"Anytime." He waits for me to situate myself behind the wheel before heading back for the building.

The drive to my apartment complex passes in a blur of headlights. Thankfully, my designated parking spot is open—sometimes when it's this late, people assume you're gone for the night and park wherever they can.

I cut the engine, take a deep breath, and pull my key from the ignition, slipping it between my index and middle fingers. I may not live in the worst part of town, but it's definitely not good either.

Mrs. Norwood—my downstairs neighbor and babysitter—opens her front door before I even raise my hand to knock. She clucks her tongue as she looks me up and down. "You're late."

"Am I?" I ask, pulling my phone from my bag to check the time. *Only by a minute.* "I'm sorry."

She shakes her head. "Time's money. You know the drill."

"But—"

"No buts. I charge a late fee. You were late. Pay up."

Tears sting my eyes as I pull my wallet from my bag. My hands shake as I peel off four twenties—three to cover my shift and one for the *late fee.*

As a single mom, every penny counts. That extra twenty could have gone to groceries or gas or rent. But I can't fault Mrs. Norwood, either. She's a widow living entirely off her late husband's pension, and while our situations aren't the same, we have one thing in common—we're both barely scraping by.

She pockets the money and then opens the door wide. "He's asleep on the couch."

"Thanks." I slide past her into the small apartment, grabbing Maverick's backpack from the coffee table before leaning down and scooping his sleeping form into my arms.

He stirs ever so slightly. "Mama?"

"Yes, baby."

"Missed you." He snuggles into me, pressing his sticky face into the crook of my neck, immediately falling back asleep.

"You working on Friday?" Mrs. Norwood asks, like she doesn't know my schedule.

I nod as I step back into the breezeway connecting the apartments.

"Figured. I can't keep him that night. Got plans."

Something inside of me deflates. Can't I ever catch a break? "Thanks for letting me know."

I turn and head up the stairs toward my apartment.

Between my bag, Maverick's bag, my keys, and my sleeping boy, it's a struggle to get up without dropping something or waking him.

The overhead light being out does little to help matters.

"Dammit," I mutter as I try to fish my phone back out of my bag.

I keep my movements small and soft, doing my best to make sure Maverick stays asleep. I swear, it feels like my fingers brush everything except my phone.

"Found it!" I can't quite reach the sensor to unlock it, but the light from the screen's just enough to see to slide my key into the deadbolt.

Inside my apartment, I place Maverick down onto our

bed and hang both of our bags on the hooks by the door before taking a quick shower and donning my favorite sleep shirt—one from Mav's dad.

My little man doesn't even stir when I crawl into bed next to him, and before I know it, I'm fast asleep with him curled into my side.

LIKE ALWAYS, Maverick wakes me up long before my alarm ever has a chance to go off. The kid's been an early riser since day one; another trait from his father, because I would gladly sleep until noon if given the chance.

"I'm hungry." He pokes my belly.

"Are you?" I poke his back, and as if to really nail his point home, it growls.

"Mmhmm." He nods. "Starving."

I check the time—it's barely six o'clock. "What sounds good?"

His hazel eyes twinkle. "Pamcakes, Mama!"

"Pamcakes, huh? Are you sure you don't want *pancakes?*"

"No." He looks at me like I'm crazy. "*Pam*cakes. Like Ms. Pam at the diner makes."

I can't help but smile. The kid's cute, and he knows it. "Pamcakes it is."

"With chocolate chips?"

"I'll see what I can do," I tell him, knowing full well we don't have any chocolate chips. "Why don't you go brush your teeth?"

"Do I have to?"

"Definitely."

He pouts but toddles off to do as I asked.

In the kitchen, I pull a mixing bowl out of the dishwasher, and then the dry ingredients down from the cabinet that serves as our pantry. But when I open the fridge to grab the milk and eggs, I realize the milk is sour and we're out of eggs.

"It's okay," I murmur to myself as I add a little extra baking soda to make sure they're fluffy. "It'll be fine." I melt some butter and mix it with water to use in place of the milk. "Everything's fine."

I'm turning the fourth pancake when Maverick flies into the kitchen. "Are they done?"

"Depends. How many do you want?"

He taps his pointer finger against the dimple in his chin. "A hundred!"

I stifle a laugh. "How about two?"

"Chocolate chips?" His big hazel eyes are so full of hope that I feel like the worst mom ever when I have to tell him no.

"Sorry, bud. We're all out."

He heaves out a big sigh before wrapping his arms around my waist. "It's okay, Mama. Maybe next time."

I hate that I'm feeling so emotional over not having chocolate chips, but I can't help feeling like, somehow, I'm letting him down on a grander scale.

"Definitely," I murmur as I plate his and top them with syrup. "Eat up—Mama has class today."

"Will I have to go to school when I'm old, too?"

"Maverick James!" I feign shock. "Are you calling me old?"

He closes his mouth around another forkful of syrupy pancakes and shrugs.

"I'm totally young—and cool!"

"Uncle Phin says if you gotsta tell people you're cool,

you probably aren't cool." He licks his fork clean and then carries his plate to the sink. "You're older than me!"

I stick my tongue out at him as I walk to rinse my plate as well. "Too true, Mav. Too true."

"Can I watch my show while you get ready?"

My eye twitches at the thought of listening to another episode of *Paw Patrol*, but Maverick loves it—not to mention, it'll buy me a few extra minutes to wash my hair. I'm pretty sure it still has glitter in it from last night.

"Yup. The remote's on the table by the bed."

"Thanks, Mama!" He crashes into me and hugs me tight before taking off for the bed. "Love you!"

My heart melts in my chest as I watch him snuggle down under the covers. Maverick is every good part of his father. Hell, the kid's every good thing in my life, period. And even though things aren't ideal right now, I'm damn sure going to hustle and make sure my kid has the best life possible. Maybe not one full of material things, like mine was, but one filled with love.

So much love.

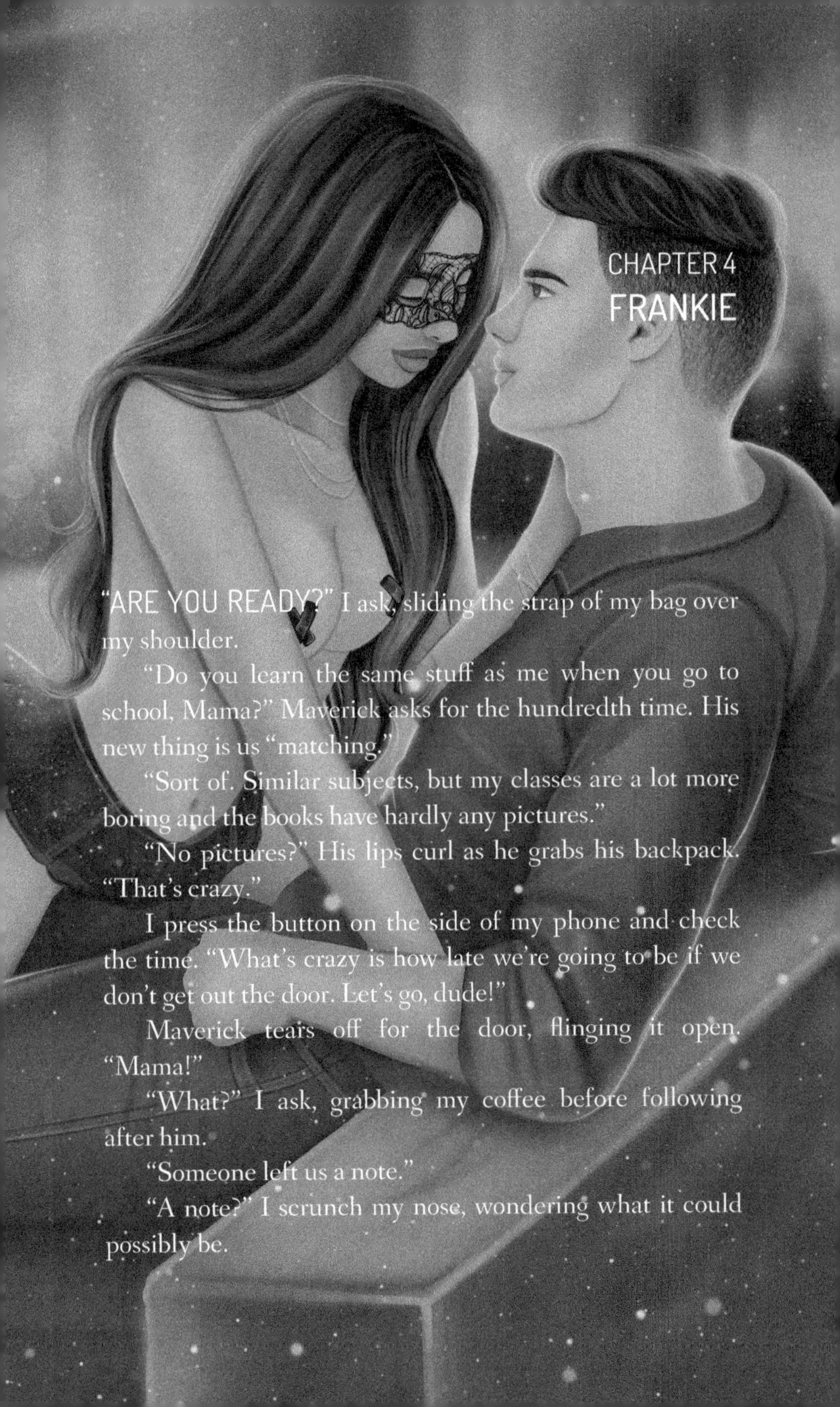

"ARE YOU READY?" I ask, sliding the strap of my bag over my shoulder.

"Do you learn the same stuff as me when you go to school, Mama?" Maverick asks for the hundredth time. His new thing is us "matching."

"Sort of. Similar subjects, but my classes are a lot more boring and the books have hardly any pictures."

"No pictures?" His lips curl as he grabs his backpack. "That's crazy."

I press the button on the side of my phone and check the time. "What's crazy is how late we're going to be if we don't get out the door. Let's go, dude!"

Maverick tears off for the door, flinging it open. "Mama!"

"What?" I ask, grabbing my coffee before following after him.

"Someone left us a note."

"A note?" I scrunch my nose, wondering what it could possibly be.

"Yeah!" He yanks it off the door right as I join him in the breezeway. "See."

I take the paper from him, my eyes immediately zeroing in on *EVICTION NOTICE* across the top in red, bold print. "Oh, God." My vision blurs as I collapse back against the door.

This can't be happening...

I bust my ass to make sure the rent is always paid. I've never even been a day late. And now, we're being thrown out? Why? Why is this happening?

"Just calm down," I mutter to myself as Maverick wraps his little arms around my middle, pressing his face into my belly.

"What's wrong, Mama?" He clutches the fabric of my shirt between his fingers. "Is it a mean note? I know hitting people is bad, but if it's mean, I'll hit 'em for you."

My lips twitch even as hot tears burn the backs of my eyes. "Let me read it one more time," I say, both to him and myself—because maybe I missed something. *It has to be a mistake, right?*

My heart is pounding and my ears are ringing as I try to reread the document. It feels like my entire world is falling apart, but I force myself to take a few deep breaths to clear my head so I can read the fine print.

Except the fine print only makes things worse—not only are we being evicted, but we have to be out in *seventy-two hours*. How in the hell am I going to find us a place to live in three days?

This is a nightmare. A certified fucking nightmare.

Maybe I could ask Phoenix—

"Mama," Maverick whispers my name and tugs on the hem of my shirt, drawing me out of my thoughts. "What's wrong?"

I suck in a deep breath and paint on the best smile I can muster. "Nothing you need to worry about." I fold the notice and tuck it into the front pocket of my bag and stand. "Let's get you to school...wouldn't wanna miss Fun Friday."

Mav cocks his head to the side, studying me with eyes far wiser than his four years. Finally, he nods once and then darts down the stairs.

"C'mon, Mama. Miss Jenna said we're doing Play-Doh today. I wanna get there before Caitlyn mixes all the colors together."

"That would be a tragedy," I murmur as I unlock my car.

He doesn't waste a second climbing into his booster seat, buckling the chest clip before waiting for me to finish. "What's tragedy mean?"

I come around to the back and clip each side of his buckle together, making sure he's snug and secure. "It means really sad."

He nods. "Yeah, it would be really sad, so come on! Let's go! Step on it, Mama!"

Despite the worry and sadness gnawing at me, I smile. It doesn't matter how bad things get; this kid is my light. He's every good thing, and no matter what my landlord says, I will find a way to make things work for us. Even if it means calling Phoenix.

Because Mav deserves it. He deserves everything.

"Mama, can we listen to *Paw Patrol?*"

I nod and grab the auxiliary cord, plugging it into my phone so that his songs can come through my car speakers.

Before I know it, we're three songs deep and pulling into the school parking lot. I snag the first space I see and cut the engine. "Ready?"

Maverick unbuckles himself from his seat and grabs his backpack. "Ready."

I walk him to the door and sign him in, pressing a kiss to his forehead. "Make good choices today, Mav."

He narrows his eyes at me and nods. "You, too, Mama."

I stand and watch until he's out of sight before turning and heading back to my car.

The drive to my landlord's office passes in a flash, and before I know it, I'm parked outside and ready to plead my case.

"You've got this," I say as I approach the mirrored glass door. "You didn't do anything wrong. He'll listen—he has to."

I suck in a deep breath and pull the door open, stepping into the musty lobby.

"How can I help you?"

"Hi." I swallow and wipe my hands on the front of my jeans. "I was hoping to speak to you about my lease."

"Complex?" I rattle off the name and he nods. "Unit?"

"Three-twelve."

"Ah, you're all set to move in Monday, but I'm afraid I can't get the keys to you until the current tenant vacates."

"I..." Dread drops inside of me like a stone sinking to the bottom of a lake. "*I'm* the current tenant."

He clears his throat. "Oh. Right. Are you here to turn in your keys early?"

I shake my head, willing myself not to cry. "No, sir—"

"Call me Chase."

"No, Mr. Chase, I'm here because I don't understand why I'm being evicted."

He clears his throat and shuffles around some of the papers littering his desktop. "Ah. You didn't re-sign your lease."

"What?" I rack my brain, trying to make his words make sense.

"It's up today, and you never re-signed."

"Are you sure there's nothing you can do?" I ask, wondering how I could have screwed up this massively. "Nothing at all?"

He leans back in his swivel chair, resting his hands on top of his rounded belly. "Wish there was, but like I said, when you never turned in your lease agreement, I figured you weren't renewing. The new tenants are moving in on Monday. My hands are tied here."

"But..." I pause and pinch my eyes shut, refusing to cry in this dingy, mothball-smelling office. "I don't even recall receiving a new lease to sign."

"Be that as it may, you still need to be out by Sunday."

"Are there any other units available?"

"Afraid not." Mr. Chase makes a big show out of checking his watch. "Now, if you'll excuse me, I have another meeting to get to."

"Right." I curl my fists and dig my nails into my palms until I feel the skin break. "Thanks."

He stands and walks me out into the lobby. "Best of luck to you."

"Yeah, sure." I shoulder open the door and step out into the parking lot. "Whatever."

If I had the time, I'd cry. But as it is, class starts in ten minutes and I'm a solid fifteen from campus. So, it looks like my impending breakdown will just have to wait until later.

Plus, it's not like crying ever solved anything. I ought to know.

I BARELY MAKE it through my first class of the day—Accounting 101. Instead of paying attention to the professor, I spent the hour obsessing over the morning's events while discreetly scrolling my phone for somewhere to live.

From the looks of things, I either need to find a way to make *a lot* more money or... well, there is no other option, because everything available costs triple what I've been paying.

Hopelessness like I haven't felt in a long, *long* time sits heavy on my shoulders as I walk into the arts building. It feels like the whole universe is conspiring against me.

"Ooh, you look extra grumpy today," Stella murmurs, falling into step beside me.

I turn and shoot her a withering glare. The last thing I need right now is little Stella Sunshine picking at the scab that is my life.

"No, wait." She grabs ahold of my wrist and pulls me to a stop. "Not grumpy. You look...*distraught*. Is everything okay?"

My initial instinct is to lash out at her, but I force a smile onto my face instead. "I'm peachy."

She crinkles her button nose. "Maybe like a Tim Burton peach. You know, with bugs and a little boy living in it?"

"I got the reference," I mutter as I take my seat.

Predictably, Stella slides into the spot next to me, and keeps right on talking. "I don't mean to be rude. I just—"

"You just what?" I cut her off, exasperated with her pep and my whole day.

"I'm just worried about you." She lowers her gaze, and I immediately feel bad. It's not her fault my life sucks at the moment.

"You don't need to worry about me, Stella. You hardly know me."

She scoffs. "You don't have to know someone to care about them."

"Pretty sure you do." I pull my sketchbook from my bag and place it on the table in front of me.

"Well, I don't," she bites back right as Professor Clayton walks in.

She doesn't waste a second and jumps right back into where we left off on Wednesday. And while sketching isn't my strong suit, I'm thankful for the reprieve from the ball of sunshine to my right.

By the time class ends, I'm pretty sure Stella's forgotten all about me. That is, until she turns and asks, "What's your next class?"

"Marketing," I mumble as I try to scoot past her.

But she's not having it. "When?"

I contemplate lying, but despite her overwhelming nature, Stella's never been anything but nice to me. "Not until two."

"Perfect." She loops her arm through mine.

"For what?" I try to tug my arm back, but she's stronger than she looks.

"For us to get lunch, so we can get to know each other better." She sets off down the hall, pulling me along. "And so you can tell me what's bothering you."

I barely manage to suppress my sigh as we wind through the quad toward the dining hall.

"Come on." Stella releases me so she can pull the door open. "I have a feeling this calls for pizza."

My stomach growls loudly at the mere thought of doughy goodness.

Stella smirks, as if to say *I told you so*. I scowl, but follow her all the same. It's just lunch with a classmate. It's pizza— not a commitment to bare my soul to her.

I mean, opening up to her a little wouldn't be the worst thing to happen, right? Maybe we could even be friends...or something.

"Let's sit by the window?" Stella asks, once we're through the line.

"Sure." I follow her to a two-seater table with a view of the quad.

I don't waste any time diving into my pizza. You'd think cafeteria pizza would be gross, but this is a slice of cheesy heaven.

Stella doesn't waste any time either—only instead of eating, she's back to prying. "So, what's going on? I'm a really good listener."

"Um." I stall by taking another big bite of pizza.

"Okay, let me share something about me first." She taps her pink-painted nail against her chin. "I'm an education major—which you know—and I've lived here my entire life. Literally, my childhood home is like five minutes down the road. I live with my best friend, and I'm dating my older brother's best friend. I've loved him my whole life, and now we're finally together. It took a long time and a lot of work, but he was totally worth all of the drama and heartache. Oh, and the sex is out of this world." She pauses, sucks in a deep breath then releases it slowly before taking a small bite of her pizza.

"Wow. That was...a lot."

"Yeah." Heat blooms across her cheeks. "But now you know me—or about me, anyway—so you're not opening up to a complete stranger."

"You are so..."

"Charming?" she offers when I trail off.

"I was going to say odd. But yeah, you're kind of charming, too."

Stella bats her long lashes and takes another bite.

"Fine." I relent. "When I left this morning, there was an eviction notice on my door."

"Oh my God!" Her eyes widen and her hand flies to her chest. "Are you okay?"

I shake my head. "No. We have to be out by *Sunday*."

"We?" she asks, leaning ever so slightly forward.

"Um." I swallow hard. "Me and my son."

"You have a son? How old is he? What's his name? I bet he's so cute. Where's his dad? Do y'all have somewhere to stay?"

"Easy, lady." I nudge her bottle of water toward her, and she takes a sip. "His name is Maverick, and he's four." I skip over her question about his dad. "And no, we don't have anywhere to stay."

My cheeks burn with shame at my admission, but I also feel lighter, simply for getting it off my chest.

"Y'all could live with me."

I choke on air. "I'm sorry, what?"

She shrugs. "I'm just saying. There's plenty of space."

"I don't even know you."

"Sure, you do. Sort of." She slides her phone out of her pocket, unlocks the screen, and then pins me with a meaningful look. "Rooming with me is better than living on the streets."

I focus my gaze on my half-eaten pizza, half-tempted to take her up on her offer. Because truly, if I don't find somewhere pronto, I'll either end up blowing my savings on a motel or calling Phoenix for help.

"Just come see it. It's in a really safe area, close to campus, and the landlord is actually my roommate's boyfriend. He lives next door and—"

"Won't your roommate have something to say about you

inviting a stranger to live with y'all? What about Maverick? Kids are loud and messy and—"

"She's actually planning on moving in with her boyfriend, hence the open room." Stella's lips quirk up into a smile. "He's been asking her to move in for forever, but she won't give in until I find someone to take over her portion of the rent. So, really, you'd be doing me a huge favor."

"Oh." What's that saying about if it sounds too good to be true? Because this definitely sounds like a dream. "Well…"

"Just come see it, Frankie. Please? I promise you won't regret it. And if it's not right for you, then no harm. I'll even help you find somewhere else, okay?"

God, please don't let me regret this, I send up a silent prayer and then nod. "Yeah, okay."

"Let's go now!"

"Now?" My eyes bug out; this is all moving so quickly. In fact, this entire day is moving at such lightning pace that it will be next week before I process it.

"Yeah, now. Your next class isn't for another hour and a half."

"Okay." I take a deep breath and then push away from the table. "Let's do it."

"ORION?" Mom's voice trickles through my closed bedroom door. "Your dad and I are going to watch a movie, and I was wondering if maybe you'd want to join us?" She pauses. "You know, like old times."

I suck in a deep breath and exhale a long sigh as I push up from my double-sized bed. The thing was too small when I was sixteen, and it's *damn sure* too small now that I'm twenty-six. "Sure, Mom."

"Oh, good!" The excitement in her voice sends a prick of guilt through me, because while she's chomping at the bit to reminisce, I'm daydreaming about hitting up ATF. It's been too long since I've seen my favorite Bluebird's hips sway. "I'll go start the popcorn."

"Be right down," I call back, resigned to spend the night either reliving my childhood or dodging setup attempts. God love my mother, but the woman's tried setting me up so many times in the last few years that I've lost count.

I set my phone on the charging dock before heading downstairs to join my parents.

Predictably, they're both on the loveseat, with a

crocheted blanket draped over their laps. There's a bowl of popcorn balanced between them and another on the coffee table, alongside three glass bottles of Coke.

"I was thinking we could watch the new *Spiderman*. You loved him growing up, and it has that Zendaya in it— she's a looker, don't you think?"

Oh, good. Tonight's going to be a two-fer. We're taking a walk down memory lane and trying to diagnose my love life. Fucking lovely.

"Yeah, Mom," I murmur, grabbing my bowl of popcorn —it has peanut butter M&Ms mixed in—and planting myself in the recliner. "She's pretty."

"Pretty enough to date?" she asks, resting her head on my dad's shoulder.

"Mom—"

"What?" She waves me off. "How can I find you a girl-friend if I don't narrow down your type?"

"Lizzie," Dad grumbles, trying to rein her in.

"I'm just saying." She sits up, grabs her Coke, and takes a sip. "At this rate, I'll never have grandbabies."

"I'm only twenty-six."

"Prime baby-making age," she counters, with her nose in the air.

"You'll be more likely to get grandkids from Stella and Samson than you are me. You know that, right?"

"This conversation is over," Dad growls, grabbing the remote and hitting play.

Mission accomplished. It's all I can do not to laugh; my dad might love Samson like a son, but even he has his limits when it comes to his daughter.

I toss a handful of popcorn into my mouth and settle in as the opening credits begin to roll.

The movie itself is pretty good, but Mom's running

commentary on how I used to pretend to shoot webs out of my fingers when I was little, and whether I think Aunt May or MJ is more attractive quickly grows tiresome.

By the time it's over, I'm damn near ready to shout that my type is petite, with dark hair, blue eyes, plump lips, and a body made for sin. But something tells me that wouldn't go over very well.

I stand and stack the empty bowls before collecting our Coke bottles and carrying it all to the kitchen.

The sound of heavy footsteps tells me that my dad is about to join me.

"You know your mother means well, right?" he asks as I drop the bottles into the recycling bin.

"Yeah, Dad." I rinse out the bowls and load them into the dishwasher. "I know."

"It's because she loves you." He leans against the island. "Wants the best for you."

"I know." And I do. Lizzie Cartwright loves fiercely and with her whole heart. She would do anything to make her kids happy. And I do mean *anything*.

Dad stares me down, searching my gaze for God knows what before finally nodding. "Good. You got any plans tonight?" he asks, simultaneously changing the subject and making me feel like a teenager begging to stay out past curfew.

"Why?" I sound defensive even to my own ears.

He holds up his hands in surrender, a wide grin splitting his cheeks. "Just making conversation, son."

I sigh. "Sorry. Being home... It's—"

His boom of laughter cuts me off. "Hard being back home? I bet."

"It's just... I keep feeling like I'm breaking rules and... yeah, it's weird."

"Your mom and I both know you're a grown man, Orion. We don't expect you to be home by any certain time or any of that. Like I said when you asked to stay with us, all we expect is for you to help out around the house while you're here and to not impregnate anyone under our roof."

I huff out a laugh, and his grin ratchets up to a full-blown smile. "Yeah, I don't think your mother would be too mad about the last one."

"Rest assured, I have no plans of becoming a daddy any time soon."

Dad tips his head at me, his expression knowing. What he knows, I have no clue, but the smugness radiating off him in waves tells me it's definitely *something*. "Never say never, son."

"I didn't." I cock my head to the side.

"Tomato, to-mah-to." He stands to his full height. "Be safe tonight."

"Who says I'm going out?"

"It's a Friday night, and you're young and single. Why in the hell would you sit at home in a bedroom that still has superhero posters on the walls?"

I smother a laugh. "True, true."

"Don't drink and drive," he says, walking back toward the living room. "And wear a condom."

I roll my eyes and head up the stairs to get dressed. Tonight was actually pretty good, but I'm more than ready to see my Bluebird's sexy little body writhing under the neon lights.

THE BASS POUNDS and the lights flash as scantily clad women work the pole, but none of them hold my interest.

There's only one woman I'm here to see and only—I check the time on my phone for the fifth time in as many minutes—ten more minutes stands between me and my VIP time with Birdie.

Swear to God, my dick's still halfway hard from watching her set on the stage, and the thought of her grinding her biteable ass down on me is pushing me into full-on tent territory.

"Hey, baby. Can I get you another whiskey?" the server assigned to my area asks.

Without even glancing her way, I nod and slide my empty glass toward the other two that came before it. I'm not normally one to drink this much, but tonight, I just need to really unwind. To relax, and lucky me, my good friend Jack Daniel's is here to help me.

She huffs out an irritated breath at my lack of interest but heads toward the bar all the same.

Moments later, she returns and places my glass down on the table to my right. "Thanks," I murmur, once again checking the time on my phone.

"Yeah, sure." She starts to walk away, but I call her back. "Yeah?"

I down the contents of my glass in two gulps. "Can I get one more and close out my tab?"

"Sure thing," she murmurs as I lift my ass and slide my wallet from my back pocket.

I pass her my card. "A double pour, yeah?"

"Mmhmm." And just like that, she's gone again.

By the time she returns, it's time for me to head back to my VIP room. I slide my card back into my wallet, sign the receipt, and stand.

My head spins for a second as I gain my bearings—those drinks must have hit me a little harder than I thought. But I shake it off and head toward the hallway at the back of the club.

The bouncer tips his chin at me as I approach. "Becoming a regular sort of thing, huh?" he asks, his voice light and his eyes hard.

During my many nights here, I've noticed the male staff really take care of the females. They're protective, and honestly, I fucking like it, because despite not knowing her real name or how she looks without a mask on, the knowledge that Birdie is safe here settles something wild inside of me... Something that snarls and rages at the thought of harm coming to her.

"What can I say, man?" I shrug. "There's something about her that keeps me coming back."

He narrows his eyes. "Far be it from me to tell you to chill, but remember, don't start no shit and there won't—"

"Be no shit. I got it, man."

"All right. Room three. Have a good night."

My lips lift in a grin as I let myself into the room. "I plan to."

The lights are low, and there's soft music playing as I settle myself down onto the center cushion of the plush velvet couch.

I sip my drink while I wait, my body thrumming with anticipation.

Luckily, Birdie doesn't keep me waiting long.

"Back again?" she asks as she slips into the room.

I drag my eyes over every inch of her body. Her black and red hair is pin straight and hangs down to the swell of her ass, which is barely concealed in a mesh skirt so short it looks more like a scarf.

"How can I stay away?" I ask, dragging my teeth over my lower lip. "You're fucking gorgeous."

Her cheeks turn as red as the streaks in her hair, and I fucking love it. It ignites something inside of me, and makes me want to know just how far down I can make that blush travel.

"I bet you say that to all of the girls," she murmurs, swaying her hips as she moves to the center of the room.

"I already told you..." I swirl the amber liquid in my glass, my eyes locked on hers. "There's only you."

She laughs lightly, like I'm joking. And honestly, I wish I was, because ever since the day I laid eyes on her all those months ago, I've become a man obsessed. I compare every woman to my Bluebird, and every single one of them is found lacking.

Their lips aren't as pouty as hers. Their eyes don't sparkle with mischief. Their bodies aren't built like hers. Their voices aren't the perfect combination of soft and raspy.

They. Aren't. Her.

Instead of replying, Birdie drags her hands up her body as she winds and twists her hips.

I watch, enthralled, and blindly place my glass on the small table; the way she moves is twenty times more intoxicating than any drink.

The song changes and she moves closer, stepping between my spread legs.

Fuck, yes.

Even though we haven't gotten quite as hot and heavy as we did my first night here, her mere presence still sets every single nerve ending in my body on fire.

"I could watch you dance for hours, Bluebird."

She leans down and braces her hands on my shoulders, pushing her perky pastie-covered breasts into my face.

I imagine moving closer, drawing one pebbled nipple

into my mouth, biting and sucking it before moving to the other. But I sit stock-still instead, because like always, she's the one in the driver's seat and I'm just the lucky schmuck along for the ride.

"Do you think about me?" she asks, swaying so close to me that her pebbled nipples actually brush against my chin. "When you're not here, I mean."

"All the fucking time," I growl, my dick officially rock hard.

"Do you ever touch yourself?" She plants her right knee beside my hip before swinging her other leg over my lap so that she's straddling me. "You know, while thinking of me?"

My willpower is a fraying thread, but I answer her anyway. "Yes."

A small moan slips past her red-slicked lips as she settles fully onto my lap. I can feel the heat of her pussy through my jeans, and the thought of ripping her little skirt off and ramming my cock inside of her is almost enough to snap the thread.

"Bluebird," I groan, clenching my hands into fists to keep from touching her.

She grinds down on me, swiveling her hips as she presses her core against my cock. "Sometimes I think of you, too."

"Fuck, fuck, fuck." *Think of something unsexy,* I command myself, but it's no use. Birdie is eclipsing every rational thought I could possibly hope to have. "Fuck!"

"Are you mad?" she asks, pausing her movements.

"God no," I reassure her. "I'm about to bust a nut in my pants like a fucking teenager."

She smiles indulgently. "Because of me?"

"Hell yeah, because of you. You're fucking perfection,

and the thought of you touching your pretty little pussy to thoughts of me is...*goddamn*."

"It's the only way I can get off," she confesses.

"Tell me." My voice is rough, like sandpaper and gravel. "Tell me everything you do."

She nibbles on her lower lip, and then palms her tits. "First, I play with my nipples." Her small fingers pluck at the hardened buds. "I pretend it's your hands, but sometimes I suck on my fingers first so that I can imagine your mouth."

I lick my lips and moan, easily falling into the picture she's painting. "Then what?"

"Then I drag my hands up and down my belly and over my thighs, and through my wetness, teasing myself until I can't take it anymore."

To my surprise, she slips one hand beneath the waistband of her skirt, and I watch, mesmerized, as she runs her index finger up and down her slit.

"What do you do then?"

She shudders as she begins to rub the little bundle of nerves at the apex of her thighs. "I gather some of my wetness on my fingers and rub my clit. I start slow, and then hard and fast, alternating between the two until I come."

"Show me," I demand, wondering what's brought about this wild side of her.

Her hand speeds up beneath the material of her skirt, and thanks to the mesh, I have a pretty decent view. She rubs at her clit like it's a genie lamp and she desperately needs a wish, until finally, she shatters, coming hard and then slumping against my chest.

By the grace of God, I manage not to come in my pants.

I gently rub her back as she comes down from her

orgasm, whispering all the while how perfect and gorgeous she is.

But when she finally sits up, she won't meet my eyes. "Hey, what's wrong?" I ask.

"I'm so sorry!" She brings her hands up to cover her burning cheeks.

"For what?" I ask, gently uncovering her face so that I can see her bright blue eyes.

"For that!" she whisper-shouts.

"Bluebird, I don't know what's going on in that pretty head of yours, but I promise, *that* is not something you need to apologize for."

She shakes her head like she doesn't believe me, so I take a chance and wrap my arms around her, drawing her close. "Is everything okay?"

She sighs. "Yeah, it's just been a weird week, and I...I don't know why, but I trust you."

I press a featherlight kiss to the top of her head. "You're always safe with me."

"Thanks." She wriggles out of my hold just as the bouncer knocks on the door. "Our time's up."

She stands and awkwardly shuffles toward the door. "Have a good weekend."

I stare at the door for a few minutes after her departure, palming my erection through my jeans, willing it to go down as I lift my forgotten glass from the table. "It's already the best," I say to the empty room before draining the last of my whiskey.

Another knock sounds, and I place the glass back on the table, knowing the staff will get it, and head out into the hallway.

I stagger a little as I cross the threshold—though, I'm not

sure if I'm drunk on lust or just plain drunk. Either way, I'm in no shape to drive.

It's late, but I dial the one person I know will answer my call no matter what.

"Orion," Stella says, picking up after the first ring, "is everything okay?"

"Yeah, but can I crash with you tonight?"

"Are you...have you been drinking?"

"Is that a yes?" I ask, ignoring her question altogether.

She sighs. "I guess, but you have to be quiet and on your best behavior. I have a new roommate."

"Emmy moved out?" I ask, meandering toward the bar.

"Just next door." I hear shuffling and then, "Do you have a ride?"

"Gonna order an Uber."

"Okay." She exhales loudly. "I'll leave the door unlocked for you."

"Thanks, Smalls." I end the call and drop down onto a barstool.

"What can I get you?" the bartender asks.

"Just a water please." I open the Uber app, request a ride, and settle in to wait.

The bartender slides my water to me and quickly moves on to help the next patron. But I don't bother drinking it—my mind's already reliving every moment from the VIP room.

Tonight, though unexpected, was a fucking dream come true—and I swear to God, I'm willing to do anything to make my dream of Birdie a reality, because as insane as it sounds, the little blue-eyed vixen is it for me.

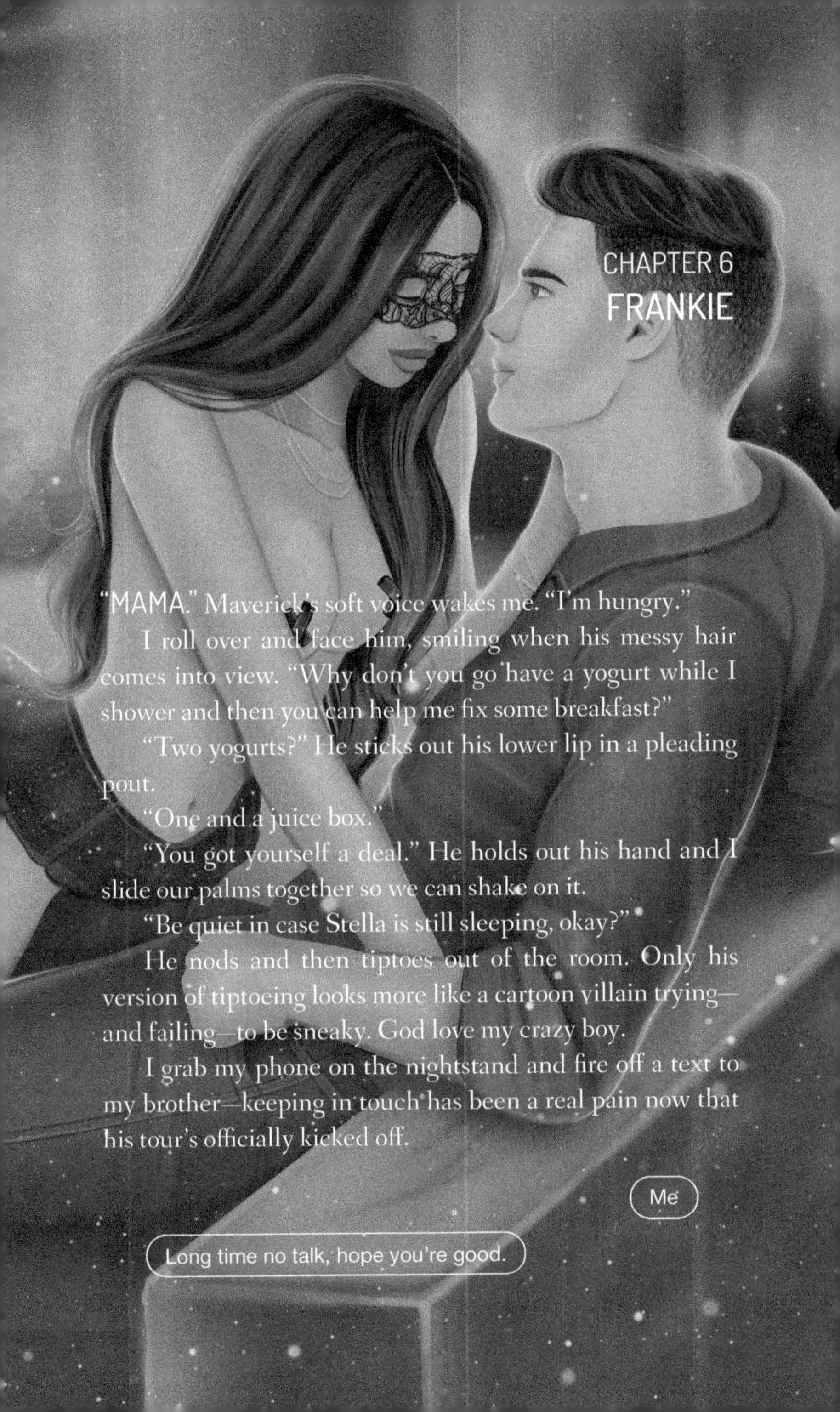

"MAMA." Maverick's soft voice wakes me. "I'm hungry."

I roll over and face him, smiling when his messy hair comes into view. "Why don't you go have a yogurt while I shower and then you can help me fix some breakfast?"

"Two yogurts?" He sticks out his lower lip in a pleading pout.

"One and a juice box."

"You got yourself a deal." He holds out his hand and I slide our palms together so we can shake on it.

"Be quiet in case Stella is still sleeping, okay?"

He nods and then tiptoes out of the room. Only his version of tiptoeing looks more like a cartoon villain trying—and failing—to be sneaky. God love my crazy boy.

I grab my phone on the nightstand and fire off a text to my brother—keeping in touch has been a real pain now that his tour's officially kicked off.

Me

Long time no talk, hope you're good.

Much to my surprise, he replies instantly.

PHOENIX

Busy. As fuck. Tired as fuck, too.

ME

Ah, such is the life of a famous rock star.

PHOENIX

I'm about to crash, so enough about me.
Tell me about you.

I gulp. This is definitely a conversation I've been avoiding. He's going to tear me a new one—all in the name of overprotective brotherly love, of course.

ME

Okay, so don't get mad…

PHOENIX

…

ME

We got evicted, but we found somewhere else to live. It's amazing Phin. Like, luxury and Stella (my roomie) even gave Mav and me the master suite. It's close to both of our schools and since Stella's bestie is dating the landlord, it's insanely cheap. See everything worked out!

My heart squeezes itself into my throat as I wait for his reply, the *typing* bubbles dancing along my screen.

PHOENIX

I'm def mad. We don't keep secrets, Frank.
But as long as you're safe…

ME

I am. Promise. Love you!

PHOENIX

You too, brat. Talk soon.

I smile to myself as I set my phone back down on the table. *That definitely went better than I thought it would.*

A yawn overtakes me as I stretch my arms overhead before hauling myself out of the bed and into the bathroom for a shower. I rinsed off last night after getting home from the club, but I'm dragging ass this morning since thoughts of my hottie kept me up most of the night.

Hopefully the hot water will finish waking me up. If not, there's always coffee.

I can't help but marvel at the events of the last week as the steamy spray sluices down my body. Despite going into this new living arrangement with low expectations, living with Stella is actually pretty great.

She's neat and tidy, and I'm pretty sure Maverick is her spirit animal. The two took to one another like they were long-lost friends.

And don't even get me started on the apartment—which isn't an apartment at all. It's a three bedroom, almost two-thousand-square-foot luxury townhouse.

It honestly blows my mind that this is the place I'm calling home. I guess being best friends with the landlord's girlfriend comes with perks, because God knows this place would otherwise be so far out of my budget it isn't even funny.

Even nicer, Stella insisted on Maverick and me taking the master bedroom—which came furnished—since there's more space and an en suite.

But still, as nice as everything is, change is hard, and my brain is struggling to cope with all of the newness raining down all around me.

After a quick wash, I shut off the water and dry myself with one of the fluffy towels. Since it's just us girls and Mav, I toss on a pair of sleep shorts, a camisole, and my robe before venturing into the kitchen.

"Can I crack the eggs?" I hear Maverick ask as I near the end of the hallway. I guess Stella's up after all. I hope he didn't wake her up.

But when a very familiar, masculine voice replies, I stop dead in my tracks. "Sure thing, little man."

"I'm not little," Maverick says, and despite my heart pounding so hard it feels like it might beat right out of my chest, I can just picture him flexing his tiny muscles. "Uncle Phin says I'm as strong as Hulk!"

What in the hell is he doing here?

Finally, my good sense kicks in and I hightail it to the kitchen. Maverick and my hottie-turned-stalker are standing together at the island, cracking eggs into a mixing bowl.

"What are you doing here?" I demand, walking over and wrapping my arms protectively around my son.

"Um..." He casts a sidelong glance in my direction.

"Did you follow me?" I take a step back toward the hall, dragging Maverick with me.

"Mama, we're making Pamcakes," Maverick whines, trying to shimmy out of my hold. But I tighten my grip, keeping his little body tucked into mine. "With chocolate chips!"

"How in the hell would I follow you?" he asks, furrowing his brow. "I don't even know you."

"Really?" I cock my head to the side.

"Lady, I don't know what you want me to say."

"I want to know why you're here!"

"Jesus fucking Christ," he mutters under his breath. "Stella didn't mention her new roommate was crazy."

I can feel my cheeks heat at his insinuation. He's either a brilliant actor or a practiced liar. I'm torn on which. "Watch your language," I growl right as Maverick flings himself out of my grip and into *his* space.

"My mama's not crazy! And my teacher says name calling is bullying. I thought you were my friend, but I don't wanna be friends with a big mean bully!" He narrows his eyes in what his four-year-old brain thinks is an intimidating glare. "Say sorry!"

My stalker-slash-hottie has the good sense to look ashamed. I guess being rebuked by a kid who's still in a booster seat will do that to a person. "You're right, bud. Name calling is shitty—I mean crappy—I mean bad. It's bad."

"So are swear words." Maverick crosses his arms, still glaring.

"Yup. Got it. No swear words." He squats down so they're eye to eye. "Are we good?"

"No!" Maverick shouts. "You didn't tell my mama sorry."

"What's going on in here?" Stella asks, glancing around the kitchen. "Y'all's yelling woke me up."

When no one immediately answers her, she shuffles over to the coffee pot and pours a cup. "Seriously, the tension's thick enough to cut with a knife. What gives?" She turns to me. "Did my numbskull brother do something stupid?"

My eyes widen as everything snaps into place. My hottie's not a stalker. No, he's something far worse—my roommate's freaking brother. *Why, God, why?*

"It was a misunderstanding," I mumble, not wanting to rehash my allegations. The last thing I need is Stella thinking I'm insane and kicking me out.

Her eyes ping-pong back and forth between us. "What kind of misunderstanding?"

"I..." I clear my throat, "I just didn't realize he was here. Surprised me, that's all."

Stella smacks her palm against her forehead. "Oh my goodness! I am so sorry. I didn't even think to tell you he was crashing here last night. It was so late when he called me and—"

"It's fine," I say, cutting off her apology. "This is your house. You don't need to ask or tell me anything—I was just caught off guard, that's all."

Maverick rolls his eyes. "Can you just tell my mama sorry so we can finish making our Pamcakes?"

My hottie rolls his eyes. "I'm very sorry for—"

"Forgiven." I'm on a roll with speaking over people today. I turn to my son. "Do you want me to help you make them?"

He looks between me and my hottie before shaking his head. "No. He can. He says he knows the top-secret ingredient."

His rejection hurts, but I quickly school my features in a pleasant smile. "Okay. Cool." Turning to face Stella's brother, I add, "Well, I'm Frankie... It's nice to meet you, I guess."

He stares at me for a minute, and for a split second I can't help but wonder if he's playing dumb. "Orion, and you've certainly made this Saturday morning interesting."

The urge to bang my head into the wall is strong, but Orion already thinks I'm crazy; no reason to add fuel to that particular fire.

"Frankie, you wanna join me in the living room while the boys cook?" Stella asks.

My heart sinks. I knew this was too good to last. Tears

threaten to fall, but I refuse to let them. "Okay." I swallow hard. "Let me just grab a cup of coffee."

Stella smiles and nods before walking toward the living room.

I skirt around the edge of the kitchen to the coffee pot, quickly pouring myself a mug. As much as I'd like to take my time before facing Stella, there's no point. This conversation is like taking off a Band-Aid...

Better to rip it off.

Hottie—I mean Orion—keeps his sharp gaze trained on me until I leave the kitchen. Somehow, it feels like he is assessing me and undressing me all at once. Which is kind of funny since he's basically seen me naked; he just doesn't know it.

Stella pats the cushion next to her when I walk into the room. "Sit, let's talk."

I inhale a deep breath and then release it slowly before joining her. "I'm sorry about this morning," I start, but she waves me away.

"Not even an issue. I know better than anyone how wonderfully frustrating my brother can be. I literally didn't have friends until college because of his overbearing ass."

"My brother's pretty overprotective, too. Or he was— he's too busy now."

She smiles and then takes a sip of her coffee. "So, I need to talk to you about something."

Here we go. "Okay, what's up?"

Stella leans forward and places her mug down onto the coffee table. "I want to preface this with you can totally say no, because I want you to be comfortable here."

"You're not kicking me out?" I blurt out, every bit as astonished as I am thankful.

"What? No. Are you kidding? Why would I?"

I shrug sheepishly and look down at my coffee.

"Anyway, I have a big ask, but like I said, you can say no."

"Okay... What is it?"

"Orion kind of needs a place to stay for a bit, and he was hoping he could stay here."

"Oh." I blink, trying to process her words.

"It's a long story, and he was staying with our parents, but he kind of feels like he's cramping their style, and our mom keeps trying to set him up with every single woman she knows under forty."

"Um." For some reason, my brain and mouth can't seem to get on the same wavelength. Because I have plenty to say, and yet none of it will come out.

"Like I said, if you're not okay with it, he'll just have to deal with living at home until he finds his own place."

It's on the tip of my tongue to tell her no, but then I hear my son's delighted squeals of joy from the kitchen and find myself saying, "It's no problem," before I can think better of it.

"Are you sure?" she asks, no doubt thinking about the tension from earlier.

Maverick laughs again, and I smile. "Yeah, I'm sure. Plus, he's your family. I'm just some girl from your art class."

Stella scoffs. "You're more than some girl. We're going to be great friends. You'll see."

"Y'all ready for some pancakes?" Orion asks, interrupting us before I can reply to Stella's bold claim.

"You mean *Pam*cakes?" Maverick shouts from the hallway.

Orion arches a brow, and I can't help but laugh. "It's a long story."

"Well, whatever they're called, they're ready."

Stella hops up from the couch and flits toward the kitchen, pausing only to jab her elbow into her brother's ribs.

"Ouch, Smalls!" he hollers, taking off after her.

"Mav Man, save me," Stella calls and my son leaps into action, placing his small body between the feuding siblings, holding his hands out to stop Orion.

"You're really gonna take her side? Bros before—"

I shuffle past him, hustling into the kitchen. "Finish that sentence and die."

Orion smiles, and I swear to God, I can *feel* an ache in my ovaries.

"What?" he asks, feigning innocence. "I was going to say bros before sisters with stinky toes."

As soon as the words pass his lips, Stella absolutely loses it laughing. "Oh my God," she wheezes, "I wish that was on video. I would literally give my left arm to have that on video."

"You're such a brat," he mutters, shoulder checking her lightly as he moves around to the other side of the island. "How many Pamcakes, bud?"

"A hundred," Maverick deadpans.

"How about two?" I counter.

He sighs but nods. "With lots of syrup?"

"Wanna know what's really good?" Orion asks.

"What?"

"Do you trust me?"

"Mister, I hardly even know you."

Turning to me, Stella cracks up again. "Yeah, he's definitely your kid, Frankie."

I shrug, even as a blush burns across my cheeks.

Orion on the other hand adopts a wounded expression and clutches at his chest. "I thought we were buds, Maverick. Bros. Best friends. And now you're acting like we're strangers. Dude."

Maverick stares at him for a minute before relenting. "Fine, but if you do something gross, you're out."

"Out of where?"

"Everywhere! You're out of everywhere!"

Stella and I hide our laughter behind our hands while Orion somehow manages to keep a straight face. "Got it."

I plate up everyone's Pamcakes while Stella grabs the butter and syrup. I'm not sure what Orion is rifling through the fridge for, but something tells me it's going to be wild.

"Y'all go on to the table, and I'll bring Maverick's plate out with me."

I hesitate, feeling slightly on edge at the thought of him caring for my son. Which is absurd, because aside from our snafu this morning, he's done nothing wrong.

"C'mon, Mama." Mav grabs my hand. "You can sit by me."

The three of us move to the dining room, leaving Orion to his own devices. I just hope he doesn't bring out some concoction loaded with sugar.

A few minutes later, he calls out from the kitchen for Maverick to close his eyes. He walks into the room with a plate loaded down with Pamcakes, layered with bananas, strawberries, whipped cream, and... *is that Nutella?*

Lord have mercy, if my son eats that, I'll... I'll kiss the man.

Well, let's be honest, I'd probably do that anyway.

"Okay, bud." He places the plate down in front of Maverick. "What do you think?"

My son's eyes widen comically. "It looks like an ice cream sundae!"

Orion smiles, his eyes already shining with triumph. "Tastes even better than a sundae, my dude. Try it."

Maverick doesn't waste a second and shovels a huge bite into his mouth. "Mama!" he shouts, whipped cream dripping from his lips like he's a rabid raccoon.

"Chew your food first, Mav."

He swallows and then tries again. "Mama! You have to try this! It's the best thing in the whole entire world. It's... it's like...*magic* in my *mouth*!"

"Magic, huh?" My lips curl into a smile, loving how excited my little man is.

"Yes, like abra-cadabra-delicious!" He wiggles in his seat and then shoves another bite into his mouth. "Try it!"

I go to fork up a bite for myself, but Orion beats me to it, extending his own fork my way.

It's no big deal, I tell myself, even though it totally feels like one. But for all I know, he goes around feeding every woman he meets.

With that thought in my mind, I lean forward and accept his offering. "Oh," I sigh as soon as my lips close around the tines of the fork.

I chew thoughtfully and then swallow. "That *is* good."

Stella clears her throat, snapping me out of my daze. "Do I need to watch the kid while you two get a room?"

I jolt back in my seat, wishing a hole would open in the pretty polished floor to swallow me up. How freaking mortifying.

"Knock it off," Orion growls, while I focus on my own plate.

"Seriously," Stella crows, "are you two going to be able to live together?"

"What?" Maverick asks, scrunching his little nose. "Live together?"

I rush to explain. "Orion is Stella's brother, and he's going to be staying here for a little while."

"Like a sleepover?" He bounces in his chair in glee.

"Sure." Orion grins. "Like a sleepover."

"Can we build a pillow fort? And tell scary stories? Can we stay up all night? Can we—"

"Slow down, Mav. I'm sure—"

"Of course, we can," Orion murmurs over my attempt to placate him. "In fact, tonight, we can even camp in the living room."

Maverick smiles brighter than I've ever seen. "This is the best day ever!"

I wish I could share my son's enthusiasm, but my heart feels like it's made of glass in my chest—thin and brittle, ready to shatter.

Because that's what men like him do. They break hearts, and something tells me he's undoubtedly going to break mine.

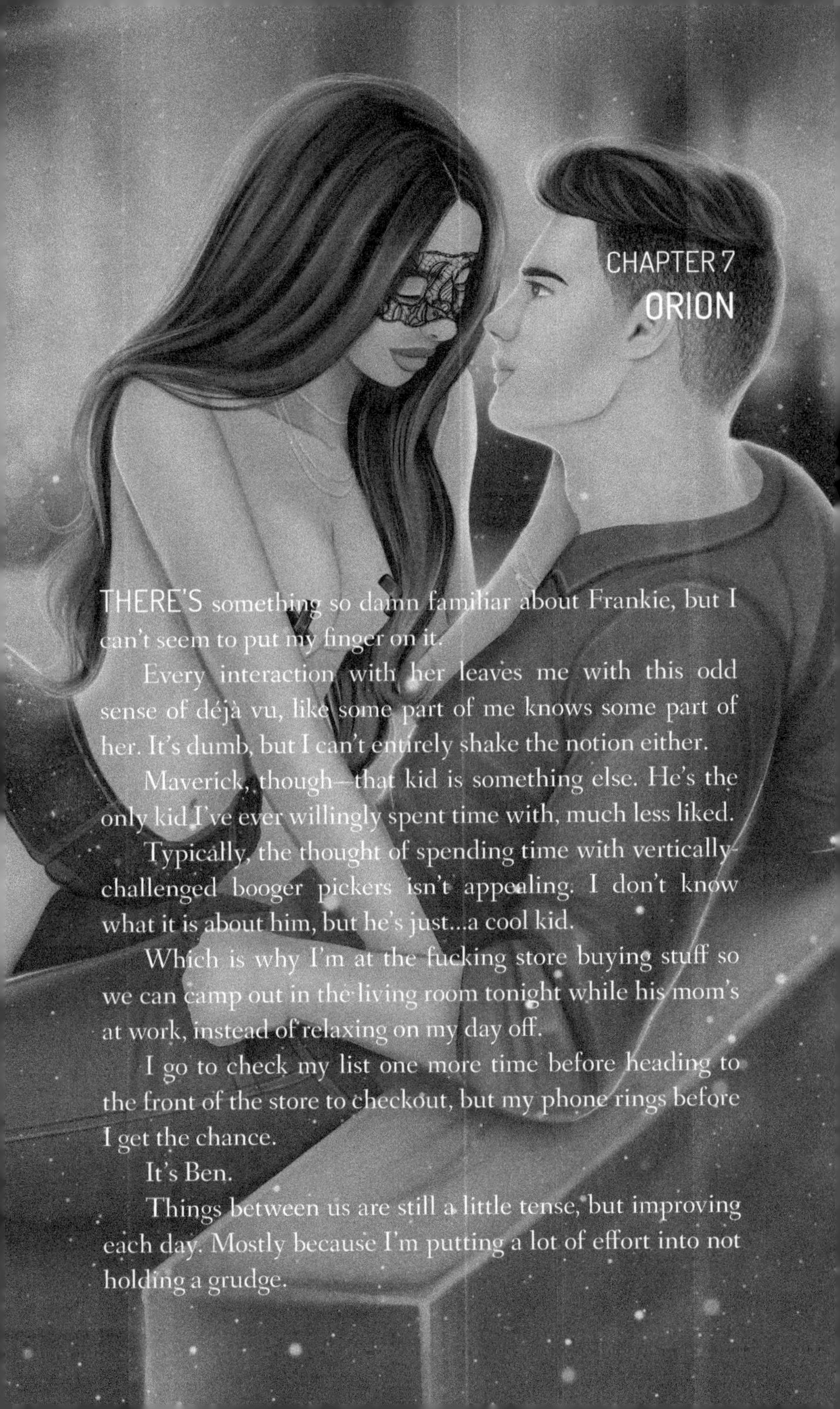

THERE'S something so damn familiar about Frankie, but I can't seem to put my finger on it.

Every interaction with her leaves me with this odd sense of déjà vu, like some part of me knows some part of her. It's dumb, but I can't entirely shake the notion either.

Maverick, though—that kid is something else. He's the only kid I've ever willingly spent time with, much less liked.

Typically, the thought of spending time with vertically-challenged booger pickers isn't appealing. I don't know what it is about him, but he's just...a cool kid.

Which is why I'm at the fucking store buying stuff so we can camp out in the living room tonight while his mom's at work, instead of relaxing on my day off.

I go to check my list one more time before heading to the front of the store to checkout, but my phone rings before I get the chance.

It's Ben.

Things between us are still a little tense, but improving each day. Mostly because I'm putting a lot of effort into not holding a grudge.

"What's up, man?" I say once the call connects.

"Just making sure we're still on for Monday."

"Yeah, we are."

"Okay, good." He exhales loudly into the phone. "Are we good, Orion? You know you're like a brother to me, right?"

It's on the tip of my tongue to—once again—tell him he has a funny way of showing it, but I swallow down the urge. "Yeah, we're good."

"Okay. Well. Why don't we meet for lunch Monday instead of at the office?"

"Sounds good," I reply distractedly, as uninvited thoughts of my new roommates creep to the forefront of my mind.

My phone beeps in my ear, and I pull it away from my face to check the screen. "Hey, Stella's calling me—see you Monday?"

"Sure—" Ben starts to say something else, but I've already swapped calls.

"Where are you?" my impatient little sister asks.

"The store," I drawl, "like I said before I left."

"Which store?"

I smirk; she's using what I call her *teacher voice.* "Target, why?"

"Oh, good—wait, why are you at Target? You hate Target."

"Um." I pause in the aisle and rub at the back of my neck.

"Oh my God!"

"What?"

"You're actually going to do it, aren't you?"

I start pushing my cart again, wandering aimlessly while Stella talks in circles. "Do what?"

"Camp with Maverick."

"So?" I cringe at the defensiveness in my voice, something I know Stella will latch onto.

"So..." she draws out the word. "I just think it's interesting, that's all."

"He seemed really into the idea. It's no big deal."

"Au contraire, big brother. It's a *huge* deal."

"Whatever. Did you need something, or did you only call to bust my balls?"

"Ew. Don't mention your balls to me. Ever."

"Stella," I growl.

"Fine, yes. I wanted to see if you could pick me up a few things."

"Of course, you do." I roll my eyes. "What do you need?"

"I'll text you a list," she says happily before ending the call.

A few seconds later, her list comes through.

STELLA

SGX NYC dry shampoo (the one with the yellow label), more coffee, and some of the Cinnamon Toast Crunch creamer.

I visibly cringe at the last item on the list—because *fucking gross*—and then I head down the aisle toward the refrigerated section, determined to finish my shopping so I can relax at least a little today.

By the time I make it to checkout, my cart is loaded down with so much shit that it's nearly overflowing. I definitely went overboard, but like I said, there's something about the kid that just tugs at me. It's like, from the moment I first saw him, something inside me decided making him smile was my new mission.

"That'll be one-fifteen even," the cashier says, both pulling me from my thoughts and shocking the hell out of me. I haven't spent this much at Target *ever*.

I swipe my card and enter my pin, all the while thinking this kid sure as hell better appreciate all of the effort I'm putting into our impromptu campout.

***

"OH, THANK GOD!" Stella shouts, the second I walk through the door. "I didn't think you were ever coming back!"

"I was only gone like two hours, Smalls."

She snatches the bag containing her coffee creamer out of my hands. "I ran out after my first cup." She widens her eyes dramatically. "One. Cup."

Laughter wells up from my chest. "Better hurry—wouldn't want you hulking out or anything."

"But Hulk is super cool," Maverick says from the couch. "And he's green." His little head pops up over the back of the couch. "That's my favorite color."

"Good choice," I murmur, walking into the kitchen.

Stella shoots me a knowing look as she saunters past, heading back to her bedroom.

I heft the bags onto the island, refusing to let her bait me, and begin sorting everything into piles.

"What's yours?" Maverick hollers.

Brilliant blue eyes flash through my mind—are they Birdie's or Frankie's? What's the chance of them both having the same hue? "Blue," I call back, because regardless of which woman they belong to, they're fucking gorgeous.

"Like Captain America's suit!"

"Sure." I toss the package of hotdogs into the fridge. "Just like that."

The sound of little footsteps echoes down the hall, and then Maverick's right there in the kitchen with me. "Can I help?"

"If you want." I nudge a bag toward him. "Where's your mom?"

He climbs up onto one of the stools and begins emptying the bag. "She's getting ready for work."

"Where does she work?" At this point, I'm not sure whether or not I'm making small talk or fishing for information.

Maverick shrugs as he surveys the contents of his bag. "You got marshmallows—the big ones—and graham crackers, and chocolate—Orion!" He shouts my name and my eyes fly up to meet his. "Are we for real having a sleepover?"

How is this kid so cute? "Yeah. We are."

Without warning, he jumps off his stool and flings himself at me. Despite his small size, the kid somehow crashes into me with the force of a Mack truck.

I stagger back as I fumble to wrap my arms around him to keep him from hurting himself.

But he just wraps his arms around my neck, hugging me like he didn't just almost bust his head open and like we didn't just meet this morning.

"Thank you! Thank you! Thank you! I'm so excited! This is—you're the best!"

Awkwardly, I pat his back. "You're, uh, welcome."

Just as quickly as he came at me, he wiggles out of my hold, landing on his feet. "I gotta go tell Mama! She told me not to get my hopes up, but you really did it, because you're the best!"

For reasons unknown, my heart squeezes in my chest as

he takes off running down the hall toward the room he shares with Frankie.

Five minutes later, everything is put away and I decide to help myself to a cup of the coffee Stella must have started. However, unlike my sister, I drink mine black.

I manage to enjoy two sips before Stella barges into my solitude, firing off one question after another.

"What's going on? You don't like kids, but you're being really nice to Mav. Are you trying to fuck Frankie? Ew, actually, don't answer that. Seriously though, what gives?"

Raising my mug to my lips, I stare at her over the rim.

"Orion!" She whines my name, sounding every bit like the brat she was when we were younger.

"Smalls!" I mimic her tone, and she narrows her eyes.

"Avoidance only means you have something to hide."

I place my coffee onto the island and throw my arms out wide. "What could I possibly have to hide?"

"I don't know." She crosses her arms over her chest. "You tell me."

"Stella." I sigh. "There's nothing to tell."

She leans a little closer and sniffs the air.

"What in the hell are you doing?"

"Yup. Just as I suspected."

"What is?" I'm half-tempted to call Samson and ask if she's taken up recreational drug use, because she's acting like a nut.

"You smell like lies. Filthy, filthy lies."

"Are you high?"

"No," Maverick scoffs. I swear, the kid is part ninja, because when he's not clomping through the house like a horse, he's noiseless. "She's short."

Stella gasps. "I prefer vertically challenged."

He shrugs and positions himself directly beside her.

"Either way, I'm half your tall, and I'm not even in big school yet!"

I don't mean to laugh, but I can't help it—the kid's got a point. "Has my sister told you her nickname?" I ask, once my laughter subsides.

"No."

"Orion," Stella growls, but she's about as threatening as a kitten.

"Smalls!" I shout, instinctually stepping out of striking range, because as I well know, kittens have claws. "You know, because she's so..." I trail off as I begin cracking up all over again.

But Maverick seamlessly picks up my train of thought. "Small?"

"Y'all are the worst!" Stella screeches, but she's smiling.

"You mean best, right?"

"Yeah!" Maverick pumps his fist into the air. "Boys rule, girls drool."

Before anyone can say anything, Frankie walks into the room, a mischievous grin twisting her pouty lips. "Maverick James, you know girls are just as good as boys, right?"

He moves to stand at his mother's side. "Yeah, Mama, we were just teasing Stella."

"Teasing or picking on?"

He tugs on the hem of Frankie's shirt twice, and she kneels so they're eye to eye. "Teasing, Mama. Because I'm not a bully."

She searches his face for a second and then presses a loud, smacking kiss to his cheek. "That's my boy."

Maverick beams under her simple praise, but just as quickly , his smile wilts. "Are you sure you gotta go to work? You're gonna miss out on the sleepover."

Frankie's frown mirrors his. "Yeah, bud. I do. But I'm off tomorrow. Sunday-fun-day, right?"

"Right," he mumbles, staring at his feet.

"Oh, Mav." Frankie's lower lip trembles as she pulls her son into a tight hug. "What if we go to the carousel tomorrow?"

He leans back, so he can look her in the eye without breaking her embrace. "Can I pick any animal?"

Frankie nods.

"And can we get food?"

I laugh, because apparently the whole *way to a man's stomach* thing starts young.

"Of course."

He licks his lips and then shocks us all. "Can Orion come?"

"Um," Frankie hedges, her blue eyes locking onto mine, silently pleading for help.

But it's Stella who comes to the rescue. "Dude, am I not invited, too?"

His little cheeks turn pink as he blinks up at her. "Oh. Yeah. You can come, too!"

Stella smiles and ruffles his hair. "Thanks, Mav."

He takes another step back, finally breaking his mother's hold. "Want me to save you a s'more, Mama?"

Sadness swims over Frankie's features as she stands—it's clear as day that she wants nothing more than to stay home with her son.

"If you want," I clear my throat, "I can send you pictures."

Frankie hesitates before pulling her phone from her back pocket; she unlocks the screen and passes it to me. "Put your number in."

I quickly add my info and fire off a text to myself so that I have her number. "Thanks."

"Why are you thanking me?" she asks.

"Just being polite." Internally, I cringe, knowing good and well I sound like an idiot. I'm usually good with the ladies, but apparently my charm doesn't apply to the likes of Frankie.

Maybe it's because she's a mom, and my brain's already placed her in the *not for you* category. Which is a real shame, because she's pretty hot.

"Right." She nods. "Well, I've got to get going, or I'll be late."

"Where do you work?" I ask before she can leave the room.

"Um." Frankie crosses her arms over her chest. "I'm a waitress."

Be a little shadier. "Where?"

She waves her right hand in a dismissive gesture. "Nowhere you'd know."

"Right." I give her a long look, wondering what kind of restaurant lets their servers work in a T-shirt and sweatpants. "Well, drive safe."

Frankie offers me a wan smile before turning back to her son, effectively dismissing me. "You listen to Stella and Orion tonight, okay, bud?"

He bobs his head. "Yes, Mama."

"And don't eat too much sugar."

"I won't."

"And don't stay up too late."

"Promise."

She exhales and pulls him into another bone-crushing hug. "I'll call you before bedtime to say good night, okay?"

"I love you. And I will save you a s'more. Orion even got the big marshmallows."

"I know. You told me." She releases him, and he scampers to my side. "If you need me, call me. If there's an emergency, call the number I gave you, Stella."

Now I want to know that number, so I can Google it to see where it goes.

She gives her son one more hug and then grabs her bag and heads for the door.

I wait for the sound of the latch before turning to Maverick. "You ready to camp?"

"Yeah! I was born ready."

Stella shoots me a grin before sneaking back to her room.

"What are we going to do first?"

"The first step of camping is to secure your shelter."

"Uh." He cocks his head to the side. "I don't know what that means."

"It means"—I grab a roll of masking tape from the junk drawer, holding it up between us like a trophy—"that we need to build a fort!"

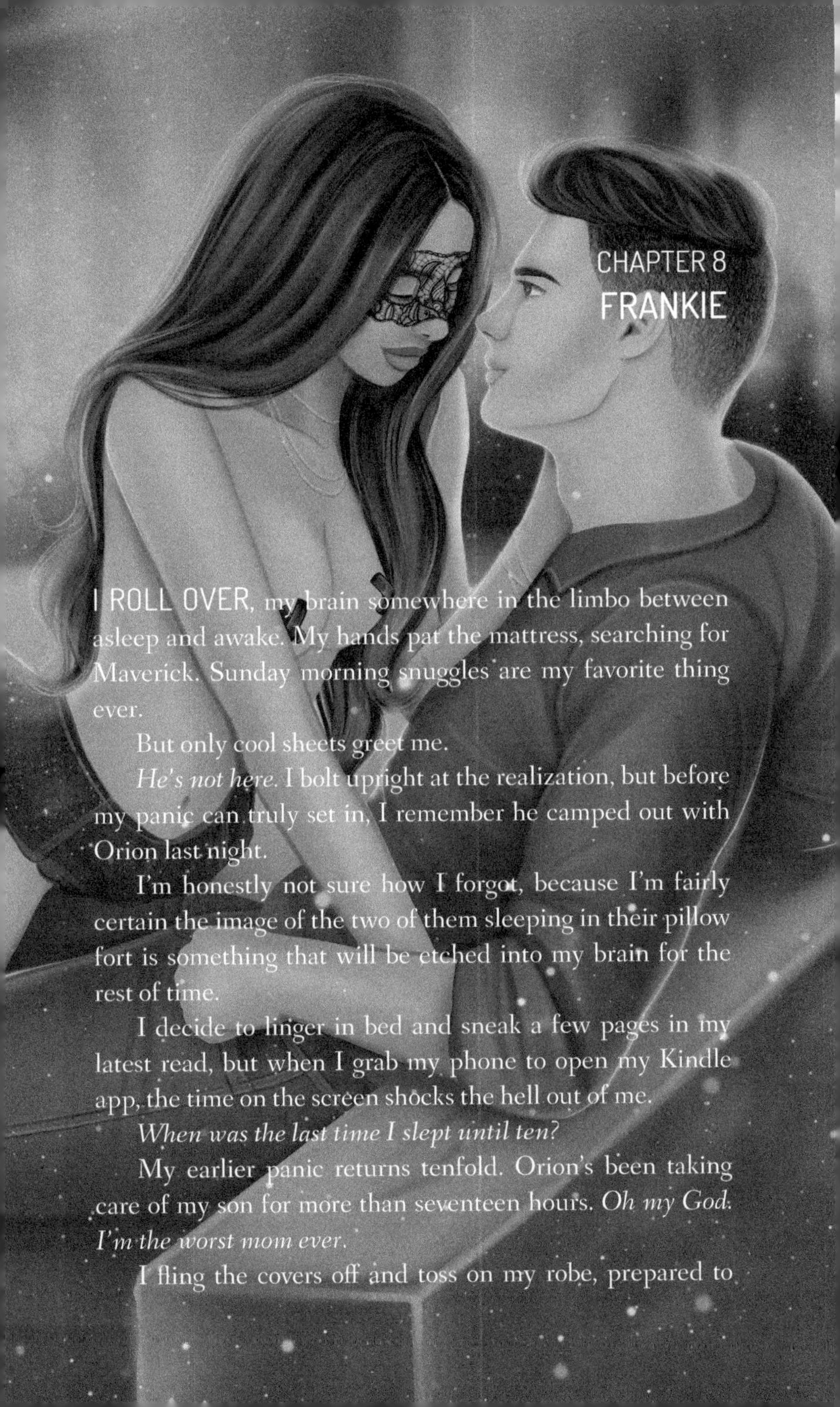

I ROLL OVER, my brain somewhere in the limbo between asleep and awake. My hands pat the mattress, searching for Maverick. Sunday morning snuggles are my favorite thing ever.

But only cool sheets greet me.

He's not here. I bolt upright at the realization, but before my panic can truly set in, I remember he camped out with Orion last night.

I'm honestly not sure how I forgot, because I'm fairly certain the image of the two of them sleeping in their pillow fort is something that will be etched into my brain for the rest of time.

I decide to linger in bed and sneak a few pages in my latest read, but when I grab my phone to open my Kindle app, the time on the screen shocks the hell out of me.

When was the last time I slept until ten?

My earlier panic returns tenfold. Orion's been taking care of my son for more than seventeen hours. *Oh my God. I'm the worst mom ever.*

I fling the covers off and toss on my robe, prepared to

beg for forgiveness. I mean, seriously, who leaves their kid with someone for that long—someone they hardly know, at that.

Sure, I'm in the same house, only right down the hall, but still. My guilt threatens to consume me.

I make a quick detour by the bathroom to brush my teeth before flying out of my bedroom.

"Mama!" Maverick calls happily when he sees me, jumping up and meeting me in the hall. "You're up!"

"I'm so sorry." I wrap him in my arms and pepper kisses all over his syrup-sticky face. "So, so sorry."

"Why?" he and Orion ask at the same time.

"For sleeping in, for making you watch him this long, for—"

"Cut it out," Orion says, all business as he stands from the couch.

"Cut what out?" I ask, fearing I've somehow made the situation worse. God, he probably thinks I'm just some user who takes advantage of the kindness of others.

"Stop apologizing."

"But—"

"But nothing, Frankie." He doesn't stop until he's directly in front of me, so close that I can smell his cologne. He smells like citrus, bergamot, and bad decisions. "I figured you could use the sleep. It's not a big deal."

"It is, though," I insist. "And I don't want you to think I just hand my kid off to whoever—"

Orion cuts me off for the third time. "You want to know what I think?"

"What?" I whisper.

"I think you need to cut yourself some slack." I lower my eyes, focusing it on the tops of Maverick's curls. But

Orion presses on. "You're a single mom, a waitress, and a college student."

He gently grips my chin between his thumb and forefinger, lifting my gaze to his. "If I didn't want to spend time with him, I wouldn't, okay?"

I swallow roughly and nod, halfway hoping he'll release me, but he doesn't.

"I want your words, Frankie," he says, stroking my jawline with his calloused thumb.

The combination of his scent and touch triggers some sort of muscle memory, and before I know it, my body's nearly quivering with need.

"O–okay." I barely manage the single word, and my cheeks flame at how raspy my voice comes out.

"Good." He strokes my jaw one last time before releasing me and taking a half-step away. "Now, go get ready, because I promised Maverick that we could try my favorite deli near the park."

"You did what?" I ask, every drop of the lust *just* coursing through me evaporating as my heart and brain are at war over this.

My heart is overjoyed at Maverick having a male presence in his life, but my brain is stomping and screaming profanities, because who is he to promise my son anything?

The man is, for all intents and purposes, a stranger. And while I might feel like I know him, the only thing I really know is that he has a penchant for strippers and enjoys watching me touch myself.

Our relationship is base level at best—no, it's less, because in the light of day, Orion Cartwright doesn't even recognize me.

I want to be mad. I want to stomp my foot and rage and

demand *how dare he!* But for some reason, I can't seem to hold onto my anger.

Orion cocks his head, studying me, trying to figure out where he went wrong. "I just figured since we were going to Coolidge Park that we could eat somewhere nearby." He raises his hands in a placating gesture. "I'm sorry if I overstepped."

"Thanks, Orion." I hang my head to hide the blush staining my cheeks. I'm so used to going it alone that I'm looking for a fight when there isn't one to be found. "We've never been there, so you'll have to tell us what's the best thing to order."

He studies me for a long minute, and it's like he can see through all of my walls, straight into my soft heart. "I won't steer y'all wrong, but get ready quick because they get busy once church lets out."

I force my lips into a smile. "Come on, Mav." I grab his hand and give it a soft tug. "Let's get ready."

Fortunately, he follows me back to our bedroom without any fight.

Unfortunately, he's far too perceptive for his age. "Are you mad?" he asks, the second I close the door behind us.

I take a deep breath, holding it for ten seconds before slowly blowing it out. "No, I'm not mad. I'm just..." I pause, because how do I explain to my son that Orion somehow activates my fight or flight instinct on a level I never even knew existed?

From our very first encounter in the VIP room, he's both set my teeth on edge and made me want to curl up in his lap like a sleepy little kitten.

He makes me want to trust him, even while erecting the walls around my heart higher and higher.

But Maverick doesn't need to know any of that, so eventually, I settle on a half-truth. "I'm just used to it being the two of us, and while I'm happy to have Orion and Stella in our lives, it's an adjustment, too."

"So, you're not mad?" he asks, his usually smooth forehead lined with confusion.

"No, baby, I'm not mad."

The way his shoulders sag with relief sends a spike of guilt through me. It's a stark reminder that I need to be more cautious in shielding him from some of the more grown-up aspects of our rapidly changing situation.

"Do you want to watch tv while I take a quick shower?"

He thinks on it for a minute and then asks, "Can I watch the Spiderman cartoon? It's on Disney Plus."

"We don't have that—"

"Yuh-huh!" he insists. "Orion showed me!"

I grab the remote from my nightstand and pass it to him. To my surprise, he expertly navigates through the various menus, until the show he wants fills the screen.

"Well, I stand corrected." I pad over to the bathroom. "Holler if you need me, okay?"

I see him nod from the corner of my eye before I slide the door closed and start the shower.

TWENTY MINUTES LATER, I'm dressed in a pair of ripped black jeans, a white thermal, and my favorite blue plaid flannel.

"Can I wear my blue shirt, too?" Maverick asks, looking up at me with big, puppy eyes. "Then we can match!"

"Of course, you can." I riffle through the hangers on his side of the closet until I find the miniature version of my shirt. "Here you go."

He slides his arms through the sleeves and then turns to face me. "Will you help with the buttons?"

"Do you want to try it first?"

He sighs but gets to work.

While he carefully lines buttons with holes, I slide my feet into my well-worn leather boots and toss my hair into a quick but cute braid. I want to look nice, but not necessarily like I'm *trying* to look nice.

Which is silly, since Orion's into Birdie and not the real me. He's into body glitter and flashing lights, not the stretch marks they both work to hide.

"I did it, Mama!" Maverick shouts, freeing me from my pity party.

"You sure did." His buttons are off by one, but he's so proud of himself that I let it go. "You look sharp, my man."

According to my weather app, it's a mild day, so I slip one of his hoodies into my bag instead of making him wear a jacket. "Ready?"

He giggles, and the sound settles the sea of anxiety churning within me. "I need shoes!"

I glance down at his feet and laugh. "I guess you do. Put 'em on."

"Can I wear the light up ones? I bet Orion will think they're so cool. And they make me run really fast."

"Go for it."

He whoops in delight before grabbing his shoes and putting them on. "Ready!"

"Good, let's go."

We find Orion and Stella waiting in the living room—well, Orion's waiting, Stella's still rocking her pajamas.

"Aren't you coming, too?" I ask, hoping like hell she says yes, because I need a buffer between me and this man. You know, other than my four-year-old, who pretty much thinks Orion hung the sun.

Stella coughs, and I swear to God, it's faker than ninety percent of my coworkers' tits. "I'm sick."

"Oh, really?"

She nods and dabs at her nose with a tissue.

I narrow my eyes and she widens hers, rearranging her face into one of pure innocence.

Oblivious to her subterfuge, Maverick gasps and runs out of the room. "I hope you feel better, but I don't want your yucky germs. We're making Jell-O at school tomorrow, and Miss Jenna is letting us mix the flavors!"

To her credit, Stella never breaks character. "I understand," she murmurs sadly, sniffling and coughing a few more times.

Orion scratches the back of his neck and then checks the time on his phone. "Well... We better get going if we want to beat the crowd."

The three of us tell Stella goodbye and then head outside.

"My truck or—"

"Maverick's still in a booster seat."

"I can put it in my truck."

"Are you sure?"

"Mama!" Maverick shouts, running circles around us. "Look how tall his truck is! I bet you'd need a ladder to get in!"

"Then you would, too." I raise my brows.

"Nu-uh!" He adopts his power pose, with one hand on his hip and the other raised with his fist toward the sky. "I have superpowers!"

I laugh, wishing he could stay this innocent forever. "I should have known."

He nods solemnly. "Now you know."

"Give me your keys, and I'll grab his seat."

"Oh. Um." Suddenly, I'm flush with embarrassment. Here he is with a jacked-up truck with all the bells and whistles, and here I am with a car that doesn't even have power locks or windows. "Sure."

Ever the gentleman, Orion doesn't utter a single word about how old my car is. He doesn't even pull a face.

I watch as he moves the seat, torn between making sure he latches it properly and watching the way his back muscles flex and bunch as he tightens the straps.

"You wanna check this?" he asks once he's done.

I snap to attention. "Yes, please." I move to step around him, but freeze at the feeling of his hands on my hips. "Orion?" My voice comes out all soft and breathy.

I swear to God, he's trying to drive me insane. He has to be.

"Just giving you a boost," he murmurs, lifting me from the ground and onto his running board. "You know, since I don't have a ladder."

Maverick giggles, and the sound instantly douses my topsy-turvy libido in ice water—*thank God.*

I take my time checking the latches, not because they're questionable, but because I know my cheeks are the color of a tomato. Finally, when I can't put it off anymore, I give my seal of approval. "Looks good."

But before I can climb down, Orion grips my hips again and lowers me to the ground. I stumble out of the way, and then he lifts Maverick into the truck and buckles him, not once hesitating.

His confidence with my son is such a freaking turn-on that I find myself zoning out, imagining we were a real family, instead of heading for the passenger seat.

Something I immediately regret when Orion steps down and grabs my hand. "C'mon, little mama, your turn."

My insides turn to downright mush at the words *little mama*, a fact I am studiously trying to ignore. I know I have no right to feel any kind of way about this man, because the months-long history we share has only ever happened in a darkened room.

And because I have the worst luck in the world, he has no idea the dancer he keeps coming to see is me.

"Oh, no." I try to step away, knowing that if he touches me anywhere else, my gooey insides will go straight-up molten. "I've got it."

"Humor me." He tightens his hold and tugs me forward.

The momentum is too much, and I have to brace my free hand against his shoulder to keep from face-planting into his chest.

"Are you okay?" he asks, close enough that I can feel the timbre of his voice all the way down to my toes.

"Frankie?" he asks when I don't reply.

I'm too busy trying to decide whether I should run for the hills or dive into the temptation that is Orion Cartwright.

"What?" I ask when I finally manage to get my wits about me.

"Let me help you into the cab," he murmurs, following my retreat. "I'd hate for you to fall and get hurt."

"Okay." I turn my head to the side and suck in a lungful of air, determined to get my body and heart under control. He's just a man—*a stupidly attractive man*—but flesh and bone, all the same.

Orion winks as he grabs my hand once again. This time, I allow him to lead me around the front of the truck.

He looks back at me with a Colgate-worthy smile before

opening the door. This time, when he grips my hips, I'm ready for him. I don't jump or gasp. I'm cool, calm, and collected as he lifts me into my seat like I weigh nothing.

My body's listening to my *heel* command—that is, until he steps up onto the running board and leans so far into my space, he's all I can see.

"Um." I swallow thickly. "What are you doing?"

"Safety first," comes his deep, rumbly reply as he grabs my seat belt and stretches it across my chest.

His hand brushes over the valley between my breasts, and I swear to God, it takes every ounce of my willpower not to scramble over the console and into the back seat.

He's freaking driving me crazy.

He clicks the buckle into place and then grins, victorious. The whole encounter is probably only seconds, but it feels like hours. "Y'all ready?"

I try to nod, but Maverick beats me to it. "Yes! I'm starving. I haven't had no food since breakfast and that was *hours* ago!"

God love him, for both his ability to lighten the mood and his bottomless pit of a stomach.

"Guess we better hurry." His body sways toward mine, and I tense. But he merely tugs on my seat belt one more time, making sure it's secure, before stepping down and heading around to the driver's side.

God help me, I say silently, because I really think I'm going to need some divine intervention to not lose my head —or my heart—around this man.

"SOOOO," Stella hums as she drops onto the barstool next to me, a mug of coffee clutched between her hands.

"So what?" I mutter, only one cup of coffee into my Monday. By some miracle, it's 6:15 a.m. and Maverick is still asleep. I guess our big day yesterday really wore him out.

Too bad I slept like shit, thanks largely to thoughts of my hottie down the hall keeping me awake.

"How was your park date?"

"Wasn't a date," I grumble, nowhere near caffeinated enough for Stella's level of pep, much less this conversation.

"Pretty sure it was." She drums her sparkly nails against her mug.

"It definitely wasn't." My prickliness puts most people off, and yet, for some reason, my little ball-of-sunshine roommate seems immune.

"Did he drive?" she asks.

"Yes."

She taps her index finger against her chin. "Did he buy y'all lunch?"

"What does it matter?" I ask defensively. So what if Orion bought our lunch, carousel tickets, and hot cocoa after?

"Oh, no." She shakes her head. "It doesn't matter. It just..."

"Just what?"

Her lips curl into a satisfied smile. "Just sounds like a date."

"Well, it wasn't." *I mean, I would know if I went on a date, right?*

"Whatever you have to tell yourself."

I want to snap at her to mind her own business, but deep down, I know she doesn't mean any harm. Teasing and meddling is Stella's love language. So, instead, I scoot my barstool back and refill my mug.

"Seriously, though, did y'all have fun?"

With my back to her, I allow the smile I've been fighting to take over. Yesterday was...*everything.*

My sweet boy had more fun at the park with Orion than he's had in...I don't know...*years.*

Don't get me wrong, he and I always have a good time, but Orion was the star of the show. He chased him faster and longer, wrestled with him, played tag, hide and seek, and rode the carousel with him—twice.

"According to Mav, it was the best day ever."

Stella hums thoughtfully. "And according to you?"

My earlier smile wilts. "It was..." I want to say confusing, but Stella doesn't need the bait. She's already relentless in her pursuit to crash through my every wall.

Not to mention, the last thing I want to discuss with her is my complicated feelings toward her brother.

"Was what?" she says from right behind me, startling me.

"Jesus Christ, are you, like, part ninja?"

"Maybe in a past life." She nudges me out of the way with her hip and grabs the carafe to refill her cup. "But we're not talking about me. We're talking about you."

"Do we have to?"

Stella places her mug down and hops up onto the counter, swinging her feet as she regards me. "Obviously."

"You're relentless," I complain, but she just smiles. "Like a tornado disguised as a sunrise."

A gasp escapes her as she presses her free hand to her heart. "That's, like, the nicest thing you've ever said to me."

"You're deranged."

"That sounds more like you."

Before I can reply, my alarm sounds. "Oh, lookie there, I've gotta get Maverick up for school."

"This conversation isn't over, Frankie."

I drain the last of my coffee, place my mug into the sink, and scurry back to my room. Because if I know Stella like I think I do, she's right...

This conversation is far from over, because she's going to hound me for details until I break.

Wearing people down seems to be a Cartwright family trait, but unlike her brother, Stella is vividly aware of her highly inconvenient superpower.

Lucky me.

BY THE TIME my art class rolls around, I'm sweating bullets.

Knowing Stella, the only reason she hasn't spent the day hounding me via text is because she's trying to lull me into a false sense of security.

Well, I'm not falling for it.

Except, in class, she doesn't so much as utter a word about her brother. She doesn't needle or pry. She doesn't even mention his name.

Clearly, she's laying a trap and hoping I'm dumb enough to walk into it.

But I know what she's doing.

"Do you have lunch plans?" she asks as the class comes to an end.

Immediately, I'm on high alert. "Why?"

She rolls her eyes. "Can't a girl ask her friend to lunch?"

"Of course, *a girl* can, but I'm wondering why *you* are."

Stella links her arm with mine. "Why does there need to be a reason? Maybe I just want to hang out."

"We literally live together."

She scoffs. "But Maverick is your priority, and I spend a lot of time with Samson and Emmy."

"Oh my God. Fine. Let's grab lunch."

"Yay!" Stella squeals, happily dragging me toward the dining hall. She makes a beeline for the burger bar. At least she's letting me get something tasty before she drags every last detail out of me.

Which she does, with both startling speed and accuracy. Or maybe I'm just that desperate for a listening ear. Who knows? Either way, I sing like a canary.

"He really played with Maverick all day?"

"All. Day. I may as well have been chopped liver with the way those two carried on."

"How does that make you feel?"

I shrug and pop a fry into my mouth. "Confused, mostly."

"I get that."

"Do you?" I ask, but she simply gestures for me to keep

going. "This probably isn't very surprising, but I don't let a lot of people in."

"No," Stella drawls, "you don't say."

"But somehow, you and Orion crept right in, and a part of me is so thankful not to be alone anymore."

"And the other part?"

I look down at the table, not wanting to see the pity on her face when I answer. "The other part is waiting for it to all be ripped away."

"Oh, Frankie." Stella clasps my hand between hers. "I hate to break it to you, but I'm a long-haul kind of friend. And like, really hard to get rid of."

Despite my best efforts not to, I smile. Because that's what Stella does—she parts people's clouds with her bright, sunshiny smile and relentless optimism.

"It's hard though, you know? I've been alone most of my life, and while I could probably handle losing y'all, I don't know that Maverick could."

"First of all, rude." Stella drops my hand so that she can count off her points, like somehow holding her fingers up as she rattles them off makes the words mean more. "Second, you would be devastated to lose me, so quit lying to yourself." She holds up another finger. "And while I can't technically speak for Orion, I'm going to anyway, and say I don't think you need to worry about losing him, either. I've never seen him act like he does with you."

"What do you mean?" I ask, my food forgotten.

"Did you know that my brother hates kids?"

"What?" Visions of him playing with Mav play like a movie reel in my mind. "He loves kids."

"No." Stella shakes her head, her eyes never leaving mine. "He likes *your* kid."

"That's crazy."

She lifts one perfectly arched brow. "Is it?"

"Definitely." I don't know if she bumped her head and has short-term memory loss or what, but from the moment they met, Orion and Maverick have just clicked. You can't fake that kind of affection.

"Ask him," Stella challenges. "If you don't believe me, ask him."

"Maybe I will." I won't—I just really want her to drop the subject, because it's making my skin itch.

"Good." Stella takes a big slurp of her drink and then turns back to me. "Oh, hey, what are you doing on Sunday? You're off, right?"

"Um, yeah." A small part of me worries something bad is coming, but I squash it down. I can't spend my whole life waiting for the other shoe to drop. Plus, friends ask friends their plans all the time. "Why?"

"My parents do a big dinner every Sunday, and I was wondering if you and Maverick wanted to tag along? They have a huge yard and my mom's food is so. Dang. Good."

"I wouldn't want to intrude..." Not to mention, what if his mom is mad he didn't make it last week?

"You wouldn't be." Stella grabs my hand again and squeezes it softly. "Promise."

"Are you sure?"

"Mom's philosophy is the more the merrier. Just say yes, please?"

"Fine. Yes," I relent, already begging the universe not to make me regret it.

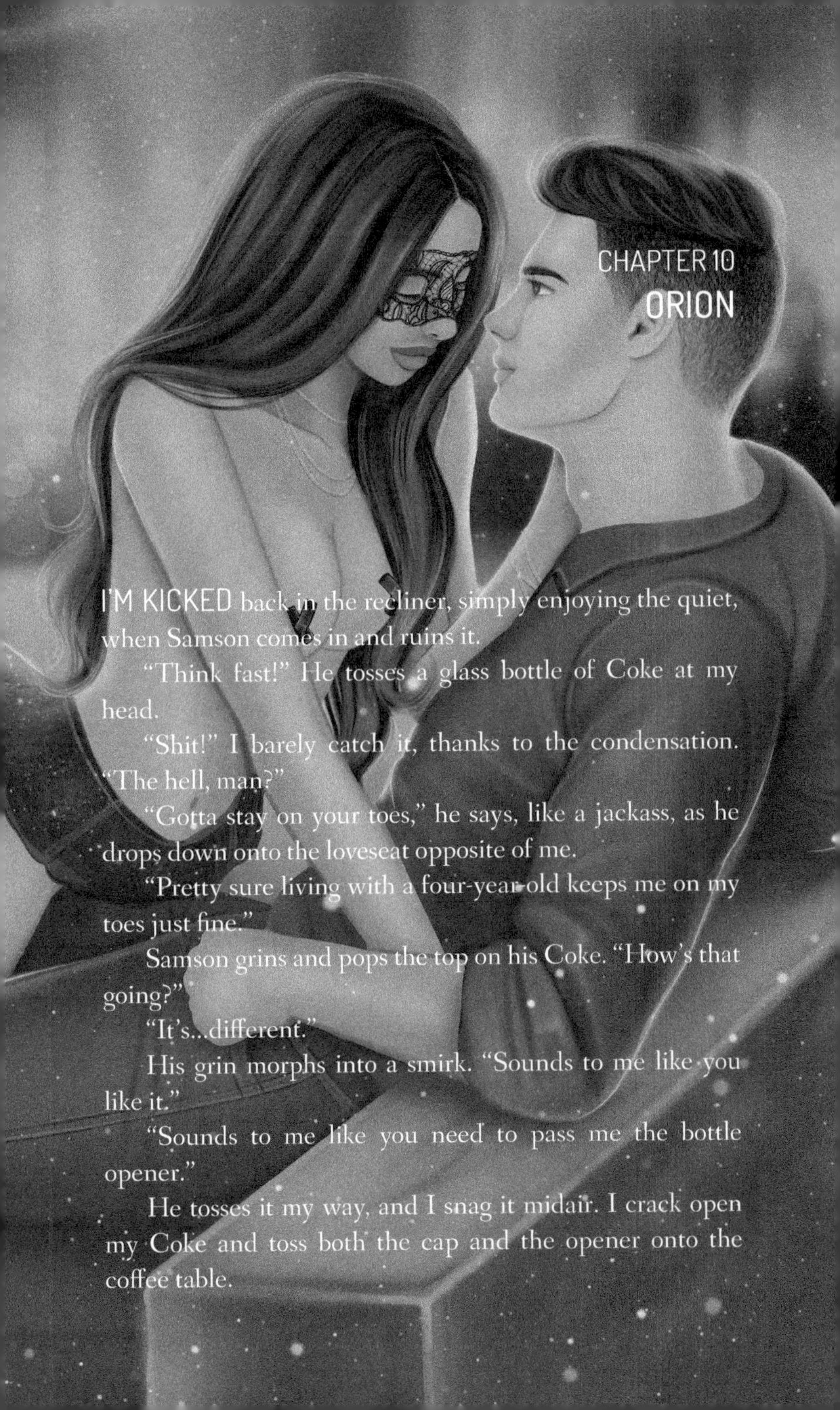

I'M KICKED back in the recliner, simply enjoying the quiet, when Samson comes in and ruins it.

"Think fast!" He tosses a glass bottle of Coke at my head.

"Shit!" I barely catch it, thanks to the condensation. "The hell, man?"

"Gotta stay on your toes," he says, like a jackass, as he drops down onto the loveseat opposite of me.

"Pretty sure living with a four-year-old keeps me on my toes just fine."

Samson grins and pops the top on his Coke. "How's that going?"

"It's...different."

His grin morphs into a smirk. "Sounds to me like you like it."

"Sounds to me like you need to pass me the bottle opener."

He tosses it my way, and I snag it midair. I crack open my Coke and toss both the cap and the opener onto the coffee table.

"Seriously, man—Stella says you're pretty gone over the kid."

"He's all right." I'm fucking lying though—Maverick's cool as hell. It's his mom that has me all twisted up.

"What about Frankie?" Samson asks, like he's able to read my mind.

"What about her?" My gruff tone isn't fooling anyone, much less my oldest friend. He knows me like the back of his hand.

"She just…" I don't even know how to put it into words. She's so fucking down to earth, and watching her with Maverick sets off some sort of caveman instinct I didn't even know I had. Every time I see the two of them, I want to claim them as *mine*, which is insane. I barely know the woman.

But at the same time, it feels like I've known her forever.

And don't even get me started on the long nights I've spent wide awake the past week, jerking off to the thought of her in her tiny sleep shorts.

Typically, a night or two at ATF would be all the distraction I'd need, but we broke ground on a big project this week, and I've been too damn tired to do anything after work.

"You like her?" Samson asks when I never finish my train of thought.

I pinch the bridge of my nose. "She's making me fucking crazy."

"They typically do."

"What's that supposed to mean?"

"You'll see." Samson shakes his head as he huffs out a laugh through his nose. "What about your stripper?"

I groan and he smiles, like discussing my fucked-up love life is the most entertainment he's had all week.

"Honestly, man? It's all a mess. I'm just glad to spend time with family tonight...to get a break from it all."

Samson doesn't say a word. Not a single word.

"Where is Stella, anyway?"

He rubs both hands over his face as he drops his head onto the cushion behind him. "You'll see."

"Not so sure I like the sound of that," I mumble to myself.

Samson barks out a laugh. "Not so sure it matters."

Before I can question him any further, the sound of the front door opening stops me in my tracks.

"Mom," Stella calls, already heading toward the kitchen. "We're here!"

We're here.

I glare at Samson. The fucker sat here and listened while I said I was grateful for a break, knowing good and well that Stella invited them to dinner.

"Oh, good," Mom calls back. "I need a taste tester for my new cookie recipe."

"Cookies?" I hear Maverick ask, his voice bubbling with excitement.

The sound of their footsteps grows closer, and even though Samson stands to join them, I remain seated with my eyes glued to my phone. Fuck this.

I wanted one night of peace, one night to get my head on straight, and here Frankie is. It's like the universe is shoving her in my face over and over, and I'm honestly not quite sure what to do about it.

Or even if I *should* do anything about it.

Instead of being the bigger person and joining everyone, I sit and stew. How in the hell did my one night of relaxation end up so off course? I mean, is a little solitude really too much to ask for?

Apparently, it is, because not even two minutes later, Maverick launches himself onto my lap.

"Orion! I didn't know you were here!" He hooks his arms around my neck and lays his head on my shoulder. "This is the best night ever."

And just like that, my frustration melts away.

"Oh, yeah?" I ask, wrapping my arms around his middle.

"Yeah! I didn't think I was gonna see you, but you're here!"

My lips lift in an involuntary smile. "I'm here."

He snuggles closer. "I missed you."

Fuck.

I'm pretty sure my heart just shattered in my chest. This kid—he's too much.

"Missed you, too," I mumble into his hair, my voice more gruff than usual.

"Mama said you was working all week, and that's why you weren't home."

"That's right. It was a busy week, but I shouldn't have to work as late this week."

He pulls back and looks at me with hope filled eyes. "You'll be home before I go to sleep?"

Another little piece of my heart just chipped off. "I'll do my best, bud."

"Okay, good." He lays back down on my chest. "Mama comes home late when she works, too, but she wakes me up and snuggles me so I know she's home. Maybe...maybe you could wake me up, too?"

Is he actually trying to kill me? He has to be.

"That's..." I swallow roughly. "Um...that's between you and your mom, okay?"

Maverick seems to think there's no time like the present

to ask his mom, because he scrambles out of my lap like his ass is on fire. "Mama!" he shouts as he hightails it back into the kitchen.

"Whoa, bud!" I jump up and take off after him.

"Inside voice," Frankie murmurs, dropping down to her knees to intercept him. He flings himself into her arms, much the same way he did to me in the living room. "Orion said I gots to ask you if he can come tell me good night if I'm already asleep when he gets home. Can he? Please say yes!"

Frankie's cheeks turn redder than the tomatoes Mom's currently chopping for the salad. "Maverick!" Her eyes are the size of dinner plates. "What?"

"It's just...you always tell me good night when you work late and I—"

"Can...can we talk about this later?" Frankie asks, an edge of hysteria to her voice.

Stella and Samson exchange a knowing glance while my mom stares me down, a million unspoken questions in her eyes.

"Dinner's ready!" Mom announces. "Maverick, would you like to help Stella set the table?"

Frankie shoots her a grateful look.

"Set the table?" Maverick's nose crinkles. "What's that mean?"

"C'mon, dude." Stella hands him a stack of napkins while she grabs the utensils and Samson grabs the plates. "I'll show you."

As soon as they're clear of the room, Frankie starts apologizing. "I'm so, *so* sorry. He's just—"

"Sweet as dang pie," my mom says, cutting her off.

Frankie nods hesitantly, but agrees. "He is sweet." Then she turns to me. "Orion, I promise you don't need to wake him up, tuck him in, any of that. I'm sorry he put you in an uncomfortable position. I'll talk to him about it later tonight, okay?"

I shouldn't—*I know I shouldn't*—and yet when I open my mouth, the exact words I didn't want to say are the ones that come out. "It's not a big deal. And if it means that much to him, I'm happy to do it."

Her eyes fill with tears, but she manages to keep them at bay. "I promise—" Her voice cracks, and I swear I feel it deep inside of me. "You don't have to."

"What if I said I wanted to?" I ask, wondering who in the hell is in charge of the words coming out of my mouth. Because none of this shit is what my brain is relaying.

My mom, to her credit, is doing a wonderful job of pretending to not pay us any attention, but the woman is like a sponge, and I know for damn sure she's soaking up every single word.

"Do you?" Frankie whispers, looking more unsure than I've ever seen her look.

No doubt, I'm about to spew some other sappy bullshit I don't want to say, but my dad walks in, thankfully putting an end to my verbal vomit.

"Smells good, Lizzie dear."

Mom smiles and meets him in the doorway. "Made your favorite."

"Lasagna." He makes a big show of patting his stomach before leaning down to press a kiss to her lips. As he pulls away, he notices Frankie standing awkwardly next to me. "And who do we have here?"

"Frankie Townsend, sir." She steps around me and holds out her hand.

I watch, amused, waiting for Dad to shake her hand, but it seems like we're all out of sorts tonight, because instead he pulls her in for a hug. "Nice to meet you."

She pats his back twice before slinking out of his hold.

"Son." The smirk on his face as he pauses tells me all I need to know. I'm not going to like whatever it is he's about to say. "You couldn't have picked a better night to bring your...*friend*." He turns back to Frankie. "My Lizzie's lasagna is the best thing in the entire world. You're in for a treat."

"Oh, um. Stella invited me, actually."

Dad looks between the two of us, and then over to my mom, the two of them having some kind of silent conversation, until finally, he nods.

"Just wait until you meet Maverick," Mom says, and then turns to me. "Orion, can you grab the pan from the oven and bring it to the table with you?"

"Sure thing, Mom."

She smiles and then links her arm with Frankie's. "Come on, let's get you seated."

"Oh, and, Michael, grab the—"

"Salad." He holds up the wooden bowl. "I know, dear."

He waits a few seconds and then spins to face me. "So..."

"So what?"

"Frankie, huh?"

"She's Stella's friend." I give him my back as I grab the baking dish from the oven.

He gives a noncommittal hum. "Whatever you say, son."

"She's—" But when I turn around, he's already gone.

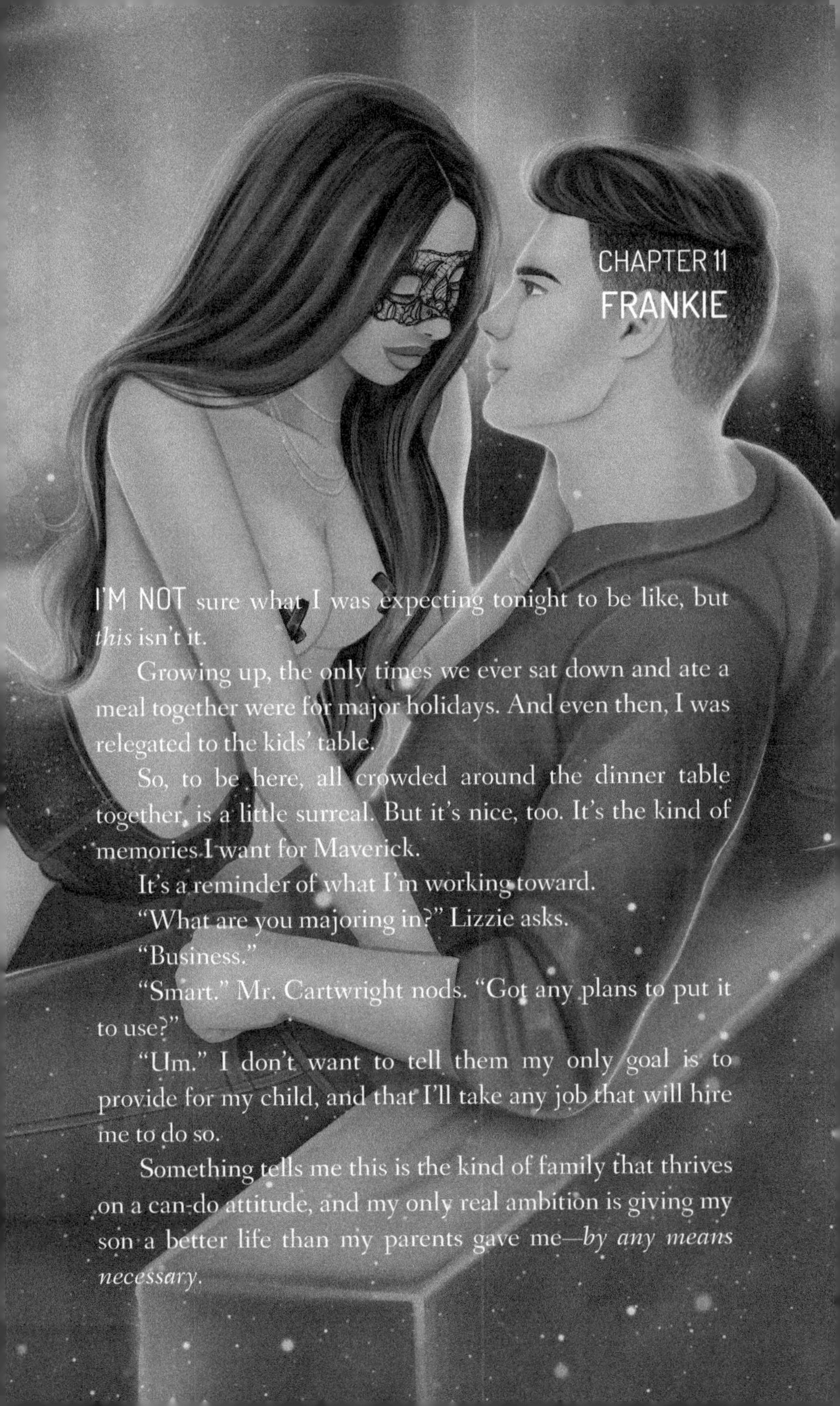

I'M NOT sure what I was expecting tonight to be like, but *this* isn't it.

Growing up, the only times we ever sat down and ate a meal together were for major holidays. And even then, I was relegated to the kids' table.

So, to be here, all crowded around the dinner table together, is a little surreal. But it's nice, too. It's the kind of memories I want for Maverick.

It's a reminder of what I'm working toward.

"What are you majoring in?" Lizzie asks.

"Business."

"Smart." Mr. Cartwright nods. "Got any plans to put it to use?"

"Um." I don't want to tell them my only goal is to provide for my child, and that I'll take any job that will hire me to do so.

Something tells me this is the kind of family that thrives on a can-do attitude, and my only real ambition is giving my son a better life than my parents gave me—*by any means necessary.*

Luckily, Orion waltzes in with a giant dish of lasagna before I can formulate a reply.

We all take turns passing around the salad bowl and bread basket before loading up our plates with heaping slices of the ooey-gooey cheesy lasagna.

The smell alone is nearly enough to make me moan in delight, but when that first bite hits my tongue, well... This certainly isn't Stouffer's.

Even Maverick is gobbling it up. And even better, we're all so preoccupied with eating that the spotlight is blessedly off me.

Until Lizzie polishes off her last bite and daintily wipes her mouth with a cloth napkin. "How old are you, Frankie?"

"Twenty-one."

"I'm four," Maverick adds.

Lizzie fawns appropriately, pressing her hand to her chest. "My goodness, I thought you were *at least* five."

My son smiles proudly. "And my favorite color is green. I like Spiderman and Paw Patrol, and my uncle says I'm as strong as the Hulk!"

"Goodness." Mrs. Cartwright smiles. "Do you see your uncle often?"

"No." Maverick's sauce-covered lips turn down into a forlorn pout. "He's on tour."

"On tour?" Stella's head tips to the side. "What kind of tour?"

"Yeah!" Mav bounces in his seat, his excitement nearly bubbling over. "He's famous! What's his band called again, Mama?"

Six sets of eyes watch me expectantly as I try to think of some way to change the subject. It's not even that I think anyone here will follow Phin's band—it's just once people realize I'm related to someone famous, it tends to be all they want to talk about with me.

I love my brother, truly, with every ounce of my heart—but sometimes it feels good not to be in his shadow.

"Um." I move what's left of my lasagna around on my plate. "He's the lead singer for My Darkest Hour."

When no one reacts—outwardly at least—I allow myself to relax back into my chair.

"What about your dad?" Lizzie asks. "Do you see him often?"

Her seemingly innocent question renders me immobile. My vision blurs and my heart pounds, my chest suddenly feeling too small to contain the jagged, battered organ. I need to inhale, to breathe, but I can't seem to remember how.

"Frankie?" someone asks, but it's like I'm inside of a bubble and everything around me is muffled...distorted.

I know I need to open up more about Tyson, to talk to Maverick about his dad, but it—it hurts. And God, I know that makes me so selfish, but the thought of Mav hurting the way I do—it's unbearable.

But then my son speaks. "He's dead." And with those two softly spoken words, my bubble pops, and everything comes rushing back.

My lungs ache as I heave in air. I went from unable to breathe to choking on every inhale. It feels like my entire chest is on fire. It feels like I'm losing him all over again.

"Excuse me." I push my chair back from the table and take off toward the front door.

The sound of another chair moving over the floor is the last thing I hear before escaping to the porch and curling into a ball in the first chair I find—an oversized rocker.

Moments later, the front door opens again, but I keep

my face buried in my knees, my tears staining my dark jeans.

"Frankie," Orion murmurs, but I don't look his way. I'm sure he thinks I'm nuts. His whole family probably does.

At the very least, they must think I'm a horrible mother. "Maverick! I just—"

Orion scoops me up into his arms and sits, arranging me on his lap. "He's fine. Stella took him to see her favorite climbing tree. It's where she met Samson."

"I just left him. I got up and ran and *left my son*."

"Baby, no." Orion strokes his hand up and down my back in a soothing motion. "You didn't leave him. You needed a minute to gather yourself, and he was in good hands. We would never let anything happen to him. You know that, right?"

I nod, because I do, but the knowledge doesn't ease the guilt gnawing away at my heart.

All I want is for Maverick to have a good life—for him to be happy, healthy, and loved, but I seem to keep screwing things up at every turn.

Maybe my parents are right about me after all...

"Right about what?" Orion asks, and my cheeks burn because I definitely did not mean to say that out loud. "Talk to me."

"When I got pregnant with Mav, they tried getting me to give him up for adoption, and maybe—"

"No!" Orion cuts me off, his voice harder than I've ever heard it. "Absolutely not."

"But—"

"Frankie, baby." He cups my cheeks and tips my face up toward his. "I need you to listen to me, okay? To really listen."

I nod.

"You are an amazing mother. You put that kid first in everything you do. Your love for him might as well be a flashing neon sign. Anyone who's spent more than a minute with the two of you knows how much you care about your son. Do not, for even one fucking second, doubt yourself when it comes to Mav, okay?"

Big, fat tears roll down my cheeks as I stare up at him, unable to speak.

"Okay?" he asks again, and this time, I nod.

"I want to hear your words. I need to know that you understand me, that you understand and *believe* that you're a great mom."

"I-I hear you." I sniffle and then let out a shaky exhale.

"Say it. Say out loud that you're the best mom Maverick could have."

"I'm the best mom Maverick could have." I say the words through hiccuping sobs, but once I do, I feel lighter. Like some of the weight pushing down on me has been lifted.

"You okay?" Orion asks, brushing his thumbs beneath my eyes to clear away the tears.

"Yeah, I think so." I offer him a weak smile. "Thank you."

He looks down at me with so much warmth in his eyes, I swear I can feel it wrapping around me like a hug. "Always, Frankie. Always."

For a second, we just sit here, with me on his lap and his hands still cupping my cheeks, and I swear it's as if time grinds to a halt. Everything else ceases to exist—it's just us.

But then, he speaks again, popping the bubble of solitude surrounding us. "You wanna talk about it?"

I try to swallow but my throat feels like it's full of

broken glass. "About what?" I don't know why I bother asking; I already know what he's going to say.

"Maverick's dad." Orion strokes his thumbs over my cheeks one last time before dropping his hands to my thighs.

His touch isn't sexual in the least, but I can feel the warmth of his hands through the material of my jeans, and it sets off a whole swarm of butterflies in my tummy.

"It's hard." I nibble my lower lip, waiting for the agony of remembering to hit. Only instead of the debilitating pain I've come to depend on, this time it's more of a prickle of awareness; uncomfortable for sure, but not all encompassing. "Tyson was my best friend in the whole world."

"Tell me about him," Orion murmurs, his voice low and soft in my ear.

"He was larger than life. The life of the party anywhere he went. We were inseparable. Everyone who knew him, loved him." I laugh, but there's no warmth or humor in it. "Except my parents. They never liked him—but they never liked me either, so..."

Orion tenses beneath me. "What's that even mean?"

"My parents are..." I suck in a deep breath and hold it as I weigh my words. "Pretentious. Judgmental. Horrible. Pick a word, they all fit. They didn't like Tyson because of his zip code."

"And why didn't they like you?" Orion's fingers flex against my hips, like he wants to hold me but isn't sure if he should.

"Long story short, Mom cheated, and I am the unhappy byproduct of her affair with my dad's old business partner. Once my dad—who I'm named after—discovered the truth, it was easier to take it out on me than on his wife. Needless to say, we aren't close."

I don't even realize I'm crying again until Orion reaches up and wipes away my tears.

"You're so damn strong, Frankie."

"Am I? Because I'm pretty sure I'm having an emotional breakdown in your lap, on your parents' front porch, while your sister watches my son."

"That's what happens when you bottle things up, baby." He hauls me closer, nestling my head into the crook of his neck. It doesn't escape my notice that he keeps calling me baby, but I'm not in the right frame of mind to figure that out. "You explode."

"I guess so." Idly, I rub the soft material of his shirt between my thumb and index finger. "We were never together, you know."

"What do you mean?"

"Tyson and me. We weren't together. He was my best friend. And we were both virgins and decided to just go for it—and then, I became the most cliché statistic ever."

"Are you telling me he knocked you up the first time y'all had sex?"

"First and only," I whisper.

I can feel Orion's throat bob as he swallows. "Like you and him only had sex once or—no, fuck it. It's not my business."

My cheeks burn hotter than the sun, but despite my embarrassment, I find myself giving him the clarification he seeks. "Meaning I've only had sex once."

"Jesus fucking Christ," he mutters. "You're killing me."

"Sorry." I try to pull away from him, but instead of releasing me, Orion tightens his hold.

"Don't apologize to me, not about this." He adjusts me ever so slightly on his lap, and I could swear something solid brushes against my ass.

But surely he isn't hard right now. *Get a grip, Frankie, it was probably only his phone.*

"Is...is it okay if I ask how he died?"

"He died the day Maverick was born." My stomach hollows, and my heart clenches in my chest. "I-I went into labor early and called him as they were admitting me." My tears may as well be twin rivers streaming down my cheeks. "He left work to meet me at the hospital, but ended up getting T-boned two blocks away."

I'm ugly crying now, heaving and panting and hiccuping as the familiar pain opens like a chasm inside of me.

"Shh, baby, it's okay," Orion murmurs, rocking us softly as he rubs my back.

"They said he died instantly. He never knew his son, and thanks to me, his son doesn't know him. God, I'm awful, aren't I?"

My question hangs in the air between us, and Orion's silence in the wake of it feels a lot like he agrees but is too polite to say it out loud. I want so badly to pull away from him, to grab Maverick so that we can run and never look back, but somehow, in his arms I feel safer and more at peace than I ever have.

Which is ridiculous.

"You're human." His voice is rough—raw—like there's sandpaper lining his throat.

"What?" I lift my face from his chest, cringing at the damp patch my tears made.

"You're not awful." This time he sounds steady. Firm. "You're human. Humans make mistakes, but you can also fix it, Frankie. It's not too late to open up to Maverick about his dad. It's never too late."

"You really mean that?"

"I really, really do."

"Thank you. For tonight. For listening. For everything."

"Anytime, Frankie." He presses a featherlight kiss to my forehead. "And I'm not just saying that either. Any time you need to talk it out, I'm here for you, okay?"

I sniffle as I nod.

"Words."

"Okay."

With soft movements, he scoots me out of his lap and helps me to my feet before standing himself. "Now, let's go find Maverick, so we can get some of the cookies Mom made."

I groan at the thought of facing everyone after the way I behaved.

"Don't worry about it. No one's gonna think any differently of you. Promise."

"You can't make promises for other people."

"Fine." He crosses his strong arms over his chest. "If anyone says shit, you can have my cookies."

Even though my sadness lingers, I feel my lips lift into a grin. "Deal."

"All right, now, let's go before Stella teaches him how to climb to the top." He starts off down the porch, and I eagerly follow. "She ever tell you how she met Samson?"

"No..."

He laughs. "C'mon, I'll tell you on the way."

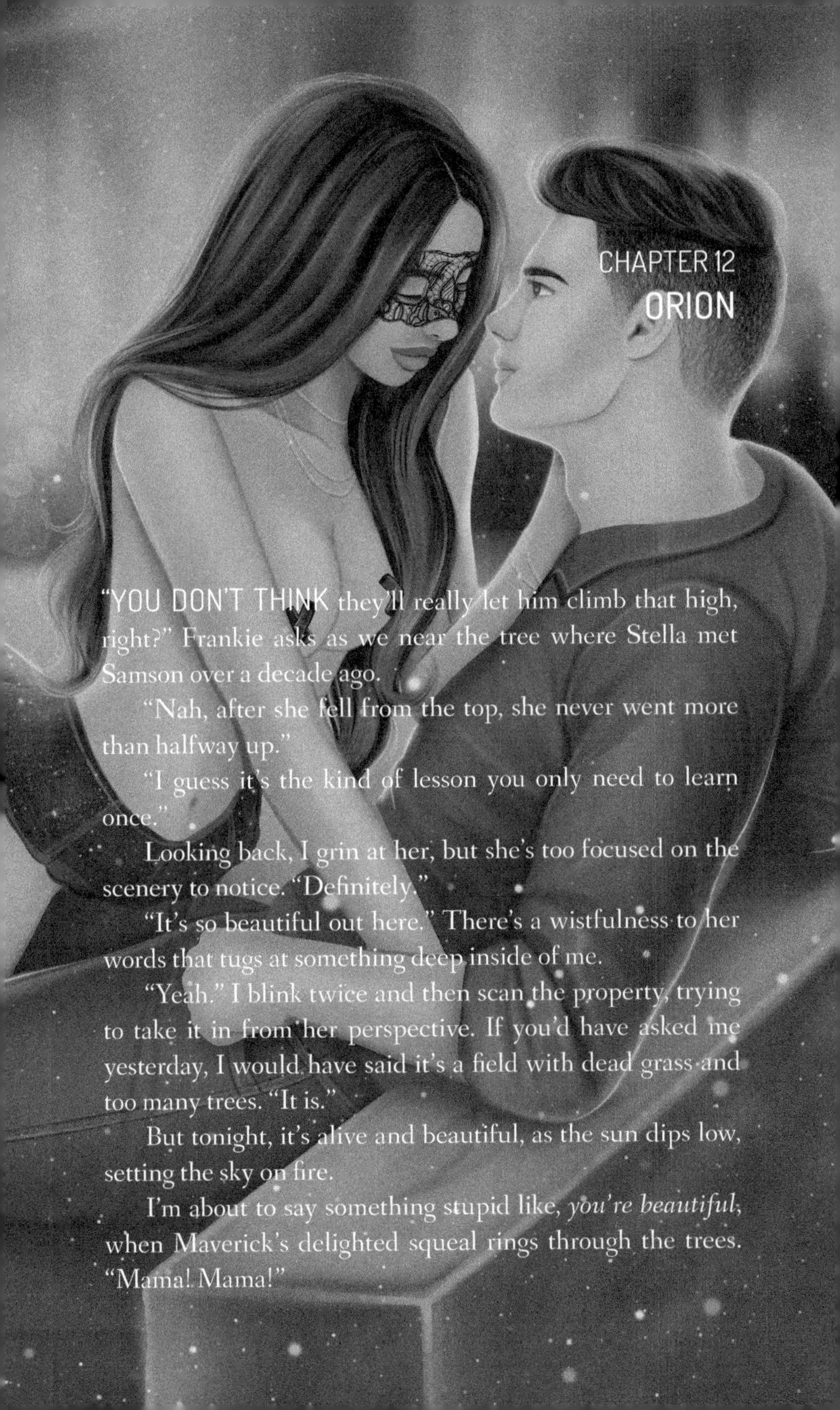

"YOU DON'T THINK they'll really let him climb that high, right?" Frankie asks as we near the tree where Stella met Samson over a decade ago.

"Nah, after she fell from the top, she never went more than halfway up."

"I guess it's the kind of lesson you only need to learn once."

Looking back, I grin at her, but she's too focused on the scenery to notice. "Definitely."

"It's so beautiful out here." There's a wistfulness to her words that tugs at something deep inside of me.

"Yeah." I blink twice and then scan the property, trying to take it in from her perspective. If you'd have asked me yesterday, I would have said it's a field with dead grass and too many trees. "It is."

But tonight, it's alive and beautiful, as the sun dips low, setting the sky on fire.

I'm about to say something stupid like, *you're beautiful*, when Maverick's delighted squeal rings through the trees. "Mama! Mama!"

Frankie's eyes widen as she looks around.

"Do you see me? Look up!"

I move to Frankie's side and direct her gaze toward the tree Maverick's calling to her from. "Right there."

She looks up and breaks out into a brilliant grin when she spots Maverick chilling on a branch with Stella bracing him.

"See how high I am, Mama?"

"I do, bud."

He turns and asks my sister something. She nods, and then the two of them start climbing down from the tree. They weren't too high up, so it's not any time before Maverick is running toward his mom.

The kid barrels into her full-speed, wrapping his arms around her middle while burying his face into her belly. "Are you still sad?"

Her entire face shutters as she sinks her slender fingers into his hair, holding him close. "I'm okay."

He wiggles his head until her hand falls away, and then looks up at her. "Promise?"

"I promise." Her throat bobs as she swallows. "And I'm sorry."

"For what?" His whole face scrunches.

"A lot of things, bud." She hugs him tight again. "For running out of there, for never talking about your dad with you. I'm so sorry, but I'm going to do better, okay?"

Maverick doesn't reply right away. I'm not sure if he's mulling over her words or if they're more than a four-year-old can comprehend.

"Can I ask a question?"

Frankie's lips quirk up into a shaky grin. "Just did."

He sighs and wiggles his whole body. "Mama!"

She releases him, and he plops onto his bottom, not caring one bit that the grass is cold and damp.

He pats the ground beside him, and without even a lick of hesitation, Frankie sits, too. "You never have to ask if you can talk to me, Mav. Anytime you want to ask or tell me something, you can. *Anytime.*" She stresses that last word.

Stella slips back into the copse of trees, and I'm half-tempted to sneak away and join her—to give Frankie and Maverick some privacy—except my feet are rooted in place. Don't ask me why, but for reasons unknown, I can't seem to walk away from these two.

Physically *or* metaphorically.

"Okay." Maverick nods a few times, like he's hyping himself up. "Did my dad like superheroes, too?"

It's nearly dark out, but there's just enough light left for me to make out the tears filling Frankie's eyes. "Batman was his favorite."

Maverick rears back, his brows nearly to his hairline and his jaw totally slack. "But Uncle Phin says Batman's a... a...*vigilante!*" Despite barely being able to say the word, he spits it out like it's a dirty word.

I know I shouldn't, but I have to interject. "Whoa, bud. Whoa."

They both whip around to face me, matching looks of surprise painting their features—almost like they forgot I was out here with them.

"It's true!" Maverick insists, jumping to his feet. "A'cause he doesn't have any powers."

"But he *is* a member of the Justice League. That's gotta count for something, right?"

"I don't know." He mulls over it, tapping his index finger against his chin. "I gotta ask Uncle Phin first."

"Mom called!" Stella hollers, stepping back into the clearing. "Cookies are ready!"

Maverick's eyes go wider than the moon overhead. "I want a cookie! Mama, please?"

Frankie nods, and he throws both arms into the air, cheering.

"C'mon," Samson says from behind Stella. "I'll give you another piggyback."

Maverick sprints over to where my sister and best friend stand, wasting no time scrambling up onto his back. "Let's go!"

Frankie watches with a wistful look on her face as the three of them trek toward the house.

"C'mon, little mama." I take a few steps closer and extend a hand down to her. "Mom's cookies are really good —especially fresh from the oven."

She doesn't hesitate, sliding her small hand into mine. Like every time we touch, a little zip of electricity moves from her skin to mine. It's fucking weird—and it's only ever happened with one other person.

Birdie.

Fuck. I haven't hardly thought about her this past week.

I shake off the thoughts of my Bluebird and focus on the woman at my side, whose hand is still in mine. Our fingers are twined together, like two middle schoolers, and yet... I don't hate it.

Not by a long shot.

We make the walk back to the house in near silence, save for the rustling of the wind and the chirping of crickets. It's a comfortable kind of quiet.

Instead of going back through the front door, I lead Frankie around back. It's closer, and the door everyone will expect us to use.

But before I can guide us up the porch steps, Frankie tugs on my hand. "You okay?" I ask, turning to face her.

She lowers her gaze and nibbles her lip. *She's nervous. Why?*

"Frankie." I release her hand and slide my fingers beneath her chin, drawing her pretty blue eyes back up to mine.

"Sorry. Yeah, I just..." She pinches her eyes closed and then blinks up at me with such a sad expression my heart fucking stutters in my chest. "I just wanted to apologize—again—for my behavior."

"I already told you that's not necessary." I stroke my thumb over the soft skin of her cheek, and ever so subtly, she leans into my touch.

"I also wanted to thank you."

"For what?"

"For being so understanding." She smiles softly. "Sweet. For being you, I guess."

"You don't need to thank me for that." I don't realize I've moved closer until my toes bump hers. But I'm fully in control as I splay my fingers from her jaw to her temple and lay my lips against hers in the softest kiss ever.

It's brief, over before it really begins, but damn if I don't feel it all the way to my toes.

"Orion." She whispers my name, sounding every bit as rattled as I feel.

I force my lips into a carefree grin and climb the steps two at a time. She watches me with wide eyes as I open the door. "Better hurry—cookies are getting cold."

AFTER A NIGHT OF SHITTY SLEEP, I'm up long before the sun. Which really sucks, because Maverick has finally started sleeping past six.

I don't know if it's because he's growing or if he subconsciously feels safer here; all I know is it's been nice waking up at a normal hour.

Thoughts of Orion plagued me most of the night—dreams of us in the VIP room mingled with actual memories, which morphed into nightmares of him realizing that Birdie and me are one and the same and flipping out.

And worse than all of that is, I swear I can still feel the tingle he caused when he kissed me last night on his parents' back porch.

What was he thinking?

I almost marched in and demanded an explanation, but after shoving three cookies down, he made an excuse and bailed, and I haven't seen him since.

So, now, it's been festering. Like an open wound.

And my mind's been picking and picking and picking at

it for so long that by the time four o'clock rolled around, I was wired.

"Fuck it," I mutter, grabbing my phone to check the time. Four-thirty.

Despite it feeling like an eternity, only half an hour has passed.

Coffee.

Coffee will make things better.

With slow, measured movements, I slide out of the bed and pad across the room. The last thing I want is for Maverick to wake up, especially before I've had a chance to sort out all of the swirling thoughts bumping around inside of my head.

I pause at the door, pressing my ear to the wood, listening for signs of life. But there's nothing. I'm good to go.

The hinges squeak as I nudge the door open, and I swear my heart leaps in my chest. But the house is still quiet.

Until I start the coffee maker. It gurgles to life, and I swear, the sounds coming from it are loud enough to wake the dead.

My heart is pounding like a kickdrum as I fumble for the cord and rip the plug from the wall, plunging the house back into silence.

After several deep breaths, I grab a bottle of water from the fridge and make a mad dash for the back porch. It's cold as hell, but my thick, cozy pajamas, along with the big fancy patio heater, will keep me warm.

I flip the switch on the heat and settle into the closest chair, drawing my legs up under me for extra heat.

The cold air nips at me as I stare out toward the towering mountain peaks, all of last night's thoughts continuing to torment me.

Namely, why on earth did he kiss me? The whole encounter was a minute at most, but those sixty freaking seconds are on a continuous loop in my brain.

How is it possible to be simultaneously filled with ecstasy and agony?

I know Orion's a good man—I've known it since the night we met in the VIP room at ATF. Most men would have tried to touch me, to take advantage, but he waited for my consent. Not just once, but every time.

And seeing him with Maverick, especially knowing he doesn't like kids, does all kinds of funny things to my heart.

Plain and simple, the man reduces me to goo.

He's a promise of happiness and a whisper of hurt all at the same time.

Risk versus reward.

Is pursuing Orion Cartwright worth risking my heart for the chance of a happily ever after?

As soon as I ask myself the question, tears fill my eyes. Because deep down, I already know the answer.

There's nothing on this earth worth jeopardizing my son's happiness.

I curl in on myself as the weight of reality crushes in on me from all sides. Orion's not mine—never has been and never will be. He's nothing to me.

He can't be.

Mav is already so attached. He would be shattered if things went poorly between us, and let's be real—they would. Everyone leaves.

And why would a man like him want to shackle himself to a woman like me? Stella said it herself—he doesn't even like kids, so clearly he's not shopping for a ready-made family.

Not to mention, aside from a brief peck on the mouth,

he's never given me—the *real* me—any indication that he's interested.

Maybe it's all in my head. Maybe I'm so desperate for affection that I'm seeing things—*feeling things*—that aren't really there.

That man could have any woman he wants, and I'd be an idiot to think for one single second that it's me.

Birdie, maybe. She's fun and sexy and bold. Confident... Everything I'm not.

Tears roll down my cheeks, dripping off my chin, as I mourn the loss of something I never had.

Stupid girl.

I know better than to let myself get attached. But it's better this way, to put him away in a box with *just friends* clearly marked on the label.

It's like my mom used to say, *there's a time and a place, Frankie, and this is neither the time or the place, so get it together.*

And so, as the sun begins to light the sky, I will myself to get a grip—on my heart, my mind, my feelings... My freaking life.

"Missing something?" a deep voice asks from behind me, sending my heart back into a frenzy.

"Orion!" I discreetly wipe away my tears as I twist around to face him. "You scared me."

"How?" He quirks a brow. "I called your name three times."

Heat rushes to my cheeks. "Did you?"

His lips kick up into a boyish grin. "Yup."

I blink twice, willing my heart to calm down. "Sorry. Is everything okay?"

"Yeah. Just figured I'd check on you." He slips past me and lowers himself into the chair to my right before placing two mugs down onto the table between us. "I figured you could use a cup. What'd the coffee maker do to you, anyway?"

My embarrassment grows. "Um." I lean forward and grab the coffee he brought me. The mug is warm against my chilled hands. I sip from it slowly, letting the hot liquid warm me from the inside out.

"Um..."

I lick my lips and divert my gaze to my lap. "It's a long story."

"One you're not going to share, huh?"

I shrug, and he huffs out a laugh.

"You're a tough nut to crack, Frankie."

"Not all nuts need cracking."

He regards me with an amused expression. "They do if you wanna get to the good stuff."

"The good stuff?" I ask, already regretting it. Curiosity killed the cat, and yet here I am, as curious as ever.

"You know..." He pins me with a loaded look. "The insides."

Something about his tone has *my* insides clenching with anticipation. Which is a no-go. Because *friends* don't evoke these kinds of feelings in each other. And that's all he can ever be to me.

If only my heart could fall in line. Stupid traitorous organ.

"Nuts are gross," I finally mutter, when nothing else comes to mind.

"Not mine." Orion's chest puffs out with the kind of confidence only men of caliber carry.

"Pervert." I force myself to sound disgusted, when really warmth is pooling low in my belly.

You'd think being a single mom, I'd have more experience with men. But I don't. I'm wildly inexperienced when it comes to men, and the thought of being anywhere near his nuts is enough to have my libido kicking into gear.

"Bet you'd like it." He keeps his voice low and his tone even, but my heart rate triples like he screamed it.

"Orion!" I wheeze his name, cutting my eyes his way.

"What?" His face is the picture of innocence. "I'm just speaking the truth."

"The truth?"

"Mmhmm." He licks his lips and leans forward, bracing his forearms on his knees.

He's looking at me like he wants to eat me alive, and if I hadn't just spent the last half hour lamenting every reason he and I would never work, I'd be tempted to offer myself up on a silver platter.

"Yeah, Frankie. The truth."

I know I'm going to regret asking him, but he has me enthralled, and he knows it. "What truth?"

"That we'd be good together," he says without missing a beat.

He's wrong though. *So, freaking wrong.* If given the chance, we wouldn't be good together, we'd be a ticking time bomb. A disaster waiting to happen.

And it wouldn't just be my heart torn to shreds in the aftermath—my son's would be, too.

Without a word, I stand on shaking legs and hightail it back inside.

"Don't run from me, Frankie!" Orion hollers after me, but I keep going.

I stumble as I cross the threshold, barely keeping myself upright, and my fingers and toes burn as the cold air gives way to the warmth of the house.

My whole body is vibrating—with anger, fear, longing,

and a whole lot of want—as I creep down the hall toward my room.

It's the anger I choose to zero in.

Who does he think he is? What right does he have to go and say things like that to me?

Mercifully, Mav is still sleeping soundly when I slip back into my bedroom. I decide to take advantage and pad into the bathroom for a nice, long shower, hoping the hot water can somehow rinse away all of my lingering doubts and fears.

It's unlikely, but I crank the knob anyway and wait for the water to heat.

I brush the snarls out of my hair and then step beneath the scalding spray. I still have about an hour until my alarm is set to go off, so I take my time, washing my hair twice before slathering it with a deep conditioner.

While it sits, I wash my body with my favorite sugar scrub and then shave everything in need of shaving—after all, nobody likes a hairy stripper.

Once I'm squeaky clean, I cut off the water and wrap myself in a fluffy towel, already feeling lighter.

This thing with Orion doesn't have to turn into some debacle.

He's a good guy, and once I lay down some clear-cut boundaries, I know he'll respect them. And then, we'll be able to be roommates. Easy peasy.

Maybe even friends.

Liar, my brain taunts. *You can't be friends with a man like him.*

"You're wrong." I speak the words out loud, glaring at my own reflection. "I can do anything I set my mind to."

I tug on my robe and roll my shoulders back, faking the

kind of confidence I long to feel, before stepping back into my room to wake Maverick.

Except, he's not in the bed anymore. He's not even in the room.

Looks like it's time to put that so-called confidence to the test.

DRESSED in a pair of thick leggings and a chunky-knit sweater, I make my way out into the hallway, following the sounds of their hushed voices.

I'm feeling good, like maybe I really can do this—until my son comes into view.

One glimpse of him cuddled into Orion's side on the couch, and my confidence vanishes quicker than a mirage in the desert.

I want to join them, but I can't. It's like my feet are cemented in place. My head and heart are waging a silent war. I wish so badly that I could listen to my heart and take a chance on what could be, but I can't. I'm not brave enough...not reckless enough.

Instead, I loiter just outside of the living room, like a total creeper.

"What's this one?" Orion asks, pointing to something out of my line of sight.

"Cuh...at," Maverick sounds out the word before confidently calling out, "Cat!"

Is he... are they...?

My heart constricts painfully in my chest as the pieces fall into place. Orion's helping my son with his spelling words. Tears burn behind my eyes, and my throat thickens with barely contained emotion.

"Good job, bud!" He points to another word on the page. "And this one?"

He's so good with him—tender and completely engaged. I know Stella says he doesn't like kids, but watching the two of them has a hope I have no business feeling blooming in my chest, no matter what my brain is saying.

"This one's hard, O," Maverick grumbles, and it takes me a second to realize he's calling Orion O. A nickname. Be still my heart, because *wow*, that's cute.

"Yeah, but you can do it." He ruffles Maverick's unruly hair. "C'mon, sound it out."

"Duh... duh... ad." He looks up at Orion with wide eyes. "Dad? Yeah, it's dad!"

"My man." Orion holds out his fist. "You totally nailed it."

They tap their knuckles together and then mime an explosion.

But just as quickly as the celebration begins, it ends. A fact that doesn't escape Orion's notice. "What's wrong, Mav? You did really good."

"I wish you were my dad." Those six little words hit me like a gut punch, knocking the wind right out of me.

I take half a step forward, ready to put an end to this whole thing, but Orion beats me to it.

"Why?" His voice comes out strong but soft. How nice for him, because I'm pretty sure I'm crumbling to pieces.

"All of the other kids have dads, and I don't, 'cause he's dead."

One million.

That's how many tiny, jagged pieces of my heart settle in my chest as I watch the object of my desire comfort my whole world.

"He may not be here with you physically, but he's always here." Orion pats his chest over his heart. "He's a part of you, and you want to know something else?"

"What?" Maverick whispers, his voice smaller than I've ever heard it.

"He loved you, so much."

"He did?" Maverick pushes away from Orion so that he can look at him. "How do you know?"

I swear, it feels like time comes to a halt as I wait for his reply.

"You're the coolest kid I know, Mav. You're smart and funny. And you take such good care of your mama. There's no way he wouldn't have loved you."

"Really?" The wobble in my son's voice sends a spear of pain through me.

"One-hundred-and-ten percent." Orion tugs Maverick into his side and hugs him tight. "I've only known you a few weeks and I love you, bud."

"You do?" Even though I can't see his face, I can picture his expression so clearly—eyes wide and his mouth slightly open in that perfect cupid's bow he's had since birth.

"Yeah." Orion knocks his shoulder into Maverick's. "Of course I do."

"Told you," Stella says from behind me, scaring the ever-loving crap out of me.

"Oh my God!" I whisper-shout, spinning to face her. "What is wrong with you?"

"Asks the creepy stalker lady."

"I'm not stalking!" I insist. "Or being a creep." *Okay, that one's a lie.*

"So, they know you're standing here?"

"Um." I wring my hands together, suddenly feeling like a fool. "I—"

"I'm joking, you're fine." She lifts her brows and quirks her lips. "You want a cup of coffee?"

"Always."

I follow behind Stella to the kitchen and park myself on one of the stools while she makes a fresh pot.

"You wanna talk about it?" she asks, once the machine begins to percolate.

"About what?" I fire back, playing dumb.

Stella blows a raspberry as she takes down two mugs. My eyes flit toward the sink on their own accord, and sure enough, the cup I left outside with Orion is there.

"It's okay, you know."

"What is?"

She pours us both coffees and takes a seat on the stool to my left. "It's okay that you have feelings for my brother."

A garbled *huh* is all I can sputter as I choke on air. Stella alternates between patting and rubbing my back.

"Is everything okay in here?" Orion asks, joining our little two-person shitshow.

"Fine," I wheeze, tears pooling from the force of my coughs.

"Mama!" Maverick rams into my back, wrapping his arms around my waist. "You need the hineylick anewver!"

"No—" I croak, but he's already squeezing.

Thankfully, Orion steps in and pries him away from me. "Your mama's fine, bud. Promise."

"Are you?" Maverick asks. "Are you fine?"

I pat my chest and nod. "Yeah, I just swallowed wrong. I'm good. Promise."

"Don't think you're off the hook," Stella warns as she rises from her stool.

A weak laugh escapes me. How silly of me to hope she'd let it go. The girl might be blonde, but she's no Elsa.

"What's that mean?" Maverick tugs on the hem of my shirt. "Off the hook?"

"It's when—"

Stella cuts me off. "It means your mama and I were talking, and she thinks because you and Orion came in here that our conversation's over. But she's wrong." She grins evilly as she refills her cup. "We're just getting started."

"Grab your backpack, okay?" I say to Maverick, expressly ignoring Stella.

I finish my coffee, refusing to make eye contact with either of the Cartwrights in the room.

It's clear neither of them are pleased with me, but Orion's much more vocal about it as he slides onto Stella's vacated stool and then gets all up into my personal space.

His nearness has my hackles up, and I freeze in place, hoping that maybe if I don't move, he won't touch me.

"How long you gonna be mad?"

"I'm not mad," I say woodenly. And it's true—at least not at him. The only person I'm really upset with is me. I know better than to let people in. I know better than to open myself up to that kind of heartache. Which is why I need to shut him out, once and for all.

And maybe, just maybe, if I'm lucky, I'll still get to keep him as Birdie. I'd rather that than for Maverick to lose him if things went poorly between us.

"Seem pretty mad to me." He leans even closer, brushing my hair away from my face so he can whisper in my ear. "You're like an angry little robot. Where's your fire, Frankie?"

My entire body is shaking—whether it's with the urge to lean into his touch or to explode like a supernova, I'm not sure. I take a deep breath and force a smile. "I don't know what you're talking about."

He leans back, crossing his strong arms over his chest. He's wearing a Henley with the sleeves pushed up. His forearms look delicious—not that I'm looking. "So, it's like that, huh?"

I shrug and avert my gaze to my coffee, studying the dark liquid like it's the most interesting thing I've ever seen.

"That's fine." He stands from the stool, and my entire body deflates. At least we're finally on the same page.

But then he moves so far into my space, I can feel the heat of his body as he leans down, bringing his lips flush with my ear. "You wanna play it cool, go for it. But I'm not giving up. Even icebergs melt, Frankie."

"Pssh. It takes months for them to melt."

"What's months when I'm thinking of years?"

"Who are you?" I demand, my frustration rising. "What is this? Why are you acting like this?"

"Like what?"

"This!" I gesture between us. "Like we're together. We're friends, Orion. Friends."

"We could be more, though," he says, right as Maverick enters the kitchen.

"You ready, Mama?"

All of my fight leaves me as I paste on a happy smile. "Ready, bud." And then I turn to Orion, my face carefully neutral. "No," I whisper, "we can't."

Stella clears her throat—and it's then I realize our entire conversation just played out with an audience. *Kill me now.*

"Y'all wanna ride with me?" she asks, her blue eyes flicking between her brother and me.

"Yes!" Maverick screeches, pumping a fist in the air.

At the same time, I say, "No thanks. I have things to do between classes and need my car."

"So, no lunch either." She eyes me with suspicion.

"Nope." I clench my hands at my sides, hating every moment of this, but it's the way things need to be. Friends. Roommates. Nothing more.

No hair braiding, no sleepovers, no spilling secrets.

No late nights, no kisses, no romance.

She and Orion exchange knowing looks, but I ignore them.

"C'mon, Mav." I usher him toward the door. "We gotta go or we'll be late."

He grumbles under his breath but does as he's told.

Friends... Roommates... Nothing more. I repeat the words in my head for the rest of the morning.

Maybe if I say them enough, they'll stick.

I DRUM my fingers against my steering wheel and try to convince myself I'm not doing anything wrong.

But fuck if it doesn't feel like I am.

"Just get out and go inside," I mutter out loud in the empty cab of my truck. But only silence answers me, and somehow, it's like it's mocking me.

It's no use though—I can't seem to make myself do it.

Except, I have to, because even though our relationship —*fuck, it's not even a relationship; I'm just her client. Most likely one of many.* But still, I can't help but feel like explaining to her that I've met someone is the right thing to do.

Even if that *person* is currently trying to ice me out.

I feel like an idiot. What kind of guy books the VIP room at a strip club just to tell the stripper he won't be coming back anymore?

Seriously, how is this my life?

"Fuck!" I groan, pressing my head into the seatback.

Maybe I should have made a move on Birdie. I've had months to do it. Why didn't I?

Better yet, what's stopping me?

No sooner than I think it does a crystal-fucking-clear image of Frankie and Maverick replace it.

They're why I won't make a move on Birdie. She's hot as hell—a literal fantasy come to life—but Frankie, she's...I don't even have the words to describe the way she makes me feel.

Birdie gets my dick hard, but Frankie lights every single nerve ending in my body on fire just by smiling at me.

Finally, I force myself to cut the engine and head inside. I don't actually have the time, but I swing by the bar first and order myself a double pour of whiskey.

I sling it back as I walk toward the hall that leads to my Birdie. The bouncer tips his head at me as I approach. "Cutting it close tonight."

"Yup."

He narrows his eyes. "You haven't been by in a while."

"Been busy."

We stare each other down for a brief moment, and then he nods and shows me to my room. "You know the rules."

"That I do."

He closes the door, and I take a seat on the couch, dread settling in my gut like a lead weight.

She probably won't even care, you jackass, my brain taunts. *You're a client with a fat wallet, nothing more.*

That's not true—I'm not crazy and I didn't imagine our connection. Birdie's not just a stripper, and I'm not just a client. We...we had sparks.

But what are sparks when Frankie's a goddamn inferno?

Usually, I'd wait for Birdie's arrival, sprawled out, anticipation thrumming through me like a live wire.

Tonight, however, I'm uncomfortably stiff, with my back as straight as a steel rod. My heart thunders, and I can't seem to stop tap-tap-tapping my fingers against the plush velvet of the couch.

My nerves are shot, and I swear to God, if teleportation was a thing, I'd be out of here.

The sound of the door opening jerks me to attention. *It's go time.*

Birdie walks in, looking like the physical embodiment of sin in a red dress that looks painted on. Her sky-high heels, glossy lips, and lace mask are all the same shade, giving her an almost devilish look.

However, there's a small frown pinching her lips, and the way she's fidgeting with the hem of her dress has me second-guessing myself. Her usual sexy-as-hell confidence is nowhere to be found.

Fuck. Am I going to make her night worse?

"Hey there," she murmurs, moving to the center of the room.

"Bluebird." *Get it together, man!* "I mean Birdie."

A ghost of a smile crosses her features. "Long time, no see."

The music starts, a deep, heady rhythm pulsing through the speakers. She begins to sway her hips, and for a moment, I watch, unable to tear my gaze away.

She twists her body and then drops her ass to the floor, her confidence growing with every move.

"Yeah." I swallow roughly. "Been busy."

As she crawls toward me, a vision of Frankie flashes through my mind, and I know what I have to do.

Because, no matter how badly I wish it, I can't have them both. I can't keep my Bluebird in a cage and my little mama on the back burner. They're both incredible women who deserve someone's full attention.

Which is why when she slithers herself between my

spread legs and uses my thighs as leverage to pull herself up, I promptly pick her up and set her on the cushion beside me.

"We need to talk."

Instantly, her entire body goes rigid. "We do?" She wraps her arms around her middle and scooches toward the arm of the couch, putting a few more inches between us. "A-about what?"

You know what to say. You have a plan—stick to the plan. But I don't. Not even a little.

"I met someone."

"Oh." Birdie's shoulders hunch, and I feel like even more of an asshole than I anticipated. "Is...is it serious?"

"I want it to be," I answer honestly.

She winces, and then carefully schools her expression before nodding. "Gotcha."

It might be a trick of the low lighting, but I swear, her eyes are brimming with tears.

"I probably won't be back." I tip my head back and laugh at my own stupidity. "Not that you care. God, how much of an ego do I have?"

"I do." Birdie reaches for me and then yanks her hands back at the last second, twisting her fingers together in her lap. "Care, I mean." She bites her lip and then sucks in a deep breath, holding it for a beat and then blowing it out. "You're not like most of the other guys who come here. They look at me and just see some nameless, faceless fantasy. I'm not even a real person to them. I'm a doll for them to throw singles at and jerk off to once they go home."

She lets out a long, sad sigh.

"But you...you see me. You always have."

"Full confession, I was borderline obsessed with you for months."

"Really?" She somehow manages to sound intrigued and condescending at the same time. "Couldn't tell, what with how often you came in."

I laugh humorlessly. "And yet I still couldn't bring myself to ask for your name."

She lifts a delicate shoulder in a shrug. "I wouldn't have told you anyway."

"Figured as much."

"It's a safety thing, you know. To protect us from guys like you." She's teasing me, and damn if that doesn't ease some of the weight bearing down on me.

"Guys like me?" I growl back.

"Yeah." She wraps her red and black strands around her index finger and twirls. "You know—obsessed."

"Smartass."

"Stalker."

I clutch at my chest. "You got me."

"Seriously though, thank you for stopping by." She stands from the couch and heads for the door. "I'll tell them to refund your money."

"No!" I shout, darting to my feet. "No, please don't. Keep it."

"Are...are you sure?"

I nod, feeling at peace for the first time in God knows how long. "Yeah, Bluebird. I'm sure."

"I'll miss seeing you..." She smiles softly, shyly. "She's a lucky girl."

I huff out a laugh through my nose. "Currently, she's not interested in giving me the time of day, but I can feel it." I thump my chest. "Right here. I can feel something between us."

She turns the knob and steps into the hallway. "Good-bye, Orion."

I lift my hand in a halfhearted wave, and then she's gone.

All in all, tonight went better than I anticipated; but now is when the real work begins, because I have to somehow convince the prickly Frankie to give me a chance —and something tells me she's going to really put me through my paces.

———

"YOU'RE HOME EARLY," Samson says, the second I walk in the front door.

I know he's here with Stella, watching Maverick while Frankie works.

Man, I wish I knew where she waitressed at because seeing her beautiful face would be really great right about now.

"Where are you?" The house is dead silent, and despite being able to hear Samson, I can't see him.

"Down here." His hand shoots up in the air. I round the corner and smirk when I find him sitting on the floor behind the couch, alone in the dark, neither Stella or Maverick in sight.

"How'd it go?"

"It went." He is well aware of where I was going when I left earlier tonight, and he's a nosy shit by nature, but I'm not sure if I'm ready to open up to him.

"You wanna talk about it?" He hauls himself up to his feet and follows me into the kitchen.

"I told her I wasn't coming back."

"Thought you were gonna marry her." His tone borders on snarky, but I know he's coming from a good place. This is just what we do.

I grab a bottle of water from the fridge and crack the lid, gulping down several sips of the cool liquid. "I know you think I'm an idiot—and I really did feel something for her. But..."

"But Frankie." He leans back against the counter, his eyes laser focused on me, gauging my reaction.

"Yeah, Frankie." I keep my face neutral. I'm sure now that he's happily domesticated, he'd love to dole out relationship advice, but I'm not sure my little sister's boyfriend—best friend or not—is the guy I want to take dating advice from.

Not that Samson cares. He's like a big, blond bulldozer, tearing shit up with no regard for anyone else. "What are you gonna do about it?"

How do I even answer that? How does one convince a single mom who's as skittish as a baby deer to take a chance?

Either way, I had to break whatever was happening between Birdie and me off. Even if Frankie never gives me the time of day, it was the right thing to do, plain and simple.

"Hell if I know."

"You're in luck, big brother," Stella says, waltzing into the room like she wasn't just eavesdropping in the hall. *How is she more annoying now than she was a decade ago?* "Because I have a sure-fire game plan to win you your girl."

"What girl?" Maverick asks, hot on her heels. He stops and wriggles his whole body like he just thought of something gross. "Girls are weird."

"The gang's all here," Samson snorts, crossing the room to wrap Stella in his arms. He rests his head on her shoulder, and something inside of me smarts at how easy the two of them make everything look.

That's not true, and you know it. They went through some shit, too.

The real question is how did I go from a content bachelor to ready to settle down?

I mean, really, am I ready to be a stepdad? And I realize, as crazy as it sounds, I am—*I really am.* Now I just have to convince Frankie.

"Mav!" Stella gives him an exaggerated pout. "Are you calling me weird?"

"Oh..." He blinks twice and then nods slowly. "You're big weird."

Stella pretends to glare and then cracks up laughing. "Yeah, you're right. I am."

"What are y'all even doing? I thought we were playing hide and seek?"

"We were, but then I heard Orion's voice and came to see what he was doing back already."

Maverick scampers over to me and wraps his arms around my leg. "You wanna play, too, O? We can be a team."

Man, this kid. He knows every right word to say. Honestly, at this point, I'm pretty sure Maverick Townsend could tell me to jump and my sad ass would ask him how high. He's got me wrapped around his little finger and doesn't even know it.

"Let's do it!" I hold out my fist for him to bump.

"Fine," Stella concedes. "But when we're done, we talk."

I grin down at my newly acquired teammate. "Let's hide somewhere really good."

"One... two... three..." Stella starts, but Maverick is already hauling me out the back door.

Hopefully the kid knows a spot she'll never find us, because as much as I want to win over Frankie, I'm not sure I want my little sister to be the one coaching me to victory.

"CAN WE PLAY AGAIN TOMORROW, O?" Maverick asks, his eyes drooping. The kid will never admit it, but after an hour of hide and seek, dinner, and reading—he's tired.

"Sure can." I reach down and lift him into the air, tossing him over my shoulder like a sack of potatoes. "If you take a quick shower and brush your teeth before bed."

He wriggles and kicks and giggles, sounding more like a hyena than a little boy. Any other kid, and I would want to cover my ears, but with Mav? It's the sweetest thing I've ever heard.

"But I don't like showers!"

I toss him down onto the bed he shares with his mother —a fact I'm studiously trying to ignore—and press my fingers into his ribs.

"O!" he screeches, trying to get away. "Stop! It tickles."

"Only way I'll stop is if you take a shower."

"Fine! Fine!" I release him and he sits up, his cheeks stained red from laughing. "But you gotta start the water. Mama or Stella usually does it so it won't be too hot."

"Grab your pajamas and I'll handle it."

We both go our separate ways—me to the bathroom and Mav to the closet—but once I'm standing in front of the shower, all I can wonder is *how hot is too hot?*

Am I going to fuck this up and burn him? He'd tell me if the water wasn't right, right? God, who knew showers could cause so much anxiety?

"Maverick," I call. "Come feel this."

He runs in, sets a little bundle of clothes on the sink, and then sticks his index finger under the flow of water. "Too hot!"

"Feel it again," I say, pulling the knob back a bit.

He shrieks. "Too cold!"

I nudge it forward. "Try it one more time, baby bear."

"That's just right, O." He turns to me. "Who's baby bear?"

"Like Goldilocks, you know?"

"Nope." He tugs his shirt off. "Do I gotta wash my hair?"

"Yeah. Hair to toes, and everything in between." I know I shouldn't laugh, but I do. I can't help it. He starts kicking off his pants and I take that as my cue to leave. "I'll wait out in your room, okay?"

"Promise?"

"Yeah, Mav." I step into the bedroom and pull the door shut behind me. "I promise."

While he showers, I sink into the chair in the corner of the room and open Google Play on my phone. Once the app I need starts downloading, I toggle over to my work calendar. It's a slow week at work, thanks to our supply truck getting delayed, but you won't hear me complaining since it means I get to be here more.

I'm pretty sure I read somewhere that repetition leads to mastery, so maybe if I keep showing up in Frankie's life, she'll let me in. Not really the same thing, but...close enough.

I know she's into me—that much is clear. I just don't know how to convince her to take a chance on me. But as far as she's concerned, persistence may as well be my middle name, because I have no intentions of giving up.

Not on her—on *them*... Not now, not ever.

After about ten minutes, I stand and pad over to the bathroom. "You okay?"

The shower cuts off. "Yeah. Almost done." His voice is tired. Maybe he'll fall asleep fast.

"Brush your teeth."

He groans, but then mumbles out an *okay*.

I turn to go back to the chair, but he stumbles back into the room before I can.

"Will you tell me a story?" he asks through a big yawn.

"Sure." I pull back the covers and pat the mattress. "In you go."

He climbs into the bed and snuggles into his fluffy pillow. "You lay, too?"

"Um." I hesitate. How would Frankie feel about me laying in her bed? Honestly, she'd probably hate it.

But when Maverick aims his puppy dog eyes my way, I'm helpless to resist. "Please?"

I toe off my shoes and lie down beside Maverick, making sure to stay on top of the covers.

"Mama was reading *Thomas the Tank Engine* to me."

"I thought I could tell you the story of *Goldilocks and the Three Bears*."

He snuggles into my side. "Okay."

I slide my phone out of my pocket and pull up the Kindle app—that I downloaded *just* so I could read him this —and then open the book I bought of kids' stories.

"Once upon a time, there were three bears—a papa bear, a mama bear, and a little baby bear."

Maverick burrows into my side, wiggling until I have one arm around him and his head is on my chest. He sighs contentedly as I read to him.

"Goldilocks is kind of naughty," he murmurs once I finish the story.

"A little bit. Curious, too."

I feel him nod. "But we're like the bears."

"We are?" I lock my phone and set it down on the table.

"Yeah. Mama's mama bear, I'm baby bear, and you... you're papa bear."

My entire body tenses as his words sink in. This kid, he has such a big heart. He's so trusting and so loving, and somehow, I'm lucky enough to be on the receiving end of it.

I tighten my arm around him and press a kiss to the top of his head. "Good night, Mav."

"Stay with me until I fall asleep?" he asks, already sounding halfway there.

Just like when he asked me to lay with him, I know it's a bad idea. I know I should tell him no, that I should get up, turn out the light, and head to my own room.

But I don't.

"Sure thing," I tell him, planning to slip away as soon as I can.

Except, his warm body and soft breathing lulls me into a state of relaxation, and before I know it, I'm fast asleep, too.

I'D LIKE to say Orion's visit earlier tonight didn't derail my entire shift, but I'd be lying. I've been an absolute mess ever since he left.

I swear, it's like the universe has it out for me. Karma. Mother Nature. Someone.

I'm too much of a wimp to take a real chance on him, so keeping him as Birdie was supposed to be my failsafe.

For the last few months, he's been my only bright spot on the nights I work, and now...*nothing*. He's just quitting me, cold turkey, and his stupid white-knight-mister-respect thing only makes me want him all the more.

Like, seriously, what kind of guy *breaks up with a stripper*? Most just stop showing up. But nope. Not Orion. He had to pay me a personal visit, to tell me he'd met some-one, and that he was going all in with her.

With me.

That's the kicker. He broke up with me, *for me*, and doesn't even know it.

I wonder how he'd react if he found out the truth?

Would he think differently of me...*less* of me? I can't imagine a guy like him would be cool with dating a stripper.

But I also never thought he'd go for a single mom, so what do I know?

"Birdie!" Walter calls my name, jerking me back to the present. "Head home."

Shit! I must be really off my game if he's cutting me.

"Walt, I'm sorr—"

"You're not in trouble." His eyes crinkle at the corners as he smiles. "Your shift ended fifteen minutes ago."

"Oh. Wow. Really?"

He nods, looking all too amused. "I've been waiting on you to clock out, but..."

"I've been in my head tonight. Distracted."

His amusement intensifies. "More like dickstracted."

I gasp. "Walter!"

"I know a thing or two about it, kid. There's a reason I only hire female dancers. Wouldn't want my Lenny worrying about my virtue in a sausage buffet."

"Respectfully," I laugh, "you're a mess."

"You say mess, I say a delight." He tosses his hands in the air. "Either way, Marcus is waiting to walk you out."

"Thanks, Walt. You're one of the good ones."

"Don't you forget it, kid," he says with a wink.

I head to the back, scrub off my makeup, and change into my sweats before heading toward the employee entrance, where Marcus is leaning against the wall, watching the club floor with steely eyes. "Sorry to keep you waiting."

"Sorry to sic Walter on you." He ducks his head. "You okay?"

"It's been a long night."

"Your boy was here." He pushes the door open and holds it for me. "Left quicker than usual. That got anything to do with it?"

"My who?"

He lifts his brows and steps back so I can lead. "You know, your boy. Dark hair, fit, is here more than I am."

"Very funny." I dig my keys out of my bag. "But yeah, he has something to do with it. But not in a bad way or anything."

"You ever need to talk, I'm here."

I unlock my door and then slip behind the wheel. "I appreciate you, Marcus."

He tips his head my way and then moves to the curb, giving me room to back out.

I'm usually anxious to get home, to see Maverick, but tonight I take the scenic route. My brain's a mess, and my heart's even worse. The walls I've spent years building feel like they're about to come crashing down.

By the time I make it to the house, my exhaustion is bone deep. All I want is to shower off, crawl in bed, and snuggle my little man until the sun rises.

I go into full-on stealth mode as I enter the house, babying the door closed and locking it before tiptoeing down the hall. I swear, I don't even breathe until I'm safely ensconced in my bedroom.

For once, things seem to be going right—until I look at my bed and see Orion and Maverick fast asleep.

All the little, mangled, pulpy pieces of my heart fuse themselves back together and then shatter all over again at the sight of my son curled around a sleeping Orion.

The two of them look so content, so peaceful, that it actually pains me to look at them.

But at the same time, I can't look away.

Does Maverick look that carefree when he sleeps next to me?

I force myself to look away and shuffle over to the closet. I grab a set of pajamas and then head into the bathroom to shower.

My mind reels as I scrub my skin clean, rinsing the night's glitter and melancholy down the drain. I stand under the steaming spray until it runs cold, and then I stand here five minutes longer, praying the icy water somehow purges the want from my body.

Or at the very least, that it gives me some clarity. Because I'm half-tempted to crawl into bed with the two of them, but come morning light, I know I'd be mortified. And the last thing I need is more regrets.

When I can't take it another second, I cut the water and wrap myself in a towel. My skin feels like gooseflesh, and my teeth chatter as I dry off. But it seems like the ice bath did the trick, because once I slip into my clothes, I hang my towel, press a kiss to Maverick's forehead, and curl up in the chair in the corner of the room.

I keep my heavy eyes trained on Maverick, watching the steady rise and fall of his chest, until finally, I lose the battle and sleep claims me.

BLINKING MY EYES OPEN, I stretch my arms over my head and then sit up, the covers pooling around my waist.

I yawn and blink again, trying to clear the fog.

Something woke me up—but I'm not sure what.

It wasn't my alarm and it wasn't Maverick, who's curled in a little ball beside me, sleeping soundly.

I reach for my phone, but it's not on my nightstand where I usually leave it.

The chair—it's in the chair, because that's where I fell asleep, because Orion was in my bed.

Orion. Cartwright. Was. In. My. Bed.

Where is he now? When did he wake up? Did he move me? Questions race through my mind as I crawl out from beneath the covers to retrieve my phone.

It's early. Not even six.

I collapse back against my pillow and suck in a ragged breath—the sheets smell like him. Spicy and citrusy with a hint of musk.

My God, I groan and force myself out of the bed.

His scent might as well be my own personal aphrodisiac.

It clings to my pajamas, and since I'm a glutton for punishment, I don't change. I like smelling like him; it makes me feel like we're closer.

This time, I don't sneak or creep. I march straight toward the kitchen, because if I'm going to make it through the day, I'm going to need coffee and lots of it.

While it brews, I decide to get a jumpstart on breakfast and grab the waffle iron—a luxury Mav and I never had until moving in here—and two cans of cinnamon rolls from the fridge.

I saw this recipe on Pinterest and have been dying to try it. Since I'm too wired to fall back asleep, I figure there's no time like the present. Plus, Mav will love them.

I'm six rolls deep when footsteps sound down the hall. "Mama!" Maverick cries when he sees me. "I missed you so much!"

"I missed you, too." I bend at the waist and smother his face with kisses. "So much."

He shrieks with laughter and wiggles out of my hold. "I had the bestest night ever!"

That makes one of us, I think sourly, before pasting on a smile. "Oh, yeah? Tell me all about it."

"Stella made a'sketti for dinner, and then we did my sight words—that part was boring—and then O came home and played hide and seek with us. And then, guess what we did, Mama? Guess!"

"Washed your stinky toes and went to sleep?"

"Yeah! But O read me a special story about some crazy girl and a family of bears and then he snuggled me." My son lets out a sigh worthy of the big screen. "It was the best. The only thing missing was you. I told O we were like the bears —Mama, Papa, and the little baby. Except I'm big!"

I suck in a ragged breath, my heart lodging itself in my throat. "Oh, Mav." I turn away so he won't see the tears dotting my lashes.

"You don't work tonight, right?" he asks, climbing up onto a barstool.

"That's right. I'm all yours."

"Can we do Taco Tuesday?"

"It's Wednesday," I tell him, placing another cinnamon roll onto the waffle iron.

He gives me a look that says *lady, I'm still learning my days of the week.* "But we can still do it, right?"

"Of course. Beef or chicken?"

"The brown one with the good sauce."

I roll my lips inward to keep from laughing. "Beef it is."

"With the sauce, Mama!"

"Tell me about this magic taco sauce," Orion says, stepping into the room.

"It's the grease," I stage whisper. "He loves it."

"Do you wanna eat my mom's taco, O?"

My cheeks burn crimson, while Orion's lips quirk up into a devious grin. "Only on days that end in Y, bud."

God, please drop a piano on me and end my suffering.

"Who's ready for breakfast?" I ask, changing the subject.

"Me!" Maverick and Orion say in perfect harmony.

I make them each a plate, adding some sliced fruit on the side. "There y'all go. I'm gonna get dressed while you two eat."

"You don't want any?" Orion asks, glancing between his plate and me.

"I ate before y'all got up." It's a lie, but my cheeks are still burning so badly, I think I might spontaneously combust if I have to stand there any longer.

He squints at me as he pops a grape into his mouth. I watch, entranced, as he chews. "We'll save you some," he says after he swallows.

It's all I can do to nod and hightail it out of there without making a fool of myself.

I pull the door closed behind me and fall back against it, my heart beating double-time in my chest.

He's clearly determined to bring his A-game, but I've got a lot more on the line to lose than he does—a fact I'd do well to remember.

For all I know, his infatuation could be about the chase. And then what—what happens when he wins? Will he cast me to the side, leaving me and Maverick both heartbroken?

I don't know. Unfortunately, there's no crystal ball I can wave my hand over and see the future. There's no guarantee we won't end up hurt.

It'd be one thing to gamble with my own heart, but with Mav's on the line, I know I need to play it safe.

I need to not only rebuild my deteriorating walls; I need

to reinforce them with concrete and rebar. Steel. I need to make them impenetrable and unscalable.

At this rate, I might even need a crocodile-filled moat.

"HEY, man, you wanna grab a drink? I'm buying," Ben says as we walk to our trucks.

Things are better between us, but only because I'm starting to understand his perspective. If our roles were reversed, and Frankie had my ring on her finger and asked for him to move out, I'd have his shit packed and at the curb in the blink of an eye.

"Nah, man, I'm good."

He casts a questioning look, knowing good and well I'm not usually one to turn down a free beer. "You sure? I'm heading over to Bandits."

"Wish I could, brother, but I got plans."

"A hot date?" He cracks up at his own joke.

I grin. "Something like that."

"You serious?" His laughter cuts off and he pins me with a searching look. "Is it serious?"

I try to play it cool and shrug one shoulder. "Too soon to tell."

"That's good, man." He tips his chin. "I'm happy for you."

"Don't break out the champagne just yet. She's...shy."

"Don't give up." Ben slaps my back as he passes me. "Macy was, too."

There's no chance of me giving up. Frankie's the real deal, and I won't stop until she's mine.

But I don't say any of that; I just lift my hand in some semblance of a wave and climb into my truck, more than ready to get home to my people.

After Frankie and Mav left this morning, I asked Stella to spend the night at Samson's. She gave me a lot of shit about it, but her car's nowhere in sight, so I'm counting it as a win.

I've only got an hour until Frankie and Mav get home, so I shuck off my dirty work clothes and hop in the shower. We may not be doing anything special, but I'm damn sure going to look—and smell—my best.

She thinks she was discreet sniffing the collar of her shirt this morning. But I saw her, and damn if it didn't stir something primal inside of me—made me want to rub myself all over her, so that everyone who came near her knew she was spoken for...that she was mine.

As the water heats, my thoughts linger on Frankie, and on what life would be like if she really was mine.

I can't help but imagine what it would be like to wake up beside her every morning—and better yet, to fall asleep with her petite body wrapped around mine every night.

Fuck yes.

I step beneath the steaming water and squirt a dollop of body wash into the palm of my hand as thoughts of her, and only her, invade my brain.

She'd sleep so good with me in her bed, because I'd wear her out every night. I'd lick her pussy until she begged me to stop, and then I'd fuck her until she was boneless. Long, hard, fast, slow...any way she asked for it, until her voice gave out from screaming my name.

Reaching down, I palm my erection and then squeeze the base.

It'd be so good between us. I know it would.

I let my imagination run wild as I jack my dick, all the while imagining it's her giving me pleasure instead of my right hand.

Bet her sweet little pussy tastes like heaven...

I brace one arm against the shower wall and quicken my pace.

Bet she'd squeeze my dick like a vise grip.

My balls tighten as that telltale tingle starts at the base of my spine . "Fuck, Frankie," I grunt, canting my hips forward as I splash the shower wall with my release.

I linger, with my forehead pressed against the tile, waiting for my body to come down. My dick, too, for that matter—because as good as jerking off to thoughts of her may be, I already know it's nothing compared to the real thing.

The sound of the front door opening rips me out of my post-orgasm stupor, and I quickly rinse off, more than ready for whatever the night may hold.

"SOMETHING SURE SMELLS GOOD," I say, ambling into the kitchen. I'm not lying, either—it smells like sizzling peppers and onions, and I am here for it.

"It's nothing special," Frankie murmurs, moving the taco meat around in her skillet with a spatula.

"That's for me to decide, yeah?" I tip my head and smirk. "Plus, Mav said your tacos are the best."

"Enough innuendos."

I take a few steps closer, shocked to see she has rice boiling in one pot, beans in another, and has two separate pans of meat cooking—one with peppers and onions, and one without.

"Never."

"You're trouble, Orion." She smiles at me over her shoulder. "With a capital 'T.'"

My heart rate kicks up, painfully thumping against my chest bone. "Don't I know it?" This playful side of Frankie makes me feel wild—reckless, even.

"Where's Maverick?"

"In our room." She wipes her hands on a dishtowel and turns to face me. "Said he wanted to color you a picture."

I try to play it cool even though I'm ridiculously thrilled at the prospect of him drawing me a picture. That must mean I'm pretty cool, right—that I have the Maverick Townsend seal of approval? Maybe it'll even earn me some brownie points with his mama.

"What can I do to help?"

"Wanna grab the plates and cups?" she asks, returning her attention to the stovetop. "Do you know if Stella will be back in time to eat?"

"Nah." I step in right behind her, nice and close. "She's staying over at Samson's tonight."

"Oh." She freezes at my nearness, at the feeling of my front pressing into her back. "Um."

I lean down, my breath skating over the exposed skin of her neck as I bring my lips to the shell of her ear. "You okay, little mama?"

She shivers and tries to step forward, but the stove keeps her boxed against me. "What are you doing?" Her voice trembles, and I swear to God, the slight shake is nearly enough to have my dick bursting through the seam of my jeans.

I bet this is exactly how she'd sound, begging me to let her come: hesitant, but hot, soft but demanding.

"Just grabbing the plates." I lean in closer and reach over her head, grabbing down three plates from the cabinet to the right of her.

"And you n-needed to b-be that close?" Her feathers are ruffled, and I'm here for it.

I step back, dragging my eyes over her tight body before placing the plates on the island. She's dressed in tight leggings and an off-the-shoulder sweater. It's casual and sexy-as-hell all at once. "Damn straight."

She huffs out an exasperated sigh and flicks off the burners. "Why are you doing this?"

"Doing what?" I give her my back and grab the cups from a different cabinet.

"This!" she cries. "Being all charming and cute and touchy. You're acting like I'm your... your... *girlfriend!*" She spits out the last word like it's sour on her tongue, but I don't let it get to me.

My Frankie is used to going it alone. She's protective and timid and guarded. She's worried I'll slam through her defenses like a wrecking ball, but she couldn't be more wrong.

I'm not going to break down her walls. I'm going to bide my time, patient if not a little pushy, until she invites me in. And mark my words, she *will* invite me in.

"Maybe because I want you to be."

She forces a laugh and turns away from me. "That's not funny."

"I'm not laughing," I say, and her shoulders tense.

"Orion—"

"Mama!" Maverick comes hurtling into the room. "Look at my picture! Do you think O—Orion! You're here!" He turns on a dime and barrels into me, knocking me into the fridge with the force of his hug. "I missed you!"

Contentment like I've never known before swims through me as I return his embrace. "Missed you, too, bud. Did you have a good day at school?"

"We painted rocks. I made mine look like Spiderman!"

"Oh, yeah?"

"Yeah!" He bounces on his toes twice and then shoves the paper he's holding into my hands. "I made you this. Do you like it?"

I take the drawing from him and study it closely. It takes a minute for the shapes to make sense, but I quickly gather the three brown ovals are the three of us, bear-family style.

"Like it?" I ask, my throat thick. "I love it." But only because he drew it. Any other kid, and I'd have tossed it. But from Mav, I want to frame it.

Frankie walks over to inspect his artwork. "Oh...um."

"It's us, Mama, see!" He points at the biggest bear-blob. "That's O." Then to the smaller one. "That's you." Last, he points to the smallest one, in the center. "And that's me! Papa, Mama, and big-boy-baby bear!"

"Mav." Frankie's voice breaks, and her eyes swim with tears. "This is..."

He looks up at his mom with wide, hopeful eyes, but she can't seem to gather her words. That's okay, though, I've got it.

"It's perfect. We love it."

"Both of you?" He whips his head back and forth, between us. "Really?"

"Yeah." Frankie nods, still reeling. "Both of us."

"Can we put it on the fridge?"

"Damn straight we can." I turn and grab a magnet, placing his paper high up on the door.

"Swear word, O."

"My bad," I say, but I'm smiling big, on cloud nine. Because my dude drew a family portrait and included me in it. If that's not winning, I don't know what is.

"Wash your hands, Mav." Frankie gives him her *mom look,* and he scampers over to the sink, stepping up onto the stool.

"Anything you need me to do?" I ask again as she grabs a bag of tortillas from the pantry, hoping this time she gives me a task.

Her shoulders tense, and a soft sigh escapes her. "Grab the cheese and sour cream?"

"Can do." I swing open the fridge door and grab our taco toppings. "Anything else?"

Her fingers are still around the plastic bag and she sucks in a deep breath before looking my way. "Napkins. We need napkins."

"You're not used to having help, are you?" There is no her giving an inch for me to take a mile. I'm fighting for millimeters when it comes to Frankie Townsend.

She slowly releases her hold on the tortilla bag. "That obvious?"

"It's okay to let people in." I take a step closer to her and our eyes lock. "To let me in."

She blinks and turns away to fix their plates, effectively breaking our connection. "Oh, and the taco sauce, please."

Her guard is up. But that's okay. Trust takes time, and I'm more than willing to put in the work.

I make my plate and then grab the taco sauce and napkins before joining them at the table.

Maverick carries the conversation for most of the meal—he's right, his mama's tacos are the best—and before I know it, our plates are clean and our bellies are full.

"Thank you for dinner." I push my chair back from the table and stand, gathering all of our dishes.

"What are you doing?" Frankie asks, reaching her hand out to stop me.

"Clearing the table." Thought it was pretty obvious, but...

"I can do them after Maverick's bath." She crosses her arms over her chest.

Don't look at her tits. Do. Not. Look. At. Her. Tits.

"Or, I could do them now, and after his bath you can relax."

"We could read a book, Mama!" Maverick rubs his hands together. "O does real good with the voices."

She looks torn, and I hate it. I hate that she's struggling with something as simple as asking for help with the dishes. A woman like Frankie deserves to be taken care of... pampered. And I'm damn sure the man to do it.

"Okay," she finally relents. "But—"

"No buts, Frankie. You cooked a good meal for us, the least I can do is clean up."

Her lip trembles but she relents, bobbing her head in a slow nod before allowing Maverick to drag her down the hall.

I make quick work of putting away the leftovers and loading the dishwasher. Maybe if I'm lucky, Frankie will let me take this for lunch tomorrow. All of the guys on my crew will be jealous fucks while they chow down on their ham sandwiches and I'm eating like a king.

I'm honestly shocked Frankie can cook like this. If I'd known, I'd have sweet-talked her into cooking for me every night. That's okay, though, it's never too late to start.

I wonder if she makes good fried chicken? I ponder idly as I wipe down the countertops.

Once the kitchen is sparkling clean, I plod into the living room and plant myself in the chair facing the hall. I want to make sure Frankie doesn't try to sneak their door closed before I can tell Mav goodnight.

He and I must be on the same wavelength, because not even a minute later, he comes barreling down the hall in a pair of green Hulk pajamas.

"O!" He flings himself into my lap, securing his arms around my neck. "Will you come read to me? Please?"

"Is your mama okay with it?" I ask, knowing damn well I need her consent. I may want to push her limits, but I'm not trying to cross boundaries and take us into hostile territory. This doesn't need to be a one step forward, two back kind of thing.

"Yeah!" He nods so fast that he looks like a bobble head. "Promise."

"Okay." I wrap my arms around him and hold him to my chest. "Hold on tight."

"For why?" he asks, right as I launch us out of the chair, tearing down the hall.

He squeals in delight as I race into the bedroom, tossing him onto the bed.

"Sure," Frankie deadpans, glaring at us with her hands on her hips. "Get him worked up before bedtime."

Maverick and I grin at each other. "You'll go right to sleep, right, bud?"

He dives beneath the covers, rolling a few times like a puppy trying to get comfortable, until he finds his sweet spot. "Promise."

Frankie rolls her eyes but smiles. She's usually so hard and prickly, but when it comes to her son, she's as soft as can be.

"What should we read?" she asks, crawling into the bed beside him.

He pats the empty mattress on the other side of him, silently asking me to join. But I'm not trying to die tonight. "I'll take the chair."

"Fine." He pouts. "But can you read the bear story again so Mama can hear it?"

"Of course." I tug my phone out of my pocket, open the Kindle app, and begin reading. Unlike last night, he's out cold before I even get to the last page.

"You're really good with him," Frankie says, brushing his hair out of his face so she can kiss his forehead.

"He's a good kid." I shrug, like it's no big deal. It kind of is, though, because before him, kids honestly creeped me out.

"Stella said you don't like kids." She glares at me accusingly.

"Well." I clench my jaw, lowkey wanting to ream my sister out for telling her that. "Mav's different."

"Right." It's clear from her tone she doesn't believe me. But it's the truth. I'm such a sucker for that kid. "Well..." She cuts her eyes toward the door, silently trying to dismiss me.

That's not going to fly, though. It's rare for us to get one-on-one time, and I'm damn sure not willingly giving it up. "Why don't we hang out? Watch a show or something?"

"Um." Her eyes flare wide, and I just know she's going to give me the brush-off.

Nah. Not tonight, little mama.

"C'mon, Frankie. Surely you don't want to sit in here alone until you're ready to go to sleep?"

She drags her teeth over her juicy lower lip, and I have to will my dick not to react.

"Please? I'll be a perfect gentleman..."

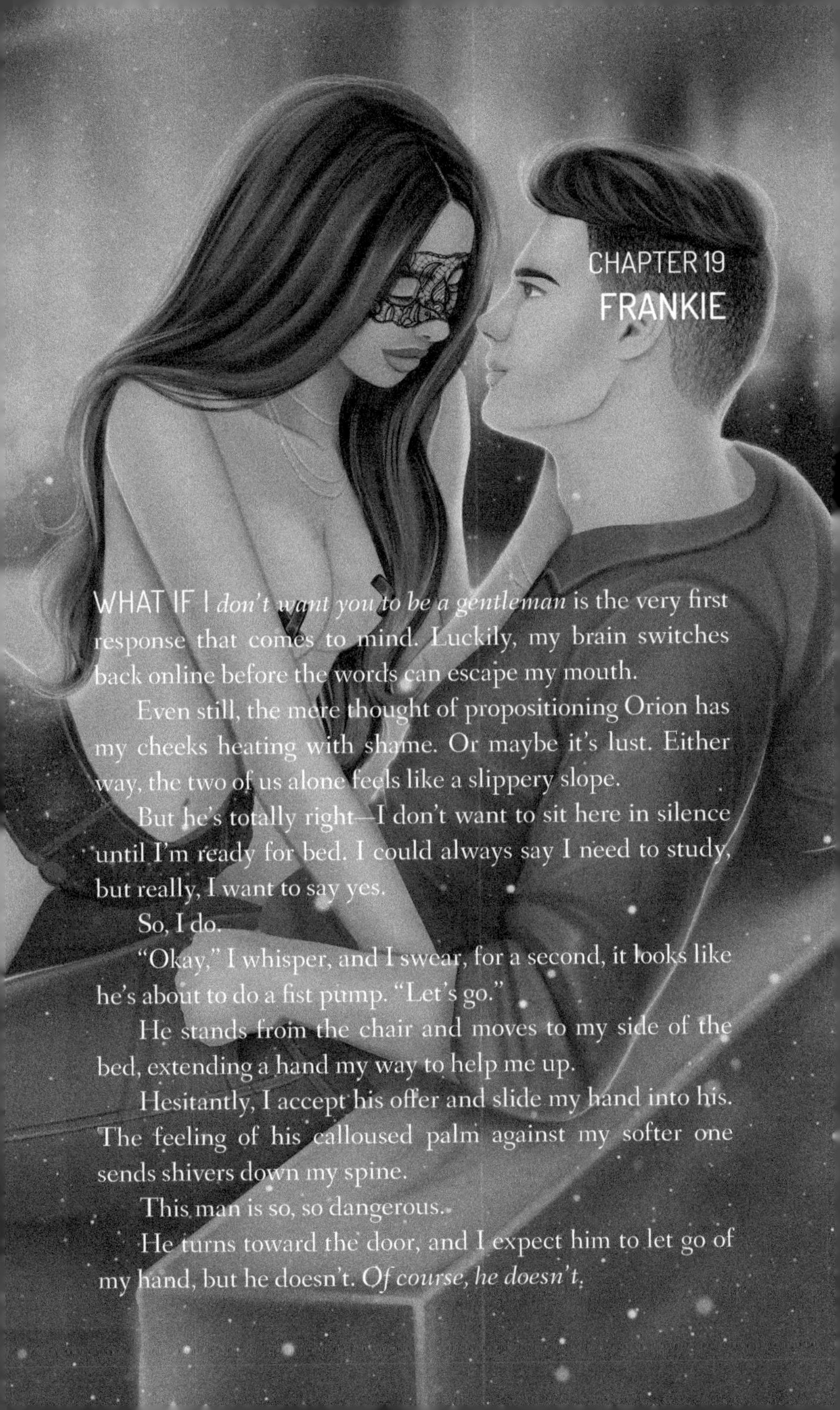

WHAT IF I *don't want you to be a gentleman* is the very first response that comes to mind. Luckily, my brain switches back online before the words can escape my mouth.

Even still, the mere thought of propositioning Orion has my cheeks heating with shame. Or maybe it's lust. Either way, the two of us alone feels like a slippery slope.

But he's totally right—I don't want to sit here in silence until I'm ready for bed. I could always say I need to study, but really, I want to say yes.

So, I do.

"Okay," I whisper, and I swear, for a second, it looks like he's about to do a fist pump. "Let's go."

He stands from the chair and moves to my side of the bed, extending a hand my way to help me up.

Hesitantly, I accept his offer and slide my hand into his. The feeling of his calloused palm against my softer one sends shivers down my spine.

This man is so, so dangerous.

He turns toward the door, and I expect him to let go of my hand, but he doesn't. *Of course, he doesn't.*

Orion's made his intentions clear; he wants me. And despite telling him that it can't happen—that *we* can't happen—over and over, here I am muddying the waters by allowing him to hold my hand.

"What do you want to watch?" I ask, once we get to the living room.

"Technically, I said watch a show *or something*." He grins, and my heart flutters in response. "I'm leaning more toward that option."

"Do I get a say?"

"Always." His voice is so serious, solemn even.

"Then give me my options and I'll choose," I tell him, taking back control of the situation.

He contemplates my demand for a minute and then nods to himself. "We can either veg out on the couch and watch a show—I'm currently bingeing *Justified*—or, I can make us some hot cocoa and we can sit on the deck and talk."

His options both seem innocuous enough, but my over-active brain and libido kick my inner-turmoil into overdrive.

Do I want to be snuggled up next to him on the couch where our bodies will be forced to touch, or do I want to have some heart-to-heart under the starlit sky?

"Outside," I say, because at least there, we won't be touching.

"Sweet." He tips his head toward the back door. "You wanna start the heater while I make us some cocoa?"

"Okay." I flex my fingers at my sides. "I can do that."

He flashes a panty-melting smile and then opens the back door for me. "I'll be right out."

"Please work fast," I mumble, powering up the heater. It was a pretty mild day, but without the sun warming the air, it's cold—really cold.

My teeth chatter as I wait on Orion. Maybe I should go back inside and grab a jacket...

But before I can, the back door opens again, and Orion walks out, his arms loaded down with all kinds of stuff.

"Here," he says, passing a balled up piece of cloth to me. "Brought you this."

I shake it out and quickly realize it's one of his hoodies. "Oh." I tug it on over my head, loving the way his scent clings to the cotton. "Thanks."

"And this." He steps closer and wraps a fleece throw around my shoulders.

"You just thought of everything, huh?"

He grins. "Nah. Otherwise, I'd have wood for the firepit."

I plop down into one of the chairs. "Can't win 'em all."

"Whipped cream?" he asks, and I jerk my gaze back toward him.

My mind swan dives into the gutter, my eyes bug out, and my cheeks burn. "What?"

Clearly, I'm in desperate need of some one-on-one time. Especially since my favorite form of relief is no longer visiting me in the VIP room.

Even worse—my desire's apparently written all over my face. "For your cocoa, dirty girl." He drags his heated gaze over my body, and I swear, it warms me up more than the giant heater between us.

What has gotten into me? *Maybe the few hits of his cologne got me high?* I'm pretty sure that's a plausible explanation. Not like stand-up-in-court-legit, unless the jury was made up entirely of women, because then they'd definitely get it.

"Yes, please," I mumble, averting my gaze to the mountains in the distance.

For a few minutes, we sit in silence and sip our drinks. If only I could get my riotous heart and brain to shut up, too. But like anytime I'm in his presence, they're battling it out, with my heart trying to get me to give in to him, and my brain reminding me of all of the reasons it's a bad idea.

"This is really good," I say when I can't take the quiet any more.

"I add vanilla." He winks. "It's something my mom always did."

"Huh. Never would've thought to do that."

"I come from a long line of geniuses."

A laugh bubbles up from deep in my belly. "Clearly," I say once I regain my composure.

"Apparently there's some comedians in my ancestry, too." He gulps down another mouthful of cocoa.

"Smartass."

"Speaking of asses, where is it you waitress?"

Tears fill my eyes as I choke on my drink. "I'm s-s-sorry," I wheeze, smacking my palm against my chest. "What? Why?"

Does he know? Has he been playing with me this whole time? Is this all just a game to him...am I a game to him?

My stupid brain fires off worst-case scenarios like fireworks on the Fourth of July.

Orion's brows dip as he studies me. "Maybe I want to come eat in your section. You said you were a waitress, right?"

"But what's that have to do with my ass?" My brain is struggling to connect the dots here. I know I'm missing something, but what?

"Is that a serious question?" He draws back and pretends to peek around to my backside, despite us both being seated. "Your ass is always at the forefront of my mind. It's peachy perfection, Frankie."

I hear his words, but for some reason, they're still not computing. Because why would he be obsessed with my ass? I mean, don't get me wrong, objectively, it's an okay ass —but I'm sure he's seen better.

"Nah," he murmurs, his voice dipping low as he shakes his head. "Your ass is by far the best. High and tight. Juicy." He snaps his teeth together. "Biteable."

"Orion!" I squeak his name, every bit as scandalized as I am turned on.

"What?" He shrugs. "It's true."

"You can't say things like that." It's one thing, under the low lights of the VIP room when I'm half-naked and wearing a mask, my identity concealed, but stick us under the stars on a random Wednesday night and suddenly it feels too intimate.

"Pretty sure I just did." He kicks his feet up onto the coffee table and smirks.

How is it possible for him to be so cool and calm while I'm over here melting down on the inside? Orion's this perfect mixture of sex appeal, confidence, and charm. It should be illegal, really.

"Well." I sink back into my chair, drawing my knees up and under the excess material of his hoodie. "Don't do it again."

"Fine, fine." He rolls his head along the back of the chair until he's staring at my profile. "I did promise to be on my best behavior. So, let's talk about something other than your hot body."

I groan and cover my face with my hands. *Why is he doing this to me?*

"You don't wanna tell me where you work, then tell me about your classes. You met Stella at school, right?"

"Yeah." I push my hair back behind my ears. "In art class."

"Are you an artist?"

Another laugh flies out of me, and I slap a hand over my mouth to muffle the sound. "That'd be a no." I risk a glance in his direction, only to find him still staring at me. "I just needed an elective."

"Stella, too. I'm pretty sure she can't even draw stick people."

We talk for hours, about everything and nothing, until I can barely keep my eyes open.

"Let's get you to bed," Orion says, standing.

"I'm good..." I protest, but it's weak. My bed is calling my name, but I'd happily forgo sleep if it means spending time with him like this.

Because in the dark of night, I can pretend he's mine.

"Nope." He reaches down and grips me under each arm, lifting me to my feet. "It's time for bed."

"Fine." I yawn and wiggle out of his hold. "But we need to clean up out here."

"I've got it, baby." And then, I swear I hear him whisper *I've got you*, but that part might have been in my head.

I stumble over the threshold, but Orion's there to catch me, hauling me against his solid chest. "Watch your step," he whispers as I sink into him.

He's comfort and safety and peril and heartbreak all at the same time, an enigma I can't seem to resist.

"Sorry." My voice is thick and heavy, tired.

Slowly, reluctantly, he releases me, swapping his hold around my waist for my right hand. "C'mon, sleeping beauty, the sun will be up before you know it."

I allow him to lead me down the darkened hall to my bedroom, nearly plowing into his back when he comes to a stop outside of my door.

"Here—" I pull my hand from his and start to take off his hoodie, but he stops me.

"Keep it."

"Are you sure?"

"Yeah." His lips kick up into a satisfied grin. "I like seeing you in my clothes."

"You like me more without 'em," I mumble, accidentally giving life to my internal thoughts.

"Yeah," he agrees easily, not catching the actual meaning. "I'm sure I would, but you took that off the table. So, for now, I'll settle on seeing you like this."

"Huh?" It sounds like he's telling me he's willing to wait to see me naked, but...

Before I can think any more on it, he leans down and presses a sweet kiss to my forehead. "Goodnight, Frankie."

My belly swoops low and my heart thumps dangerously in my chest as I let myself into my room. "Goodnight," I whisper back.

I skip my bedtime routine and crawl straight into my bed. Maverick immediately curls into me, but I can't seem to fall asleep.

Because as I lie here, next to my son, wrapped in Orion's sweet scent, I can't help but wonder if a little danger is exactly what my life needs.

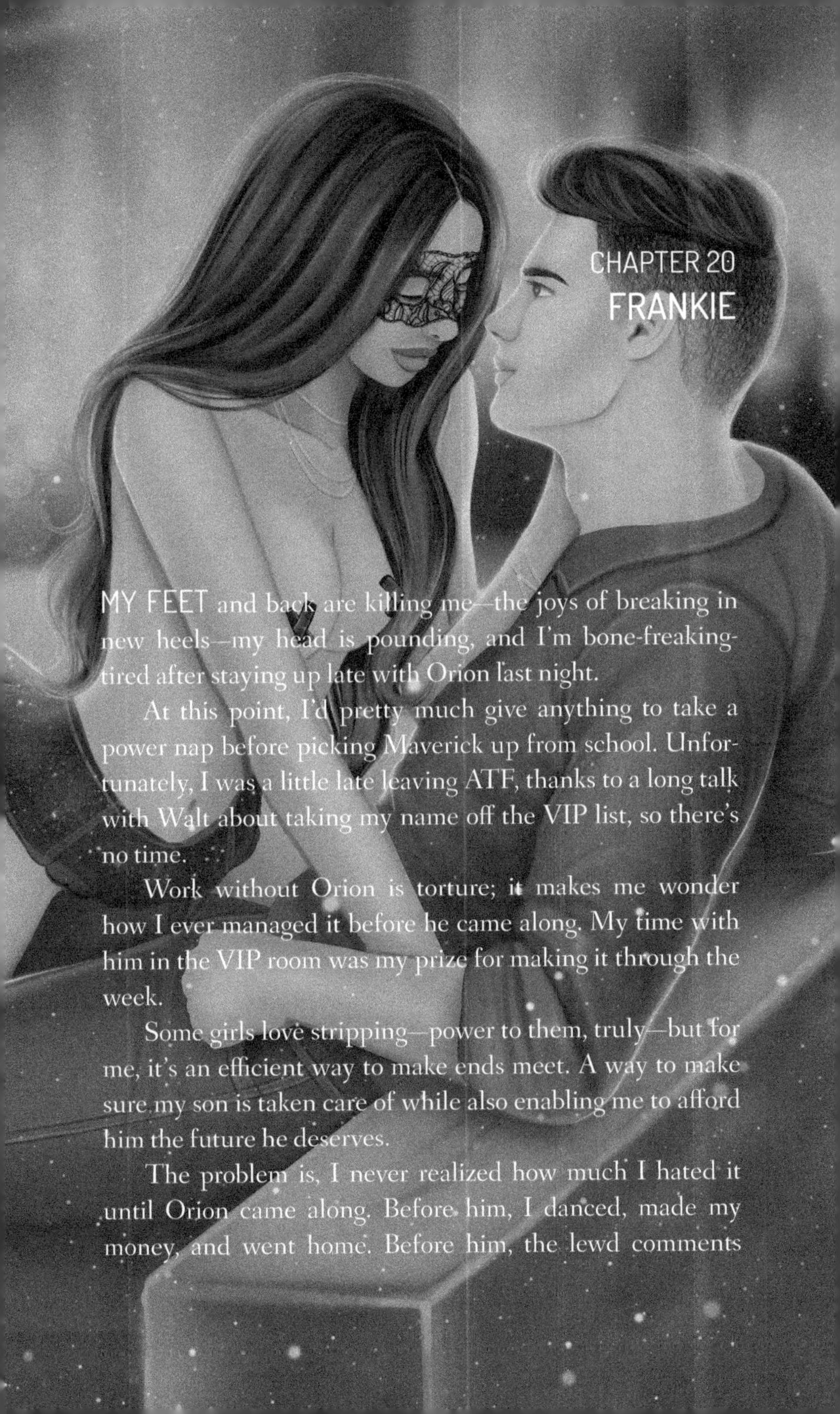

MY FEET and back are killing me—the joys of breaking in new heels—my head is pounding, and I'm bone-freaking-tired after staying up late with Orion last night.

At this point, I'd pretty much give anything to take a power nap before picking Maverick up from school. Unfortunately, I was a little late leaving ATF, thanks to a long talk with Walt about taking my name off the VIP list, so there's no time.

Work without Orion is torture; it makes me wonder how I ever managed it before he came along. My time with him in the VIP room was my prize for making it through the week.

Some girls love stripping—power to them, truly—but for me, it's an efficient way to make ends meet. A way to make sure my son is taken care of while also enabling me to afford him the future he deserves.

The problem is, I never realized how much I hated it until Orion came along. Before him, I danced, made my money, and went home. Before him, the lewd comments and hungry eyes didn't bother me—but now, it just makes me feel dirty.

Better suck it up, Frankie, because until you get your degree, dirty *pays the bills.*

Either way, it's a problem for future Frankie to deal with, because tonight is going to be all about Maverick and studying. Worrying can wait.

I make it to the car line with seconds to spare, which is fine with me, since I always have to get out and help Maverick buckle. A lot of times, other moms honk at me, but not today—perks of being last, I suppose.

"Did you have a good day?" I ask, once I'm back behind the wheel.

"Yeah!" He kicks his feet and his toes tap against my seatback. "We got to finger paint!"

That explains the new additions to his shirt. "What did you paint?"

"Us, Mama. Our family."

"You and me?" *Please say yes, please.*

"And O, Mama. He's my papa bear."

"Mav, baby," I say, though I can barely hear my own voice over the sound of my heart disintegrating in my chest. "You know Orion's not your dad, right?"

I wait with bated breath and a white knuckle grip on the wheel for his reply. But he's in no hurry, and by the time he finally answers me, we're nearly home.

"I know, Mama, but we never talk about my dad, and I like O. He's real nice. And he's smart and funny and strong. He'd be a good dad."

How many times can a heart break?

"I'm sorry, Mav," I whisper, pulling into my designated parking spot and throwing the car into park. "Ask me anything."

"What was his favorite color? Did he like broccoli? Was he tall? Will I be tall? Did he really love me—like a lot? Who was his favorite Batman baddie?"

"Slow down, bud." I turn off the radio and unbuckle, twisting around to face him. "His favorite color was green—like the color of the Hulk. But despite loving the color green, he hated *all* green food. Lettuce, broccoli, green beans—he hated all of it. Your daddy was tall."

"How tall?" Maverick interrupts. "Like taller than Uncle Phin?"

"About the same height, so even though I'm short, I bet you'll be tall."

"Yes!" He pumps his fist into the air. "One day you'll need a stool to be as big as me!"

"Definitely. And, Mav, your dad loved you so much. From the moment we found out you were growing in my belly, he was excited. He actually picked out your name. He was so excited to be a dad—to be *your* dad."

"For really?" He leans forward as far as his car seat harness will allow.

"Really." I glance away from him and pinch the bridge of my nose, willing my tears away. "And, Mav, I'm sorry I haven't talked much about him, but I want you to know, you are always—and I mean *always*—welcome to ask me anything about him."

He crosses his arms and narrows his eyes. "You forgot to answer one of my questions."

"Did I?"

"His favorite Batman baddie!"

"Oh." A half laugh, half sob lodges in my throat. Maverick's innocence is truly a thing of wonder. "He loved the Joker."

"Me, too!" Maverick screams. "We're just alike, huh, Mama?"

More than you know, my sweet boy, I think, my tears flowing down my cheeks unchecked. Talking with him like this has been a long time coming. And while it hurts me to even think about Tyson, Maverick deserves to know his dad.

He deserves to know what a wonderful, kind, caring, and compassionate man his father was.

"You are, Mav. Your dad was my best friend in the whole world, and while losing him was so hard, you healed me, bud. You are every single good part of him, and anytime I miss him, I know I can snuggle you."

My son's nose crinkles. "Is that why you hug me so much?"

"Yeah, baby." I sniffle and wipe beneath my eyes. "And just because I love you."

"I love you, too." He tugs at his buckle. "But I'd love you even more if we could go inside and have a snack."

Leave it to a four-year-old to make me laugh and cry in the same conversation. "You got it."

"How about yogurt?" I ask, unclipping his harness. He passes me his bag and scrambles out of the car.

He pauses, one foot on the asphalt and one on the sidewalk. "Strawberry but with Goldfish."

"Sure," I reply, internally cringing, because I already know he plans to dip the crackers into the yogurt—the little weirdo.

"You're the bestest!" Maverick takes off down the sidewalk, running toward the front door like a pint-sized man on a mission.

I make it to the door less than thirty seconds after him, but with the way he's hopping and bouncing around, it looks like he's been waiting for hours.

"Hurry, Mama, I'm starving."

"Didn't you eat lunch?" I swipe my key fob over the sensor and then open the door.

"Yeah." He rushes past me, heading straight for the kitchen. "But that was forever ago!"

"You're home!" Stella shouts, barreling into me.

"Thanks for the freaking heart attack," I mutter, trying to pry her octopus arms off of me.

"I've been waiting on you forever!" She tightens her hold, rocking us back and forth with the energy of a labradoodle playing tug-o-war. Seriously—what is it with dogs, kids, and Stella all having this much energy? What's their secret?

"I was at work... you literally saw me this morning before I left."

She finally releases me, taking a step back while her lips turn down in an exaggerated frown. "I know—it just feels like we never spend any time together."

Guilt slams into me even harder than Stella did, because she's right—we haven't really been hanging out. When I'm not working or in class, I'm either with Maverick, which I know she gets—or with her brother.

I'm totally a shit friend.

"I'm sorry, Stella."

Her lips twitch before pulling down into a pleading pout. "I know how you could make it up to me."

There may as well be a flashing sign over her head that reads: *Warning! This bitch is up to no good!*

But still, my curiosity wins out. "How's that?"

"Come out with us tonight." Her blue eyes twinkle with mischief as she clasps her hands under her chin and bats her lashes. If I didn't know better, I'd say she looked angelic.

"Who's us?" I ask, assuming she means her and Samson. Maybe even Orion. "And what about Maverick?"

"That's where I come in," Orion says, joining us in the foyer. "Made Mav his snack by the way—did you know he dips his Goldfish crackers into his yogurt?"

"Yup. He also likes peanut butter and mayo. He definitely got his tastebuds from Tyson, because ew."

"The fuck?" Orion whispers, disgust lining his every feature.

"Yeah, super gross." I shrug, because really, what can I do?

"Yes, gross." Stella grabs my hands and tugs me toward her. "Back to me."

"I don't know... I'm kind of tired."

"Please, Frankie?" There's that stupid puppy-pout again. "I promise it'll be fun!"

It's on the tip of my tongue to say no. All I want to do is crawl in bed and catch up on my reading; maybe watch a movie with Maverick. Instead, I find myself asking, "What exactly do you have planned?"

"Nothing crazy." She's smiling like she's already convinced me. "Just some pizza..."

From her pink cheeks to her pitchy voice, it's obvious she's not telling me everything. "And what else? Because whatever you're trying to sell right now..." I wave my hand in her general direction. "I'm not buying."

"Okay, fine. There's something else, but it's a surprise for you and Emmy—she's coming, too. I promise it's not a party, club, bar, or anything involving alcohol or being outside."

I glance toward Orion, but he just smirks back at me like he knows I'm going to say yes.

But then Maverick joins us, sliding across the floor in his socks. "Why are y'all standing around here by the door?"

"We're talking," I tell him, opening my arms to him for a snuggle, which he readily accepts. I'm already dreading the day he doesn't want my hugs and kisses.

"'Bout what?" he asks, worming out of my hold in favor of climbing all over Orion like he's his own personal jungle gym.

My cheeks heat as soon as the thought enters my brain, because, *same kid, same.* Although, I'd prefer to do it somewhere a lot more private and with a lot less clothes.

"About whether or not your mama should come to dinner with Emmy and me tonight," Stella helpfully supplies.

"Whatcha gonna eat?" He crosses his arms over his chest as he waits for her answer.

"Pizza."

Maverick's brows dip low. "What kind?"

"Whatever kind your mama wants."

"Who's going with you?" he asks, and I swear my stupid brain immediately conjures up an image of him asking a younger sibling these same questions before a night out. My boy's protective nature is pure instinct, and God if it doesn't make me feel all gooey.

Stella rolls her lips inward to keep from laughing. "Me, your mama, and Miss Emmy."

"That's good." He nods and then freezes. "What about me? Where will I be? I like pizza, too!"

Orion drops down to one knee. "I thought you could hang out with Samson and me. Let the girls have their thing and we can have ours. I'll even order pizza."

Mav's pensive gaze flip-flops between Orion and me. "Add ice cream and you've gots a deal."

Stella does a quiet little happy dance while I roll my eyes. Who knew my big protector could be so easily swayed?

"Name the flavor and I'll make it happen, bud."

"The kind with the cookies in it!" Maverick shouts.

"Cookie dough?"

"Yuck." He sticks out his tongue. "No. The chocolate cookies. The ones Miss Emmy likes."

"Oreos?" Stella asks, but I'm still wondering how my son knows what kind of cookies our neighbor likes.

I guess she is Stella's best friend, and she lives next door, so she's probably over here a lot when I'm at work. But still—hearing him say it threw me. *I wonder if he knows my favorite flavor?*

Orion snaps his fingers. "Cookies and cream?"

"Yes!" Maverick tosses his hands in the air and spins in a circle. "Best night ever!"

"I thought camping was the best night ever?" Orion asks, his brows pulling low as he pretends to be offended.

I don't know how I'm expecting Maverick to respond, but when he scrambles into Orion's lap and wraps his arms around his neck and says, "Every night with you is the best night ever, O." I'm surprised to say the least.

Surprised, and an emotional wreck. Maverick loves Orion so much, and I can't help but worry I'm making a colossal mistake by letting him become so attached.

What if he leaves? Mav would be heartbroken—I'm talking utterly devastated. But I know I can't lock him away in a tower to shelter him from every potential hurt either.

I know he needs to experience life—the good parts and the bad—even if the thought of him hurting for a split second makes me feel like I can't breathe. My mama heart wants to shrink him, bubble wrap him, and carry him in my pocket forever. But I can't. He has to grow up, and instead of living in fear, I should count us lucky that we've somehow managed to find us a little makeshift family of our own.

My son is happy, healthy, and so freaking loved; that's what matters. And if for some reason, Orion leaves... well, I'll cross that bridge when we get to it.

"Yeah, bud," Orion murmurs, his voice deeper than usual, "right back atcha."

Stella sniffs loudly, and I look up just in time to catch her wiping beneath her eyes. "Well, let's get ready then. I told Emmy five."

***

"THIS IS THE BEST EVER," Stella mumbles around a mouthful of pizza.

Emmy and I exchange knowing looks, totally on the same page.

The two of us are cut from the same cloth—both introverted and wary of newcomers.

We've only met a handful of times, but she's always been nice enough. Her boyfriend is kind of intimidating though, what with him being tall, dark, and growly. Luckily, I pay Stella and she handles paying the rent, because I'm pretty sure I'd just throw the money at him and run, like a total loon.

"Yeah, it's good," Emmy finally agrees, dabbing at the corner of her mouth with a napkin.

A look of betrayal crosses Stella's face. "Good is an understatement, my friend."

I don't mean to laugh at her antics, but I can't help it.

When we first met, I straight up told Stella she was *a lot* —meant it then, mean it now. But I love her for it, too.

"Dramatic," Emmy singsongs, wriggling her brows.

Stella heaves out an Oscar-worthy sigh. "Why do I even keep you around?" She tears off another bite, chews, and swallows before pointing at me. "Both of you! Y'all're impossible!"

"Impossibly awesome, you mean?" I ask, causing Emmy to laugh.

"Oh, sure, laugh at her." Stella crosses her arms over her chest. "Traitor."

"Sounds like you girls are having fun," a masculine voice says, seconds before arguably the tallest man I've ever seen plops down next to Stella like he has every right to be there.

"Damnit, Gabe!" another deep voice hollers, seconds before an attractive black man with long dreads slides into the booth next to Emmy. "What on earth is wrong with you?"

"With me?" the jolly blond giant asks, one golden brow lifted. "Not a thing. You, on the other hand, may just be beyond help."

I swear to God, it's like we're in some sort of alternate dimension, because in what freaking universe do total strangers just crash someone's dinner?

More importantly, what's up with Stella and Emmy, because while my brain is literally short circuiting due to our interlopers, they both look like this is an everyday occurrence.

"There's nothing wrong with pineapple on pizza, Gabe."

"Eeeehrr!" the blond one—Gabe—imitates a game show buzzer, "wrong answer. It's abhorrent. Seriously, how did you manage to hide this from me for so long? Ugh." He drags his gaze up and down the other man, somehow managing to look both turned on and repulsed at the same time before turning to Stella. "How can someone be so close to perfect only to ruin it in the blink of any eye?"

She smiles brightly and shrugs. "Men, am I right?"

"I'll show you perfect, jackass," Dreadlocks mutters. "Just wait until we get home."

I'm trying to keep my cool, since Stella and Emmy aren't freaked out, but hello, *stranger danger*.

Out of nowhere, Dreadlocks' gaze snaps toward me. "You're Frankie, right?"

"Um." I press my lips together and nod. "Yes."

"I'm Zach." He leans around Emmy and thrusts his hand toward me. "It's so nice to meet you."

"You..." I wipe my hand on my jeans before offering it to him. "You, too. I'm Frankie. But apparently, you, uh, already know that."

"Aren't you just a little raincloud." I yank my hand back and whirl around to face Gabe.

"What?"

"It's fitting really. Stella's a ball of perpetual sunshine and you're a juicy little raincloud."

Emmy hmmphs under her breath.

"I didn't forget you." He winks at her. "You're my sweets."

"I'm sorry, but who are y'all?"

Gabe and Zach's gazes clash, and then Gabe says, "You mean you've never heard of us?" He looks back to Zach. "I always thought our reputations preceded us."

Zach rolls his eyes. "Yours maybe."

"Apparently not." He focuses on me again, and my head's spinning from all of the back and forth. "I'm Gabe.

Daddy to Emmy, bestie to Stella, and giant-two-headed dragon to Mav-a-doodle-do."

"My son?" I ask, planting both palms on the table. "You know my son?"

Gabe quickly realizes I'm neither smiling nor joking. "I do. He's a great kid."

I swallow roughly, trying not to let my emotions get the best of me. "How?"

"We're at Emmy's a lot," he says, his once loud voice now calm and pacifying. "At first, I only met him in passing, but Stella's brought him over with her a few times. We played knights." He flicks his eyes to Stella. "Zach was the noble steed, I was the two-headed dragon, Emmy was the good witch, Stella the princess in the tower, and Sterling was... Sterling."

Vaguely, I remember Mav telling me about a dragon and a princess, but I thought he was talking about a book Stella read him.

Don't flip out, Frankie. I count down from ten in my head. *You know, love, and trust Stella. She's good people and if she approves of Gabe and Zach, then they're probably also good people.*

The tension surrounding our table is so thick, I'm sure we could slice it with the pizza cutter. "Okay." I nod. "Well, it's nice to meet y'all."

Gabe and Zach both audibly exhale their relief.

But Stella's cheeks are red and her eyes glassy. "I'm so sorry, Frankie."

"It's—" I pause, because while I'm not mad, it's not really okay either.

"No, truly." She reaches across the table and takes my hand. "I should have talked to you first, let you meet them. I'm so sorry."

"I forgive you," I say, meaning it. I know her heart was in a good place, and having never been a mom, how could she really know?

"Thank you." Stella squeezes my hand softly before letting it go.

"Quick question though, and I mean no offense..."

She quirks a brow as her lips turn up into a barely there smile.

"I thought you said this was a girls' night?" I feel rude asking about the guys crashing, but at the same time, I was promised a girls' night and I'm not sure how I feel about sharing it with two ginormous, strange men.

Gabe widens his eyes and presses his hand over his heart. "You mean... I'm not... one of the girls?" he asks, batting his too-long-for-a-guy lashes.

"This feels like a trick question," I mutter to myself.

"Chill, rainy day, I'm just giving you shit. We may not be chicks, but we are definitely into dicks. More specifically, each other's. You feel me?"

I press my lips together and nod. "Totally feel you, J-B-G."

He rears back. "Excuse me—what does that mean?"

I suck down a gulp of my drink, suddenly feeling totally at ease. Gabe and Zach lowkey remind me of Walt and Lenny, and I love it. "Don't know what you mean."

"Those letters!" He pounds his fist against the tabletop, and we all giggle—especially Zach. "Tell me!"

"Jolly." I pop the last bite of pizza into my mouth and chew thoughtfully. Slowly. "Blond." I take another sip of my drink. "Giant."

For a moment, silence engulfs our table, the two of us engaging in a battle of wills. But then, he laughs. Hard.

"Oh, shit, that's good." Gabe knocks his shoulder into Stella's. "Priceless."

Her blue eyes flit back and forth between us like we're both off our rockers—probably because I'm laughing and joking with a virtual stranger when it took me forever to open up to her.

I don't know what it is; there's just something about Gabe that puts me completely at ease.

"Y'all are weird."

"Takes one to know one." Gabe claps back, looking all too pleased with himself.

"Whatever." She throws a wad of cash on the table, and Emmy and I follow suit, making sure to leave enough to cover our meal and the tip. "Are y'all ready for the best part of the night?"

"If by ready you mean terrified?" Emmy asks. "Then sure."

"Great!" Stella nudges Gabe out of the booth and pops up to her feet. "Let's go!"

We all file out of the pizzeria, but instead of heading for where we parked, Stella guides us in the complete opposite direction.

"You're really not going to tell us where we're going?" I ask, rubbing my hands over my upper arms for warmth.

"We're here!" she says, gesturing game show style to the big building behind her.

"Are you for real?" Gabe asks, excitedly knocking his shoulder into Zach's.

"Yup." She rocks forward on her toes. "I figured we could all blow off a little steam."

"Stell..." Emmy hedges, her brown eyes ping-ponging between her best friend and the illuminated sign over head that reads: Sky High Trampoline Park.

"Have I ever steered you wrong?" Stella steps forward, slinging an arm around Emmy's neck. "Seriously, have I?"

"I guess not."

"It's just some good old fashioned bouncy fun. C'mon!"

Emmy looks toward me and I shrug. "I mean, it sounds kind of fun..." Even if I do feel a little guilty about being here without Maverick.

She turns to Zach for backup, only to find he and Gabe are already heading for the door.

"C'mon, sweets." Gabe crooks his finger at Emmy. "Let's jump the night away."

Emmy sucks in a deep breath and then links her arm with Stella, who links hers with mine, and together, the three of us head inside, ready to cut loose and relax, if only for a little while.

IT'S BEEN about an hour since Frankie and Stella left, and for nearly all sixty of those minutes, Mav and I have been snuggled up on the couch watching *Spiderman.*

He's a little clingier than usual, laying completely on top of my lap with his arms around my neck and his head on my chest. The kid looks like he's about two seconds away from conking out for the night.

"You ready for dinner?" I ask, running my fingers idly through his messy hair. "Samson should be here soon."

"O," he groans, snuggling closer. "I feel funny."

"Funny like what?" I press the back of my hand to his forehead like my mom used to do to me. He feels clammy more so than warm; that means he's not running a fever.

At least I think it does. Right?

"I don't know." His voice sounds smaller than I've ever heard it. Puny even, and nothing like the larger-than-life Maverick I know. "Bad." His tummy gurgles right then, as if to say *see...bad!*

"Maybe I should find you something to eat instead of pizza?" I try to ease out from under him to see if we have any soup, but he whimpers and clutches at the fabric of my shirt. "You want me to stay?"

"Yeah."

Settling back against the couch, I carefully readjust Maverick on my lap. I know I should call Frankie, but my phone sits just out of reach on the coffee table.

But Samson should be here any minute. I'll call her then.

I try to focus on the show, knowing all I can do is wait, but worry for Mav crowds my brain, forcing out all other thoughts.

Thankfully, a few minutes later, the front door swings open and Samson struts in. "Who's ready for guys' ni—"

"Shh!" I cut Samson off, holding one hand up in the air, quickly curling my fingers into a closed fist. "Maverick's sick."

"Damn, really?" he asks from somewhere behind me.

"Yeah. Can you hand me my phone?" I nod my head toward the coffee table.

"Let me set this stuff down in the kitchen."

I press my hand to Maverick's forehead again, and then his cheek. *Shit.* He definitely feels warmer than he did last time.

A minute or two later, Samson joins us, passing me my phone before dropping down into the chair on the other side of the room. "He okay?"

"I don't know, man. He's warm and says he feels bad."

"O!" Maverick cries my name—and that's all the warning I get before he vomits all over me, and my phone.

"Holy shit!" Samson gags, leaping from his chair like his ass is on fire and running out of the room. "Is he possessed?"

"He's sick, you jackass!" I shout after him. "Grab a towel and some cleaning stuff."

The smell is fucking awful, but Maverick's soft cries steal all of my attention. "Are you okay, bud?"

"I'm s-s-sorry," he says, hiccuping. "I d-didn't mean to."

"Hey, no. Shh. It's okay. You're okay."

He sniffles and then wipes his nose on what might be the only clean part of my shirt. "I want my mama."

"I know you do, bud. Let's get you cleaned up and I'll call her, okay?"

Samson walks into the room with a bath towel draped over his shoulder, a roll of paper towels tucked under his arm, cleaning spray in one hand, and the other plugging his nose. "Here." He sets everything down and scuttles back into the foyer.

"Thanks." I roll my eyes. "Call my sister while I clean him up."

"You got it."

"Oh, and start a bath for Mav, too. Warm but not hot."

"You want me to go into Frankie's room?"

"Jesus," I mutter. "Yes, Samson, I want you to go into her room and start the bath."

"Fine."

I glance over my shoulder in time to see him press his phone to his ear as he walks away.

"C'mon, bud." I press Maverick into my chest, internally cringing at the feeling of my puke-soaked shirt sticking to my chest. "We gotta get up."

He wraps his arms around my neck, clinging to me as I stand. I secure him to me with one hand and grab the towel Samson brought with the other, tossing it down onto the couch, hoping it will absorb some of the mess—the rest will have to wait.

"Think you can handle a bath?" I ask, striding toward his room.

"Yeah," he mumbles. "But will you stay with me?"

"The whole time."

Samson meets us in the hall. "Did you get ahold of Stella?"

"No." He steps back, giving us a wide berth. "She didn't answer."

"Damnit."

"Swear word," Mav mumbles weakly.

"Gotta set you down, okay?" I ask as we step into the bathroom.

He nods and I gently place him on his feet.

"Think you can get undressed?"

"Yeah." Another nod. "I think so."

I check the temperature of the water; it feels okay. "Alright, in you go."

He shuffles past me and steps into the tub. "You won't leave, right?"

"I'm not going anywhere, bud, promise." I wait a minute to make sure he's okay in the tub, turn off the water, and then strip off my puke-covered shirt. "Do you know where your mama keeps washcloths?"

"Under the sink." He's reclining against the back of the tub with his legs straight out in front of him, with his wiggly toes poking up out of the water.

I grab two washcloths from the cabinet, one for him and one for me, and turn on the sink faucet.

"Can you wash up all by yourself?" I ask, waiting for the water to warm up.

"Yeah, O. I'm sick, not a baby."

Smirking at his inherent sass, I grab his shower gel and place it on the side of the tub. "Here you go."

He sets to work scrubbing himself clean, and I do the same at the sink.

The first pass of the wet cloth over my chest feels like heaven, but I make sure to keep my relief to myself; the last thing I want is for Maverick to feel bad. It's not like he can help getting sick.

"You ready to get out?" I ask, once my chest is no longer sticky.

"Yeah."

"Are you clean?"

"Promise."

I start to unplug the tub, but stop and grab the towel instead. When I was his age, the sound of the water being sucked down the drain terrified me.

He climbs out of the tub and wraps the towel around his shoulders, but doesn't make any effort to dry himself off.

"How about you tell me what drawer your pajamas are in and I'll grab them while you dry off?"

"The second one, but my undies are in the first."

"Got it." Turning on my heel, I head into the bedroom toward the dresser.

By the time I make it back into the bathroom, Maverick's mostly dry, but shivering like crazy. "You okay?" I ask, my worry coming back tenfold.

"I'm c-cold and my mouth tastes bad."

I press my hand to his head again, he feels normal, but don't baths skew things?

"Get dressed and I'll get your toothbrush ready, okay?"

He nods and takes his clothes from me.

Once his teeth are clean, I hang the towel, scoop him into my arms, and carry him to the bed.

Maverick instantly rolls to his side and snuggles into the covers. "I want my mama, O."

"I know, bud. Let me grab my phone and I'll call her, okay?"

He tries to nod, but his movements are sluggish at best.

I check my pockets for my phone, but it's not there—I must have dropped it in the living room.

"I'll be right back, bud," I murmur to Maverick, but he's already out like a light.

I find Samson in the kitchen stuffing his face with pizza. "Seriously?"

His mouth is too full to talk, so he shrugs. "How's Maverick?" he asks, once he swallows.

"Asleep. Feels a little warm. Did you ever get ahold of Stella?"

He shakes his head and a prickle of worry zips through me.

"I'm going to call Frankie, clean up, and change. Keep an ear on Mav for me?"

Samson nods, already tearing into another slice of pizza.

Luckily, my phone is sitting on the floor right next to the couch. I quickly wipe it down and then dial Frankie's number. But the call goes to her voice mail.

I try her a few more times as I clean the couch and floor, but she never answers.

I'm officially freaking the fuck out. What if something happened to her?

I decide to try Stella's phone after changing into a pair of sweats. She doesn't answer either.

Maybe they're somewhere loud and can't hear their phones? They have to be. It's only the reason that doesn't threaten to send me into a panic.

"Samson," I call, walking back into the kitchen. "You have Sterling's number, right?"

"Yeah, man." He tips his head my way ever so slightly.

"Call him and see if he's heard from them. Frankie's not picking up either."

"You think they're okay?" Samson pushes his plate away, his attention solely on me.

"Fuck, man, I hope so." I run a hand through my hair, tugging on the ends until my scalp stings. "Hey, do you know where Stella keeps the thermometer and shit?"

"You live here, not me." His tone is easy going, but I can see the worry he's trying to hide.

"Helpful, real helpful. Call Sterling. I'm going to sit with Mav."

"On it."

I try Frankie one more time on my way back to her bedroom, but still, no answer.

Maverick whimpers in his sleep, and I rush to the bed, pressing my hand to his forehead. His cheeks are candy-apple red, and he's burning up. *Fuck.*

With Frankie not answering, I call the only other person I can think of, and she answers on the first ring.

"Orion, is everything okay?"

No, I want to shout, *nothing's okay!*

But then, Mav reaches for me in his sleep. "O, you're back," he mumbles, wrapping himself around me.

"Maverick's sick, Mom. He's burning up."

"Where's Frankie? How high is his fever? Other symptoms? There's a nasty bug going around."

"I don't know. Stella took her for girls' night and neither of them are picking up their phones. He threw up earlier and now he... he has to have a fever, but I don't know where Stella keeps her thermometer. I think he needs medicine, but I don't know what he can take. What do I do?"

"Do you need me to come over? I can be there—"

"You don't have to do that, Mom. I wouldn't want you to get sick. Just tell me what to do."

I swear I hear her sniffle just before she asks, "Do you have a pen and paper?"

"I can make notes in my phone," I tell her, switching the call to speaker.

"First, you need a thermometer. I always let you kids sweat out your fever, unless it was over one-oh-two or you were in pain. Either way, you'll want to get some kids Tylenol and some Motrin. You can alternate them. He can also take lukewarm baths to bring his fever down. You said he threw up?"

"Yeah, just once," I reply, steadily tapping her advice into the notepad on my phone.

"Okay. Get some Pedialyte and popsicles just in case."

"Any kind of popsicles?"

"Yep. Any kind."

Maverick slings his arm over my middle, burying his head into my armpit.

"Do you need me to run to the store? I really don't mind."

"I know you don't, Mom. But Samson is already here. I'll just send him."

When she doesn't reply right away, I know it's killing her not to be able to help. She's been ready for grandkids for years, and Maverick's the closest thing she's got.

"Okay. Tell him Gigi loves him."

"I will. Oh, and, Mom..."

"Yeah?"

"I love you."

"Love you, too, Orion." She sniffles again. "So much."

I end the call and then dial Samson.

"Are you seriously calling me from the other room?"

"Did you figure out where they are?" I ask, ignoring his smartass question.

"Nope. But Sterling said he'd call Gabe and Zach."

We're playing the world's most fucked up game of telephone. "I need you to run to the store."

"Yeah, man. Sure. Just tell me what you need."

I rattle off the list and then end the call right as Maverick's lids flutter open. "Where's Mama?" he rasps.

"She'll be home soon, bud. Don't worry."

A riot of emotions explode inside of me as I watch his eyes fill with tears. The kid's miserable. My heart aches for him. All he wants is Frankie, but he's stuck with me.

"You'll stay with me, right?" His voice wobbles as he scooches impossibly closer to me.

"I won't move a muscle until your mama's here."

"No." He wraps his pinkie finger around mine. "Stay then, too. I need you, too, O."

This kid, man. He's killing me.

"I'll be here." I press a kiss to the top of his head and draw the covers up to his chest. "Try to sleep."

He yawns and nestles into my side, his skin practically searing mine, he's so hot. "Love you, O."

That's it. Game over. TKO. Stick a fork in me, I'm done.

"Love you, too, Mav," I murmur, my whole fucking heart lodged in my esophagus as I run my fingers through his hair.

"OH MY GOD," I say between panting huffs, "that was way more fun than I thought it would be."

"See!" Stella shouts victoriously, skipping ahead of us toward the wall of lockers where we stashed our belongings.

"You really did it now." Emmy brushes her shoulder against mine as she passes me.

"Did what?"

"Told her she was right," Gabe says, pulling his shirt away from his body in an effort to cool down. "She's never going to let that go."

"Hey, guys…" Stella's voice trembles. "I have like a million missed calls from Samson."

"Oh, I have three from Sterling," Emmy says.

"I have two from him—I think we might be in trouble, Sweets."

Zach rolls his eyes, trying to go for calm, but I can see the worry radiating off of him.

I'm the last one to grab my phone, and when I unlock the screen, there are countless missed calls from Orion. "Oh, God—Maverick!"

I hit redial, but he doesn't answer.

"Guys, we have to go. I... I don't know what's wrong, but I need to get home to Maverick. Now."

"Gotcha." Stella nods. "Let's go." We all quickly slip on our shoes and jackets, and then race to our cars.

"Let us know what's going on," Zach says as we go our separate ways.

"I will." I climb into the back seat and secure my seat belt. My heart feels like it's beating ninety-miles-a-minute. I don't know how I know, but Mav needs me. My son needs me, and I'm not there.

Guilt like never before gnaws at me, eating me up from the inside out as Stella drives us home.

"I didn't get any texts," Stella muses, rolling to a stop at a red light. "So, maybe they're just lonely or something?"

"I don't know." Emmy turns slightly in her seat to look at Stella. "Sterling texted me, but he didn't say what was going on. What about you, Frankie?"

"No texts." I wring my hands together in my lap. "What if something happened to Maverick?"

"I'm sure everything's fine," Stella says, but I can tell she doesn't truly believe her own words. "Orion would never let anything happen to him. He loves that kid."

"Accidents happen." My voice breaks, but I manage to keep my tears at bay.

Stella hits the gas. "We're almost home, Frankie. It's okay. Everything's going to be okay."

Thankfully, we don't hit any other red lights and make it home in record time.

The second we park, I'm unbuckled and out of the car, hauling ass toward the front door. Stella and Emmy are hot on my heels.

"Where have y'all been?" Samson whisper-shouts the

second I unlock the door. "And why weren't you answering your phones?" He pinches the bridge of his nose and mutters something unintelligible under his breath.

"What's going on?" Stella and I ask at the same time.

"Maverick's sick. He has a fever and he threw up."

My guilt from the car returns tenfold. Mav's only ever been throw-up sick once before, and the thought of him going through that without me makes my knees weak.

"Is he okay?" I whisper, hot tears gathering in the corners of my eyes. "Where is he?"

"He's good. Orion gave him some Tylenol and they're asleep."

"He gave him medicine?" *How did he know what to give him? He doesn't know his weight, so how did he know how much?* One after another, questions shoot off in my brain like fireworks.

"His mom." Samson moves to Stella and tugs her into his embrace. "He called her and she talked him through it and I went out and bought everything. Anyway, they're uh, in your room. Asleep."

"Thanks," I whisper, guilt and gratitude threatening to crush me under their dual weights.

"I'm going to go," Emmy says. "See y'all later."

I toss a wave over my shoulder as I head down the hall toward my room; I need to see with my own two eyes that my son is fine.

Seeing the two of them curled around one another in my bed does all kinds of funny things to me. A hope I have no business feeling begins to mingle with my guilt, warming me from the inside out.

"Oh, Mav." I cross the room and press my hand to his forehead. Sure enough, he's burning up.

"Mama?" he whispers groggily. "You're here."

"I am. I'm so sorry, baby."

"It's okay." He rolls onto his side so that his back is tucked against Orion's chest. "O tooked good care of me."

Is it possible for your heart to grow and break at the same time? Because if the pressure behind my ribs is an indicator, that's exactly what's happening right now.

"Lay down, Mama." Maverick blinks slowly, his eyelids heavy with sleep. "Snuggle me."

My eyes flit over to Orion and then back down to my son. It's not like I can wake him up and kick him out—especially after he spent the night caring for Mav. Plus, it's not like we'll be sleeping *together*-together. Maverick will be in between us the whole time.

"Okay, baby. Let me get changed."

I grab a pair of leggings and a T-shirt and head into the bathroom to wash my face, brush my teeth, and change.

Nerves flutter in my belly like butterflies taking flight as I approach the bed. Which is dumb. All we're doing is sleeping, with a kid between us, and he doesn't even know I'm here.

But still, climbing into bed with a man who's watched me masturbate while sitting on his lap feels reckless. Like I'm not only inviting trouble into my life, but holding open the door and throwing a dinner party in its honor.

Or maybe I'm just tired and not thinking straight. All I know is, when it comes to Orion Cartwright, more and more, I find myself wanting to take chances.

SUN PEEKS in through the gap in the curtains and consciousness begins to slowly filter in.

Maverick's curled in a ball, with his head under my chin and his knees against my chest. He's still burning up.

I am too, but for a completely different reason...

One that involves the man wrapped around me from the other side. Orion has one arm wrapped around my middle and his chest is pressed tightly to my back. But what really has me hot and bothered is the big, thick erection digging into my ass.

Why is this my life?

Luckily, Maverick's presence keeps me grounded, because let's be real—if he wasn't here, I'd be tempted to throw myself at the man groaning in my ear like he's dreaming about something naughty.

"Fuck," I mutter, realization dawning that if the sun's up, we majorly overslept. Which I guess doesn't really matter since Maverick's clearly not going to school today.

If anything, I need to get up and call the pediatrician's office to see if they can work him in today.

"Mmm," Orion rumbles, low and dirty. "Fuck's right."

My entire body warms, every bit as embarrassed as I am turned on. I need to put a stop to his wandering hand and thrusting hips—the man's still sleeping for Pete's sake.

"Wake up," I whisper, trying to wriggle free of his hold, but he only tightens it. "Orion, get up."

"Shh." He presses his lips to my shoulder.

"No." I crane my neck forward. "Not happening." Even though I really, *really* wish it could.

I try once again to free myself from both Orion and the covers, but it's no use. I may as well be a fly in a freaking web.

His hold on me is so tight, I can't even roll over. I swear, this is the kind of shit that only happens to me.

It's like the universe was all... *Oh, you like him? Well,*

now you live with him! Oh, and he's into you, too, but you're keeping a secret from him and let's be real, it'll never really work, but temptation be thy name—have fun though!

Maverick's still sleeping soundly, curled in a ball at my side. The last thing I want is to wake him, but I also don't want him to wake up and see Orion cuddling me.

That would lead to questions I'm in no way prepared to answer.

"Orion!" I try one last time, but he only nuzzles his face into the crook of my neck.

I'm weighing my options when his hand leaves my hip and presses into my soft belly, his fingers dangerously near the waistband of my leggings.

Temptation is definitely thy name.

His index finger slips beneath my leggings, and I panic, yanking on his arm hair.

"Shit!" he hisses, bolting upright in the bed.

"Shh!" I smack a hand over his mouth and cut my eyes toward Mav, who is still sleeping.

"What the fuck, Frankie?" he whispers, glaring at me.

"You were two seconds away from shoving your hand down my pants! I didn't know what else to do!"

"Oh." He coughs and looks away, his cheeks turning a deep shade of scarlet. "Uh. Sorry about that."

"It's..." I run my hands through my tangled hair. "It's fine."

"How's Mav?"

"He's still running a fever." I draw my legs up to my chest and rest my head on my knees.

"Damn, poor kid."

"Thank you for taking such good care of him."

"Don't mention it."

"But I have to, Orion." I sit up straight and lock my eyes

on his; I need him to see how much I mean this. "I have to, because what you did, the way you cared for him, it means everything to me. He loves you so much and I—"

"You what?" he asks, leaning toward me, his gaze laser sharp.

Was I about to tell him I loved him, too? I don't think I was... but... *fuck.* "I appreciate you."

"Right." He pulls back, propping himself up against the headboard. "Well, I *appreciate* y'all, too."

We sit side-by-side, with only the sound of Maverick's deep, steady breaths filling the room—until Orion lurches toward the nightstand and grabs his phone.

He taps around on the screen a few times before cursing under his breath.

"What's wrong?"

"Well, aside from missing your call last night." His voice is soft, but I can hear his regret so clearly. "I've missed three from Ben this morning and one from a supplier."

"I'm sorry." And I am, too—sorry I missed *all* of his calls and sorrier still that he feels guilty for missing mine. He has nothing to feel bad for, not a single thing.

"Don't." He leans forward and grips my chin, tilting my face toward his. "Don't apologize. It's not your fault I overslept."

I tilt my head, loving the way his rough fingers feel against my skin. "Eh. It kind of is, you know since you spent the night taking care of my sick kid."

"Frankie." The way he says my name is toe-curling.

"What?" I whisper, leaning farther into his touch.

"This is going to sound crazy." He hesitates briefly before sliding his hand up from my chin to cup my cheek. "But—"

"Mama," Maverick calls out, patting the bed in search of me.

"I'm here, bud." I smile softly before rolling to face my son, knowing good and well that I'm going to obsess over whatever he was about to say. "How are you feeling?"

"Bleh." He lifts his head and sticks out his tongue before flopping back against his pillow. But just as quickly, he pops back up. "O! You're still here!"

Orion scoots closer to me and peers at Maverick over my shoulder. "Of course, I am. I promised you I wouldn't leave last night."

Maverick looks up at him like he hung the freaking moon. "Love you, O."

"Love you, too, bud."

"Can I stay home today, Mama?" Maverick asks, tugging the covers up to his chin.

"Yeah, but I need to call the doctor's office and see if they can work you in."

Mav's entire body tenses. "Will I have to get a... a shot?"

"I doubt it."

"But what if I do?" he wails, clutching the comforter to his chest.

Orion answers before I can. "If you do, you'll handle it like a champ because you're big and brave. You have super powers, remember?"

"Yeah, you're right. I'm strong." He yawns. "And tired. Can I go back to sleep, Mama?"

"Of course, you can." I brush his messy hair off of his forehead. "I'll wake you up when it's time to get ready."

"I guess I better get out of here. Ben's already going to kick my ass."

I know it's not his intention, but his words send another

ping of guilt through me. If I'd have been home last night, he wouldn't have overslept this morning.

"Stop it," Orion softly commands, as if he can hear me berating myself. "I love y'a—that kid. I'm exactly where I want to be, and the only thing I'd change is Mav being sick. Do you hear me?"

"I hear you." I nod and he climbs out of the bed. "Have a good day."

The crazy thing is—I think he means it. With me—*with us*—is exactly where he wants to be.

"You, too." He pockets his phone and moves across the room toward the door. "And, Frankie?"

"Yeah?"

"Text me and let me know what the doctor says, okay?"

"Okay," I whisper, my eyes glued to his retreating form until he's out of sight.

ALL I'VE DONE today is put out fires. Between getting Ben off my ass for oversleeping, to getting a shipment rescheduled, to an issue with a permit, it's been one thing after another.

It doesn't help that I'm fucking exhausted. Which doesn't make any sense, seeing as I was out cold before nine and slept in a good two hours past my normal. If anything, I should be rested.

But I'm not. I'm bone-tired and have a headache forming right behind my left eye.

At least it's Friday, I guess, but damn what I wouldn't give to spend the night with Frankie and Maverick. Turns out there's some twenty-four-hour bug going around and he's pretty much feeling back to normal.

But the way things are going, the only thing I'll be doing tonight is sleeping. And I highly doubt Frankie's going to let me crash in her bed again.

A guy can dream though, I think, waving my key fob to unlock the door.

Inside, I'm met with the sounds of whatever cartoon

Maverick's watching and the smells of whatever Frankie has simmering on the stove.

"O!" Maverick shouts. He pauses his show and jumps up from the couch, heading straight for me. "You're home! I missed you all day."

I brace myself for impact, but it's no use. I feel like crap and the kid hits me like a ton of bricks, knocking us both to the floor. "Shit," I wheeze, my body absorbing the impact of both the floor and Maverick.

"Is everything okay?" Frankie asks, rounding the corner.

"Fine." I carefully sit Maverick upright. "Totally fine."

"I'm sorry," he says, his lips turned down in a frown. "I just really super missed you."

It takes me a minute, but eventually, I haul myself back up to my feet. "It's okay. I missed you, too."

"Any big plans tonight?" Frankie tugs Maverick into her arms and tips forward to press a kiss to the top of his head.

"Nah. I'm probably going to grab something to eat and go to bed. I'm exhausted."

Her big, blue eyes cloud with guilt. "I hope you're not getting sick…"

I wave her off. "I'm sure I'm fine. Just tired. It was a long day."

"Well, at least let me feed you. I made Maverick's favorite day-after-sick dinner."

"Grilled cheese!" Maverick grabs my hand and tugs me toward the kitchen. "They're the best. Mama uses magic to make 'em extra tasty."

"He calls it magic; I call it mayo."

My face must show my apprehension, because Frankie laughs. Seriously though, what is it with this family adding mayo to sandwiches where it has no business being?

"Just try it. It's the only way."

As on the fence as I am over mayonnaise in my grilled cheese, I'm all for time with my two favorite people. "Alright, but if it's gross—"

"I'll make you one without it if you hate it. Promise."

The three of us head into the kitchen. Frankie moves to the far side of the island, where all of her ingredients are out and waiting, while Mav and I each grab a stool.

"Did everything turn out okay at work?" she asks, turning on the front burner and then adding a pat of butter to the pan.

I sigh and prop my elbows on the counter, resting my head in my hands. "More or less. Ben was agitated with me, but he can take a big ass step and get over it."

"Swear word," Maverick mumbles, his attention split between our conversation and the piece of paper he's coloring on.

"Sorry, bud."

We lapse into a comfortable kind of silence, with Maverick drawing up a storm and Frankie flipping and frying out sandwiches. I know I should offer to help, but I'm so tired, I can barely keep my eyes open.

"Here you go," Frankie says, and I jump in my seat.

"What? I'm up!" I look around the kitchen, shocked to see Maverick happily munching away on his grilled cheese.

"Are you sure you're okay?" She nudges my food closer to me, and then grabs her plate and plops down onto the stool beside me.

"Honestly?" I grab one half of the sandwich—it's cut diagonally, which is the only acceptable way—and lift one shoulder in a half-hearted shrug. "I feel horrible."

She wipes her hands on her napkin and then presses one to my forehead. "Oh, Orion, you're burning up! Let me get the thermometer."

I'm tempted to argue, but she's already halfway down the hall.

I force myself to take a bite while I wait for her; much to my surprise, the mayo works.

Unfortunately, my tastebuds and stomach are not in agreement.

Fuck.

Slapping a hand over my mouth, I shove back from the bar and haul ass to the bathroom, dropping to my knees just in time to empty the contents of my stomach into the toilet.

"Orion…" Frankie's voice filters through the partially open door. "Are you okay?"

"Yeah." I swipe the back of my hand over my mouth and flush. "I think so."

"I, um, have the thermometer, whenever you're ready."

Pushing myself back up to my feet, I grunt out some kind of reply and then turn on the faucet, splashing my face with some water before brushing my teeth.

When I open the door, I'm shocked to find Frankie lingering right outside, worrying her lip between her teeth.

"I'm so sorry Maverick got you sick."

"It's fine, Frankie." Obviously, I'd rather not feel like shit warmed over, but I'm not mad about it either. It's a part of life with kids and I have a feeling this won't be the last time Mav passes his germs my way.

"Stick it under your tongue," she murmurs, pressing the *on* button and passing the thermometer my way.

"Yes, ma'am," I mumble around it, causing her to grin.

Seconds later, it beeps, and she pulls it from my mouth. "One-oh-one. Mav definitely gave you his bug."

"I'm sorry, O." He peeks around the corner. "Do you still love me?"

"Always, bud. Always."

His little shoulders slump with relief. "You gotta gets some rest. Right, Mama?"

She smiles at him. "That's right."

I brace myself on the doorframe. "I think I'm going to call it a night."

Frankie takes a step closer to me and then stops. "If you need anything, don't hesitate to let me know."

"I'll be okay," I tell her, meaning it. It's been a helluva long time since I've been sick, but I'll make it.

"I mean it." She's got her mom face on, so I know she's not playing around. "If you need anything, text, call, shout really loud—whatever works, and I'll be there."

"Thanks, Frankie. G'night."

She blinks up at me with those big blue eyes of hers. "Don't mention it."

I slip back into my bedroom and collapse onto the unmade bed pulling the covers up to my chest.

For the longest time, thoughts of Frankie and her hauntingly familiar blue eyes keep me tossing and turning, until finally, my body gives out and sleep takes me.

***

I'M NOT sure what time it is when I wake up, but the sun is shining bright and I only feel a little bit like shit. A definite improvement to last night, anyway.

Stretching my arms over my head, I listen for any signs of life in the house, but it's quiet. Makes me wonder if I'm here by myself.

Stella's been staying at Samson's place more and more. She thinks she's slick, but I know what she's doing. My little sister is pushing hard for me to pursue Frankie, and while I know she loves spending the night with her boyfriend

—*fucking gag me*—I also know these recent sleepovers have been as much for my benefit as they have hers.

I lie around for a few more minutes before finally forcing myself out of the bed. A quick glance at my phone screen tells me it's nearly lunchtime .

Damn.

It's been years since I've slept this late, but I guess I needed it.

After a quick shower, I dress in a fresh pair of sweats and venture out into the kitchen for some water, but stop in my tracks when I see Frankie standing at the stove with her back to me.

She's stirring a large pot of something, softly humming to herself. Watching her, it does something to me. It's almost like she's unleashed this dormant domestic side of me I never knew existed.

It sounds dumb—I know, but before her... before Maverick... my life was late nights and random hookups. But now, I'd rather stay in and watch the fucking Disney channel with Mav. It's like some *Freaky Friday* shit, only I like it.

Realization dawns... I like the man I am with Frankie. Without even trying, she brings out the best in me. I want more of that, and I want it forever.

"Mav-oh!" She whirls around, presumably to call for Maverick. "You scared me. How are you feeling? Did I wake you?"

"Better, but not great. And no, you didn't wake me." I breathe out a laugh and shuffle further into the kitchen. "I actually thought I was home alone, it was so quiet."

"Oh, good. Mav's watching a show on my phone with some headphones. I told him you needed to rest."

Something inside of me warms at her thoughtfulness. She's a nurturer by heart. "Whatcha cooking?"

Her cheeks go rosy. "Some chicken noodle soup. It's what I like when I'm sick, so I figured you might..."

"You made me soup?" That warm feeling grows, spreading throughout my entire body.

"Um, yeah." She locks her hands together and rocks back on her heels. "I also ran to the store this morning and got you some Gatorade."

"You didn't have to do that."

"I know." She turns and grabs three bowls from the cabinet. "But you took such good care of Mav, I figured it was the least I could do."

I want nothing more than to cross the room and sweep her into my arms, to hold her close, to make her really and truly understand that she doesn't need to keep thanking me for taking care of Maverick. I know he's not my son, but in a way, it also kind of feels like he is. I damn sure know I love him like he is. That kid is one of the best things to ever happen to me.

But I know *telling* her is pointless; I have to *show her*.

Instead, I grab a Gatorade from the fridge and plant my ass on a stool. "I appreciate you, Frankie," I say, knowing good and well I mean something else.

Judging from the blush painting her cheeks, I'd say Frankie knows it, too.

She places a steaming bowl in front of me. "If you don't like the soup, I can make you something else."

With my eyes locked on hers, I drag the spoon through the broth and then bring it to my lips. I groan in delight the second it hits my tongue. It's warm and buttery and creamy with hints of garlic. It's fucking delicious.

"I take it that means you like it?"

"It's delicious." I make a show of licking my lips before taking another spoonful. "I *appreciate* it."

Frankie's cheeks go from rosy to beet red and I fucking love it. "Um." She flexes her fingers at her sides. "Let me just... Maverick! Let me get Maverick."

She bolts from the kitchen, leaving me smiling into my soup, because yeah—she totally knows.

A few minutes later, Maverick hops up onto the stool beside me. "You all better, O? Mama said I had to be extra quiet so you could sleep." He blinks twice. "You sleeped for a really long time."

My shoulders shake with silent laughter. This kid is just too cute. "Yeah, bud. I'm feeling better than I did last night. Still tired though."

He nods like he totally gets it, and to be fair, I guess he does. "Mama says rest is how the body cooperates."

"Recuperates," Frankie corrects, sliding a bowl of soup in front of him.

"Yeah, that."

I finish off the last of my soup and yawn. "Makes sense."

"What are you doing for the rest of the day?" Maverick asks, trying his hardest to rock his stool closer to mine.

"Resting." I reach out and tug him closer. "That's about it."

"Wanna watch a movie?"

"Oh, Mav, he probably—"

"Absolutely. You can even pick what we watch."

"But you have to finish your soup," Frankie adds, giving him her mom-eyes.

My dude nods rapidly and then picks up his bowl and drinks the soup down like it's his favorite flavor milkshake. "Done! Can we watch *Toy Story*? I know they aren't super heroes, but..."

"They're still super cool. Let's do it."

Frankie throws her hands in the air. "I guess we're having a movie day."

"Can we have popcorn?" The kid's practically vibrating, he's so excited.

"Not this time, bud. You and Orion are still recuperating."

"But hey." I nudge him with my elbow. "Next time, I'll show you the best way to eat popcorn."

"Huh? Like with a fork?"

A laugh bursts out of me, leaving me winded. "What? No. With peanut butter M&Ms."

His little nose scrunches. "I don't know about that, O."

"Listen, I tried your mayo-grilled cheeses, so you can try this, yeah?"

He heaves out a sigh that's nearly bigger than he is. "Fine. But can we watch it in bed?" Maverick turns his pleading look on Frankie. "Please?"

She rolls her eyes like she's annoyed, but the brilliant smile on her face says otherwise. "Fine, yes, in the bed. But only if Orion's cool with it."

He turns his big, round eyes on me, his lower lip pushed out in a pout. I was already down for whatever, but seriously, how could anyone say no to this kid? "Works for me."

He jumps up from his stool and takes off toward their bedroom. "I call middle!"

"How are you so good with him?" Frankie asks in his absence.

I don't reply right away, mostly because I don't know what to say. Loving Maverick—and his mama—comes as natural as breathing, but she's not ready to hear that.

Instead, I say, "He's Maverick. To know the kid is to love him."

She gives me a look I can't quite decipher, but doesn't

press the issue further. "Well, thank you." Frankie holds her hands up, silencing me before I can correct her. "I know, I know. *I don't need to thank you.*" She drops her voice low, mimicking me.

"Smartass."

"Jackass." She transfers all of our bowls to the sink and begins rinsing them, treating me to a delectable view of her backside.

"Cute ass."

"What?" She whips around to face me, her eyes wide.

Smirking, I stand from my stool. "You heard me."

"You're impossible."

"No arguments there. You need any help?" I tip my head toward the dishes.

"I've got it. You need to rest. Why don't you go lay with Mav and I'll be right there?"

"If you're sure..."

"Sure that you're a pain in my ass," she grumbles good naturedly.

"Back on the ass again?" I ask, making a big show of checking hers out.

"Go!" She flicks her hands in a shooing motion. "Get out of here, Orion Cartwright. I literally cannot deal with you right now."

"That's a damn lie. I'm delightful and we both know it." She grins and I swear, it goes straight to my dick. "However, I'm still exhausted, so I will go lay down." I step into the hallway, giving her one last look. "Because I want to, *not* because you told me to."

"Sure, sure," she murmurs, sending me on my way with a megawatt smile.

"ARE you sure you're feeling up to going to Lizzie—I mean Gigi and Pop-Pop's house?" I ask Maverick as I wrap a section of my hair around my curling wand.

He's keeping me company while I get ready for dinner with Orion—he's insisting on taking me out to thank me for taking such good care of him while he was sick. Kind of ironic, what with his insistence that he needed no thanks for doing the same.

"Uh, yeah!" he shouts, running from the bathroom door-frame to the bed, and back again, like a puppy with the zoomies. "Stella said she made cupcakes and I love cupcakes, Mama. Love. Them!"

"I know you do, but please don't eat too many. I don't want you upsetting your stomach."

"I won't. I promise." He makes another lap. "What are you doing tonight? Why does your face look like that?"

"Like what?" I ask, inspecting my reflection in the mirror. All I'm wearing is a little blush, some bronzer, mascara, and lip gloss.

He scrunches his nose and points at me. "Your lips are shiny and there are sparkles on your cheeks."

"You don't think I look pretty, Mav?"

My sweet, innocent, brutally honest son tips his head to the side. "I guess so."

All I can do is laugh. "Thanks for the vote of confidence, bud."

He beams like he just won free toys for life. "You're welcome, Mama. I'm gonna go see if Stella's ready to go."

"Be care—" I start to say, but he's already gone.

I finish curling my hair and then get dressed. He said to wear whatever, which is the most typical guy response ever, and so incredibly unhelpful.

Eventually, I settle on a pair of black jeans and a dressy black top. Casual but cute—and the V-neck makes my tits look great.

"Frankie," Orion calls, sending all of the butterflies roosting in my belly into a frenzied flight. Dumb, I know, since we're just going to dinner. But for some reason, tonight feels important...

Like it's the start of something amazing.

Fingers crossed, anyway.

"Almost ready!" I call back, spritzing myself with my favorite perfume before venturing out in search of everyone.

I find them all congregated in the kitchen, with Maverick trying to convince Stella to give him a snack and Orion watching, his lips kicked up in an amused grin.

"Maverick James, did you tell me Gigi was making cupcakes?"

"Yeah!"

"Then why do you need a snack? If you eat now, you'll be too full."

"Oh." He crosses his arms and glares at Stella. "Why didn't you just say that?"

Stella throws her arms up in the air and then jumps at Maverick, digging her fingertips into his ribs.

"You little rascal!" she shouts, but the sound is barely audible over his hysterical giggles.

"Mercy, Stella! Mercy!"

She gives him one last tickle for good measure, and then slings an arm around his shoulder, pulling him close. "You ready to go see Gigi and Pop-Pop?"

"Yeah!" He wriggles out of her hold and runs over to me, throwing his arms around my middle. "I love you, Mama."

"Love you, too, bud. Be good, okay?"

"I will." He releases me, turning to pounce on Orion, but he's ready for him and scoops him up into his arms.

They whisper to one another with their heads bent together, leaving Stella and me in the dark, until finally Orion presses a kiss to Mav's forehead and sets him back down on his feet. "Have fun, bud."

"I will, O. Love you."

"Love you, too."

Stella grabs Maverick's backpack and then they're out the door, leaving only Orion and me.

"You look..." He drags his eyes over every inch of my body. "Fucking stunning."

"Thank you." I feel my cheeks warm as I return the favor, looking him up and down. He looks like a freaking dream in a pair of dark jeans and a gray button-down with the sleeves rolled. "You look nice, too."

"Just nice?" He arches a brow, clearly fishing.

Too bad I'm hook, line, and sinker for this man—if only I could find the courage to tell him.

"You look... really good." *There. That's better.*

Orion pouts. "I was hoping for hot. Sexy. Jaw-droppingly handsome." He's definitely teasing me, but he is all of those things.

"D," I say, clasping my hands behind my back. "All of the above."

He flashes me his best panty-melting, heart-stopping smile "That's more like it."

"So, what are we doing tonight, Mr. Secrecy?"

"I know I asked to take you out, but I was actually hoping we could stay in?"

"Um." I blink twice, wondering if I misread the situation. *No, Frankie! He's dressed up, too. Get out of your own damn way.* "Sure."

"Good." He claps his hands once before rubbing them together. "I was going to take you to 1885, but then decided I'd rather cook for you. I'm not great in the kitchen but I know my way around a steak."

"I'm not one to turn down steak." I nibble my lower lip. "What about sides? I'm happy to help..."

Orion's eyes light up. "I was hoping you'd say that. I bought a few different options—asparagus, sweet potatoes, brussels sprouts, and some bread, too."

"Mmm." I pat my belly. "Mashed sweet potato and brussels. Yum."

"Okay." He grabs the cast iron skillet from the cabinet and ignites the burner. "Let's do this."

We move around each other in the kitchen in perfect harmony, like we've been cooking together for ages.

It's domesticated and thrilling and almost feels like a glimpse into the future we could have.

Between the scents of garlic and rosemary and all of the

little touches as we cook, I'm brimming with want—for both the food and the man searing steaks at my side.

He grins at me and then slowly licks his lips, sending my libido into overdrive. Luckily, the timer for the bread sounds before I can do something stupid—like offer to let him feast on me instead.

"Let's eat," Orion murmurs, pulling down two plates from the cabinet.

I grab the bread and then we work together to plate everything.

"Table or bar?" I ask, wishing it was warm enough to eat outside. Even with the heater, it's too cold tonight.

"Table works for me." He grabs both of our plates and strides toward the dining room. I grab us each a drink and then hurry after him.

"Orion!" A gasp slips past my lips followed by a moan of delight as I swallow my first bite of steak. "Oh my God. This is... *mmm.*"

My praise is met with dead silence, and when I look up at him, he's frozen solid, with his fork halfway to his mouth.

"Are you okay?"

He sets his fork down on the edge of his plate and swallows roughly, his Adam's apple bobbing. "Frankie."

"What?" I ask. "What's wrong?"

"You really don't know, do you?" Disbelief tinges his voice.

"Know what?" I blink innocently. "Did I do something wrong?" I definitely know—it was the moan. But hey, the steak really is *that* good and teasing him really is *that* fun.

"You... Um." He reaches up and tugs at his collar. "Sound like you're enjoying yourself."

"Oh, yeah, I am. The food is amazing." I pop another

bite into my mouth and moan again, licking my lips this time. "Best I've ever had."

"It's like you're trying to kill me," he mutters under his breath.

"If you don't want me to tell you how delicious your meat tastes in my mouth, I won't." I pout my lower lip and take a silent bite.

"You're something else." He shakes his head, but he's smiling. "I'm over here thinking you're some innocent little lamb, when you were fucking with me the whole time."

I hold up my index finger, signaling for him to wait while I chew. "Not the whole time. It really is amazing. Juicy and so flavorful."

"Thanks." He forks some mashed sweet potatoes into his mouth. "The sides really made the meal though. You and I... we make a good team."

I want to take those words and pick them apart. Does he mean we make a good team as friends or as something more? I know he's expressed interest in me, but how deep does his desire run? Am I making something out of nothing? Or is he as into me as I am him?

"Yeah, we really do," is what I settle on. "Wanna help clear the table and clean up?"

Orion slides his chair back. "We both cooked, so we both clean. I like it." He grabs my plate and stacks it on top of his. "I like you, too."

I trail behind him, blushing like a schoolgirl.

"What now?" he asks, once the kitchen is sparkling clean.

"Now you let me thank you for such an amazing night." I step into his space and press my lips to his cheek in a quick kiss. "Thank you."

"Not so fast." He hooks an arm around my waist,

preventing me from retreating. "If we're doling out thanks, I owe you some, too. Hence the whole reason for this dinner."

I look up at him just in time for his mouth to come down on mine. His lips are soft yet insistent and I can't help the gasp that escapes me.

Orion seizes the opportunity and slips his tongue into my mouth, tangling it with mine as he kisses me like I'm the dessert he's been waiting all night to savor.

He tunnels his fingers into my hair, no doubt messing up my curls. Using his newfound leverage, he tilts my head, deepening our kiss.

With every skilled swipe of his tongue, my body aches with the need for release. Since moving here, my poor showerhead has been put through the ringer, but right now, my body wants the high only Orion can give me.

"Fuck, Frankie," he murmurs, breathless as he breaks our kiss and releases his grip on my hair.

I touch my fingers to my still-tingling lips. "That was..."

"Fucking perfect," he finishes for me. "You're perfect."

"No." I shake my head. "I'm really not."

"You're flawed, sure. We all are. But, Frankie, you're... you've been through so much but you still shine so fucking bright. You're an amazing mother, a good friend, and just..."

"Just what?" I whisper, my entire body on tenterhooks as I wait for him to finish his train of thought.

"Fuck, this is going to sound crazy." He tugs me even closer; so close I can feel how fast his heart is beating in his chest. "I want you, and I know you and Mav are a package deal. So yeah, I want him, too."

His fingers flex against my hips, like he's trying to hold himself back. "And I know he's got a dad, but, Frankie, I fucking mean it."

"What?" I can barely form the word; my brain and

mouth are not on the same frequency. His kiss must have rendered me dumb, because surely, he didn't just say what I think he did.

"I'm. All. In." His tone is unyielding, and before I can even begin to think of a reply, his lips are once again on mine.

I want so badly to throw myself into this, to greedily take all he's offering.

But I can't.

Not until he knows the truth.

"Orion." I pull away from him and step out of his embrace, putting some much needed but unwanted distance between us. "I... I feel the same, but we need to talk."

He gulps. "That sounds... ominous."

I smile weakly. "Why don't we go to the living room?"

"After you." He steps back and lets me pass.

My fight or flight is pushing hard for me to make a break for the front door, but I don't. Orion Cartwright is a man worth fighting for, even if he sends me packing once I'm done.

Orion's dark stare never strays as we settle down onto opposite ends of the couch.

"Well?" he asks when I don't say anything.

"I'm not really sure how to tell you," I mutter, more to myself than to him. "It's just that... well..." *Come on, Frankie, rip off the Band-Aid.* "You remember how we met?"

"In the kitchen my first morning here."

"Right." I nod and force myself to stop fidgeting. "And what did I ask you? What was the very first thing I asked you?"

Orion's eyebrows slant down in confusion, but he answers my question. "You asked what I was doing here."

"Right. And then what?"

"Didn't realize we were playing twenty questions."

"I know this is weird, but just... I... humor me, please?"

He scratches the back of his neck. "You asked if I followed you, which was weird, because I didn't know you."

"Where were you the night before that you could have followed me from?" I ask, trying to get him to connect the dots without me straight up saying it.

He crosses his arms over his chest, his lips pressing into a thin line. Clearly, he's not going to make this easy on me. But his stubbornness is one of the things I like the most about him.

"Come on, Orion. We both know where you were..."

"How do you know?" he asks, still not admitting it.

"I was there, too," I whisper. "I was there with you."

"You were where with me? Just spit it out, Frankie. Please?"

I suck in a deep breath and slowly exhale it before replying. "It's me—well, she's me. Or maybe I'm her?"

"Frankie!" His tone is sharp; frustrated but not quite angry.

"I'm Birdie, Orion."

"Bullshit." His instant reply makes my heart sink. He doesn't believe me. Why would he? Birdie is bold and sexy, while I'm... *me*.

"I'm not lying." Silently, I beg him to believe me. "I'm your bluebird."

He exhales sharply at the use of his nickname for me. "What did you just say?"

"I'm your bluebird."

"Holy shit." He pinches the bridge of his nose and scrubs his hand over his face. "Don't take this the wrong way, but—"

A bitter laugh escapes me, eclipsing his words. "Trust me, I know. Birdie is a lot different than Frankie. We're the same person, but we're not the *same* person."

"Holy shit!" he says again, louder this time. "The last time I came to ATF you called me by my name. I kept thinking maybe I just forgot telling it to you, but I didn't. I never did."

"Yeah." I wrap my arms around my middle. "I definitely slipped up."

"This is... but your hair," he says, as if he can't comprehend the difference.

I lift my long, dark hair from my shoulder and inspect the strands. "I wear red extensions when I'm working. It helps with anonymity. Between the mask, the hair, and the makeup, I really do look like a different person."

For a minute or two, neither of us speak; the silence is crushing.

Finally, I can't take it anymore.

"I, um, I'm sure you're upset, and probably no longer interested in pursuing anything more with me." Tears burn my eyes, but I'll be damned if I break down in front of him. "I'm sorry, you know, I'm really sorry for lying to you. I hope you can forgive me. But if not, well, I wouldn't blame you."

I want to beg him to understand my side of things, to forgive me, to still want me, but my pride won't allow it.

Instead, I bolt from the couch, craving the privacy of my bedroom, where I'll be able to let myself fall apart.

I STARE after Frankie for all of two seconds before shooting up from the couch after her.

"Wait up," I call after her, but she doesn't even look back.

Luckily, I manage to wedge my foot into the doorway, blocking her from shutting me out.

"Just let me go," she pleads, but there's no way that's happening. Hell, I don't think I could let her go even if I wanted to.

"Don't run from me, Frankie." I get it, she thinks I'm mad. I'm not though. This is a literal *have your cake and eat it, too,* situation.

"Orion." My name falls from her lips on an anguished cry. She thinks this is the end of us. But she's wrong; it's only the beginning.

"Talk to me, baby, please?"

"Are you mad?" She's still pressing her body into the door, not shutting me out, but not letting me in either.

"No," I answer honestly, hoping like hell she believes

me. "Surprised, not mad. C'mon, Frankie, talk to me. Let me in."

"Fine." She steps back and I swing the door fully open, scoop her into my arms, and cross the room to the chair on the far side.

I position her sideways on my lap with my arms wrapped around her waist. I hold her close, fearful that if given the chance, she'll bolt again.

Her posture is rigid, and I hate it.

"I'm really not mad. Not at you."

"Then who?"

"Myself, mostly."

"What?" She whips around to face me. "That doesn't even make sense."

"Sure, it does. It kills me that I didn't put two and two together on my own. What kind of man doesn't recognize the woman he—" I clamp my lips shut, but it's too late.

"The woman he what?" Frankie asks, her entire body trembling.

I swallow roughly around the lump in my throat, deciding I may as well lay it all out there for her. "Loves. The woman he loves."

"You love me?" she asks, a bewildered look on her face.

"Of course, I love you."

"Why?" Her voice shakes with the threat of more tears.

"You're it for me, Frankie. Don't you see it?"

"Please don't say it if you don't mean it."

I grab her chin and bring her face to mine, rubbing my nose along hers before placing a soft kiss to the corner of her mouth. "I mean it with every ounce of my being. I love you. I love Maverick. Y'all are the future I want."

She sucks in a ragged breath, before releasing it slowly. "I'm scared." Her voice is so small, so fragile.

"I know you are, but I've got you. I won't let anything hurt you, not even me." I stroke along her jawline with my thumb. "Don't you know, I'd kick my own ass before hurting you."

The smallest laugh I've ever heard slips past her lips, and for the first time since dinner, I feel like maybe we're back on the right track. Like maybe this thing between us is going to work.

"Do you love me, Frankie?" I need her answer more than I need my next breath.

But she takes her sweet time replying. So long that I start to worry I've pushed her too far, too fast.

"Yes," she finally says.

"Yes what?" I have to be sure.

"I love you. I have for a while, but I was too scared to let myself believe we could have any kind of future together."

I cup her cheeks with both hands. "The only future I want is with you and Maverick."

She nods. "You said you were all in..."

"I am." One-thousand-fucking-percent.

"What about me working at ATF? Does that... change anything?"

"Frankie baby, I will never come between you doing what you need to do to provide for your son. Never."

All of the breath wooshes out of her, as if she can't believe what she's hearing. "Really?"

"Really." I lean forward and kiss the tip of her nose. "I do have one request though..."

"What?" Her whole-body tenses, like this is the part where the other shoe drops.

"Would I be out of line to ask you not to do VIP?"

The most beautiful smile takes over her whole face. "I already asked them to take my name off the list."

"Are you serious?" I ask, hardly able to believe things are falling into place this easily.

"Yeah. This past Friday, you were my first and only VIP client."

Unable to help myself, I wind my fingers through her long locks. "I love you, Bluebird—fuck! Can I... can I call you that?"

She bites her bottom lip as she smiles up at me. "You wouldn't believe how much I've missed hearing it."

I give her hair a firm tug, guiding her mouth back to mine. "I love you, Bluebird," I say again, just because I can, before claiming her with a searing kiss.

Frankie groans, and the raspy sound heats my blood as I alternate between sucking and nipping at her pillowy lips.

Bracing herself on my shoulders, she swings a leg over my lap so that she's straddling me, instantly taking our kiss from hot to scorching as she rolls her hips, grinding herself against my rapidly growing erection.

"Orion." I swallow her whimpered plea as she trails her fingertips over my shoulders, up my neck, and curls them into my hair. "I—"

Whatever she was about to say is lost in a throaty moan as I release her hair and palm her ass, pulling her tightly against my rock-hard cock.

"I've got you, Frankie." I kiss my way down her jaw to the soft skin of her neck, licking and sucking, eagerly marking my claim on her pale skin. "Fuck, you taste like heaven."

It's probably only my overly active imagination, but I swear I can feel the heat of her pussy through the denim of our jeans, and I want nothing more than to rip away the offending material, because how dare it keep me from her.

I want to feel her wetness coating my fingers... my cock. I want to taste her release as she screams my name so loud our neighbors can hear it.

"I'm so close," she says between little pants and sighs of delight, every bit as desperate for her release as I am.

My only goal right now is to make Frankie fall apart. To make her shatter into a thousand tiny, pleasure-filled pieces.

"Can I touch you?" I ask, hoping like hell she says yes.

"Please, oh God, please?"

I pop the button to her jeans and tug down the zipper before sliding my hand beneath the material. My fingers meet nothing but smooth, slick, sloppy wet skin.

"You're soaked." I draw my index finger up and down her slit three times before pressing my thumb to her clit.

"Orion!" She wraps her arms around my neck, pressing her forehead into mine.

"I can't wait to be inside you. To stretch you and fill you up with my cock. Do you want that, Frankie? Do you want to be full of my dick?"

"Yes, yes, yes," she chants the word like it's a sacred prayer.

What it really is, is music to my ears. My Bluebird's as wild for me as I am her.

"Come for me. Come all over my fingers."

She grips the back of my shirt for leverage as she moves her hips in tight little circles, rubbing her clit against the pad of my thumb.

"That's right, Frankie. Just like that."

"Kiss me," she begs, her entire body shaking. "Oh, God —I'm come—"

I seal my lips to hers, swallowing down her soft cries and moans as she rides out her orgasm.

"Oh, wow," she murmurs, slumping against my chest. "That was…"

"A practice round, Bluebird. The real thing and you won't be able to walk."

"Promises, promises." She clucks her tongue at me and then presses one last quick kiss to my lips before climbing off of me.

"Next time," I tell her, sucking my index finger into my mouth, "I'm gonna eat that pretty pussy before I fuck you."

"Orion!" Her cheeks flame bright with a heady mixture of embarrassment and desire. "You can't just say things like that."

"Just did, Bluebird. I just did."

She opens her mouth, undoubtedly to fuss at me—but my phone rings before she can.

Groaning, I dig my phone out of my pocket. "Hey, Mom."

"I. Adore. This. Kid, Orion. Do you hear me? I adore him."

"He's a good kid," I agree, transferring the call to speaker phone. "What's up?"

"Well…" I can tell from the tone of her voice that she's up to something. "Maverick asked if he could sleep over. It's fine with me, but I told him he needed to ask his mama."

Frankie worries her bottom lip between her teeth. "It's not that I mind, because I know he'd be in good hands, it's just… it's a school night and—"

My mom's soft laughter cuts off her anxious rambling. "Mom to mom, I understand. My kids couldn't do sleepovers on school nights either."

"Um." Frankie clears her throat and flexes her fingers at her sides. She's clearly bothered at having to turn my mom down.

But I might just have the perfect plan. "Hey, Mom, can I put you on hold for a second?"

"Oh, sure."

I mute the call and tug Frankie into my side. "I know you just took this weekend off since Mav was sick, but do you think you could take next weekend off, too? I feel like a shit even asking, but—"

"I try not to dip into it, but I have enough in savings that it would be fine. Why though?"

"My parents have a lake house here in town. I was thinking maybe, and only if you're comfortable with it, Maverick could stay with my parents this weekend and we could go to the lake. Just you and me."

I shove my hands under my thighs to keep from fidgeting while waiting for her reply. *Fuck, I hope I'm not asking for too much, too soon.*

"I think..." She licks her lips. "I think I could manage that."

Hell. Yes.

"You still there?" I ask, unmuting the call.

"Yep."

"Do you think Mav could stay with y'all next weekend?"

"Of course! Oh, we can make an apple pie and some brownies. Does he like meatloaf? What about grits?"

Frankie laughs, and I swear, I would bottle the sound if I could. It's like a straight shot of serotonin, from her lips to my brain.

"He likes all of that, Lizzie. He's going to have a blast, I'm sure."

"I'm so excited. He likes superheroes, right? Orion, I bet I still have your old sheets somewhere..."

"Hey, Mom, one more thing?"

"What's that?"

"Could I take Frankie up to the lake house?"

Mom falls quiet. So quiet, I actually check my phone to make sure we're still connected.

"It's happening!" she murmurs, her words barely audible. "It's really happening!"

"Are you okay?" I ask, wondering what exactly is happening.

"Orion Michael Cartwright, you are finally settling down and I—I'm just happy, son. Let me be happy."

Frankie smacks a hand over her mouth to muffle the sound of her giggles, while I groan in embarrassment.

You gotta love mothers.

"So, is that a yes?"

"Of course, it is, son." A loud beeping sound comes through the line. "Oh, the second batch of cupcakes are done! Gotta go. Love you."

"Love you, too," I say, but she's already ended the call.

"It sounds like they're having fun," Frankie says, her lips tugging down into a small frown.

"That's good, right?" I hedge, not sure why she's upset.

"It's great. Really, it is. It just breaks my heart that my parents will never know how amazing he is."

Man, fuck her parents. "Their loss, Bluebird. It's their loss."

"I know." She tips her head to the side and shrugs. "Really, I do. It's just... before you and your family, I was all Maverick had. I thought I was all he needed, and seeing how happy he is... what if we never met? What if he never got to experience this kind of love?"

I haul her back into my lap, and she snuggles in, tucking her head beneath my chin. She fits so perfectly against me, it's like we were meant to be.

"Mav was never lacking for anything, especially not love. The way you are with him, you really are a mama bear, Frankie. Fierce and protective. You put him first in every-thing you do. So, while I'm glad as hell we met—trust me, I'm the real winner there—don't doubt for a single second that he'd have been just fine if we hadn't. Because you'd have made sure of it."

She sniffles and clutches at the material of my shirt. "You mean that?"

"I do." I smooth her hair away from her face. "And he has your brother, right?"

"Yeah, he loves his uncle Phin. Doesn't get to see him much, but they really are two peas in a pod. Mav pretty much has Phoenix on a pedestal. The man can do no wrong."

I press my lips to the top of her head. "Well, if Maverick likes him that much, I can't wait to meet him."

"So, we're really doing this, huh?" A hint of vulnera-bility creeps into her voice.

"I guess I haven't made myself clear." I shift her so that she's once again straddling me, her brilliant blue eyes locked onto mine. "Hell, yeah, we're doing this. You're mine, Frankie. And you be damn sure, I'll spend every day showing you just how much I mean those words. I said I loved you and I meant it. So, yeah, we're fucking doing this."

"Okay." Her lips twitch, as she tries to hold back her laughter, but it's no use. And it's definitely not the response I was looking for either.

"What's so funny?" Because seriously—*what the fuck?*

"It's just... I totally love you, too, and am totally here for this, for you, but..."

"But what?" I lean in for a quick kiss, mashing my lips against hers. "Spit it out."

Her nose crinkles and her eyes dance with mischief. "What if the sex is bad?"

"The fuck did you just say?" A growl rips loose from my chest. "How is that even a question?"

She shrugs, a coy smile playing at her lips. "I'm just saying…"

"Our chemistry is explosive, Bluebird, and I can guaran-goddamn-tee that when we fuck, it will be so damn good. I'm talking seeing stars and talking in tongues good."

Frankie lifts one shoulder in a delicate shrug. "Promises, promises."

"Five days and that ass is mine, Frankie." I wrap my arms around her waist and pull her body snug against mine, snapping my teeth playfully against her throat. "Five days and I'll show you just how fucking good we are together."

"Why wait?" she asks, rolling her hips against mine.

For a half a second, I'm tempted to take what she's offering, to throw her down on this bed and fuck her brains out. But I won't. "Because from now until then, I want you to think about it. To imagine it."

I press my lips to her collarbone, nipping at it, before licking a path up her neck with the tip of my tongue.

"When you're alone in the shower, with your pussy aching and begging for my touch, I want you to rub your clit just like you did in the VIP room; I want you to touch yourself and pretend it's me. I want you on edge, desperate and begging for my cock."

"Orion," she whimpers as she tries to rock against me. "Please."

I still her hips and give her one last kiss before sliding out from under her. "C'mon, Bluebird, we better get Maverick. It is a school night, after all."

Frankie gives my tented jeans a pointed look. "You sure you don't want me to take the edge off?"

Smirking, I reach down and readjust myself. "As tempting as that sounds, good things come to those who wait."

THIS WEEK HAS SOMEHOW FLOWN by while also being the longest week of my life.

I've also spent the last five days horngry—yeah, horny and angry. Well, not angry, but frustrated. Ever since last Sunday, Orion has managed to keep me on edge.

He's been all little touches, lingering looks, and filthy texts. He also came to ATF and booked me in the VIP room —something Walt had a field day over, God love him—but even there, in the low lights with me half- naked, he wouldn't take my bait.

And believe me, I tried.

"You all ready for a long weekend with my brother?" Stella asks, immediately cringing. "Nope, don't answer that. Brain bleach!"

Orion laughs. "Now you know how I feel."

She rolls her eyes and hops up onto the island, her feet swinging back and forth over the ledge. "Whatever."

"I'm just saying, Smalls. What goes around comes around. You ended up with my best friend, so it's only fair—"

"Hold up. I am not your consolation prize because your little sister is—"

Orion steps into my space and presses his lips to mine, silencing my protest. "You're a prize period, Bluebird."

"O!" Maverick yells as he bounds into the room. "Did you just kiss my mama?"

This isn't how I wanted to tell him. I mean, the kid's intuitive, so I'm sure he has an inkling, but now...

"I did," Orion says, dropping down to a kneeling position in front of my son. "Are you okay with that?"

Mav taps his index finger against his chin. "Why'd you do it? Do you love her? 'Cause on tv people kiss when they're in love."

"What would you say if I told you that I do in fact love her?"

The biggest smile I've ever seen takes over his face. "I'd say *finally!*"

See, intuitive.

Orion opens his arms and Maverick tackle-hugs him to the floor. "Glad you're okay with it, bud."

"You are?" Mav rolls off of him and rearranges himself so that he's sitting cross-legged on the floor.

"Of course," Orion says, also sitting up. "You're the most important thing in the world to your mama, and knowing that you're okay with me loving her, too... that's important to me."

Oh my God, my heart can't take this. My chest aches, like the organ behind my ribs is tripling in size with the overload of love pumping through it.

"Good." Maverick nods and then pops up to his feet, turning to, with his eyes wide. "Mama, we gotta call Uncle Phin! I tolded him this was gonna happen and he said no way!"

Orion arches a brow as I press my palms into my burning cheeks, as I recall the silly argument my brother and son had over whether anything would happen between Orion and me.

Maverick was adamant, whereas Phoenix flat-out said *'There's no way your prickly cactus of a mama is falling for anyone, Mav.'* I zipped my lips during that call, and good thing too, because I'd definitely be eating crow.

"Oh, Maverick," I murmur, looking to Stella for help. But she's too busy batting away pesky tears to come to my aide. *At least I'm not the only one feeling a little emotional.*

"Is it time to go to Gigi and Pop-Pop's yet?" Maverick asks, no longer interested in why Orion kissed me.

My whole-body warms at the knowledge how loved my son is, at the family we've found.

She smiles down at him. "Sure. Go grab your bag and we'll hit the road."

"Yes!" He jumps up, waving his hands over his head before taking off down the hall to get his bag.

Seconds later, he flies back into the room. "Okay, let's go!"

Stella hops down from the island. "Don't you want to tell your mom bye?"

"Oh!" He runs over and wraps his arms around me, hugging me tight. "I love you, Mama."

"I love you, too, Mav. Be good, okay?"

"I'm always good." He beams up at me. "Pop-Pop says I'm the bestest boy!"

Orion stands, rolling his lips inward to keep from laughing. "Does he now?"

"Yup!" Maverick hugs Orion, too, and then he and Stella are on their way, leaving just the two of us.

"Are you ready to go, too?" Orion asks, crowding me

from behind. He moves my hair off of my neck and skims his nose over my sensitive skin.

"Yes."

"Then let's go." He starts for the door.

"I need my bag!" I laugh, heading down the hall to my room.

"Do you though? And here I thought I'd just keep you naked and in bed with me the whole weekend."

"I'm not opposed to the idea." I drag my teeth over my lip and clench my thighs together, already picturing the rumpled sheets. "But I'm still bringing clothes."

In my room, I double check that I have everything I need packed—including something extra special for Orion. I quickly grab my phone charger and toothbrush, tucking them both into the front pocket of my duffel before rejoining Orion in the kitchen.

"It seems you packed a bag, too." I arch a brow.

"Doesn't mean it's clothes. For all you know it could be full of sex toys." He winks, and I laugh.

"You're a mess. Let's go."

"I'm *your* mess," he corrects, taking my bag from me.

"WHOA," I breathe as the house comes into view. When Orion said his family had a lake house, I pictured a quaint little cabin on the water, not... *this.*

The house is huge, with a wide wrap-around porch and floor-to-ceiling windows. Honestly, it looks more like a farm-house than a lake house, but what do I know?

"It's been in our family forever," Orion says as he pulls to a stop at the end of the winding drive. "I'm pretty sure my great grandpa and his brother built it. Mom spent a lot of time modernizing it once it was passed down to her and Dad."

"It's amazing." I grew up with wealth—well, around it anyway—but this place is something else entirely. It's somehow opulent and understated at the same time; like you'd pay five figures a night to vacation in it, but feel right at home during your stay.

"Let's take our things inside and then we can grab some dinner?" He cuts the engine and hops down from the cab.

I'm more than capable of getting out on my own, but I know he likes helping me, so I hang tight and wait.

It also doesn't hurt that he's handsy as hell whenever he helps me down, making sure to brush his hands along my thighs and ass.

This time is no different, and the second his knuckles brush against my bottom, I'm ready to go off like a bottle rocket.

Seriously, do we really *need food? Really?*

Except, my stomach rumbles—*loudly*—telling me that we absolutely need to eat.

"I guess we need groceries, huh?" I try to think of how close the nearest store is, but the only one I can think of is at least twenty minutes back the way we came.

He smirks and lets down his tailgate. "Got a cooler in the truck bed."

"Look at you thinking a step ahead."

"Bluebird, I'm ten steps ahead. All I've been able to think about for the past week is getting you naked. I damn sure wasn't going to let getting groceries keep me from tasting your sweet pussy."

My cheeks blaze and my core clenches. "Oh my God! You can't just say things like that."

He shrugs and grabs the cooler from his truck. "Just did, now let's get inside."

I grab both of our bags from the truck while he unlocks the door and hauls the cooler inside.

The interior is probably the prettiest place I've ever seen. It's just... perfect. Light and bright and open.

Until this moment, I've never, ever imagined myself getting married, but now, I can't help but wish it could happen here.

"What do you think?" Orion calls from the kitchen.

"It's gorgeous."

"Let me give you a tour on the way to our room." He takes his bag from me and starts toward the stairs.

I follow behind him, taking in every detail on my way up.

"The master bedroom is downstairs. Stella's is to the left of the landing and mine is to the right. There's a shared bathroom in between. There's also a guest room at the end of the hall on my side, but it rarely gets used. Especially now that Samson and Stella are together."

"This place really is magical," I say, as Orion opens the door to his room. It's spacious with a king-sized bed and a picture window that faces the lake.

"You know, I guess I've kind of always taken it for granted, but you're right. It's really nice."

"Of course, I am. I'm always right."

He lunges for me and I dart back out into the hall, narrowly escaping him.

"You'll pay for that, Bluebird."

"Sure, sure. But feed me before you punish me."

His eyes darken, and a grin that promises payback curls his lips. "That can be arranged."

"The food part, right?" Although, with Orion, I'm not so sure I'd mind being punished. In fact, something tells me I'd probably like it.

He shrugs. "Guess you'll have to wait and see."

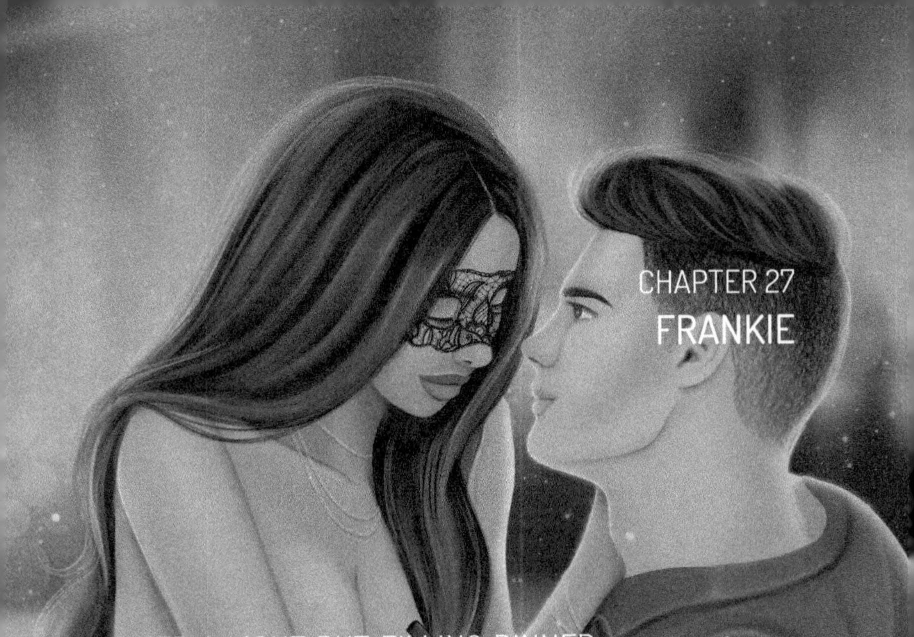

AFTER A LIGHT BUT FILLING DINNER, there's only one thing on my mind—getting Orion into bed.

Except, I can't just point blank ask him if it's time to fuck. At least, I don't think I can. Unfortunately, my lack of experience puts me at a distinct disadvantage when it comes to seducing him.

Dancing in a dark room, I've got it on lock. Asking for dick in the kitchen after dinner, I'm a damn mess.

"So," I draw out the word, hoping he'll take the hint. "What now?"

He stretches his arms overhead and arches his back, causing his shirt to ride up and show a sliver of his delectable abs. "I was thinking we could watch a movie."

I pout. "I was thinking we could go to bed."

"You tired?" he asks, a wicked gleam in his eyes. The ass, he's totally playing me.

Two can play this game, sir.

I fake a big yawn. "Mmhmm, exhausted."

Orion shuffles closer to me, wrapping his arms around my waist and tugging me close. He presses a soft kiss to my collarbone and then skims his nose up my neck before flicking his tongue against my earlobe.

An embarrassing moan slips past my lips and Orion chuckles. "Tired my ass."

You know what—fuck this. I am an empowered woman and I can absolutely ask for what I want; it's not like I can actually die from embarrassment. "You're right. I'm not tired. I'm horny."

To his credit, Orion only chokes a little.

"I mean, you talked a big game all week. You told me over and over how good it was going to be and how you were going to fuck me until my legs turned to jelly. But we've been here for hours and you haven't touched me."

"Frankie, baby—" he starts, but my hornger—horny anger—is back full-force.

"Nope. Don't you *Frankie, baby,* me. Fuck me. Strip me naked, put your mouth on my pussy, and then fuck me." Even as I say the words, my cheeks burn. My *whole body* burns like I'm standing right in front of a bonfire. Only, the heat is coming from inside of me.

And the way Orion's looking at me, as though it's taking every ounce of his self-control to not do exactly as I said right this very second—well, that's just freaking gas on the fire.

"It's like that, huh?" He reaches around and grabs the back of his shirt, tugging it off. Strong and lean with bronzed skin, the man's body is what dreams are freaking made of.

"Yeah." I nod my head, refusing to back down. "It is."

He pops the button on his jeans and kicks them to the floor, leaving him in only his boxers. His thick erection stretches the cotton to its limits, making my mouth water.

I've never had a dick in my mouth, never really wanted

one there either, but all of the sudden, the only thing I can think of is how he tastes.

I take a step closer to him, trailing my fingers over his chest. His pectoral muscles flex under my touch and gooseflesh covers his skin.

"Orion." His name is a whispered prayer as I sink to my knees.

"What are you doing?" he asks, a slight tremor to his voice.

Licking my lips, I reach for the waistband of his boxer shorts. "I want to taste you."

"Fuck, Frankie, baby." He curls his hand around mine. "You don't have—"

"I want to." I wiggle my fingers trying to dislodge his hold. "But fair warning, it might be awful. I've never... um."

"You've never, what?" His eyes widen as realization sinks in. "Never sucked dick?"

I shake my head, hoping he's not turned off by my lack of experience. "Is that okay?"

Instead of answering, Orion bends down, scoops me into his arms, and then heads straight for the stairs. "What are you doing?" I shriek, bouncing with every step.

"The first time my dick is in your mouth, you aren't going to be kneeling on the hard floor."

"Where will I be?"

He sets me down at the foot of the bed and sinks to his knees in front of me, slipping his thumbs beneath the waistband of my leggings. "You'll be sitting on my face."

"What?" Now it's my eyes that are wide. Surely, he doesn't mean that literally. Right?

"You trust me?" He flexes his fingers and his knuckles brush against my skin.

"I do."

Apparently those two words are all he needs, because with one solid yank, my leggings are bunched around my ankles.

"No panties?" he growls, sounding more animal than man.

"Not with leggings."

"Fuck, Frankie. Hold onto my shoulders."

I do as he says, allowing him to finish removing my pants.

"You're so perfect." He presses a kiss right above my right knee, and then another to my left, alternating until his lips are poised right over my pussy. "Gonna kiss you here now, okay?"

My entire body is shaking like a leaf, but I manage a nod. But Orion wants more.

"Need your words, Bluebird."

"Okay. Yes. I want this." I tunnel my fingers through his hair. "I want you."

Without warning, he surges forward, sealing his lips around my clit, sucking hard.

My back arches as I try to process. It's like someone stuck me with a cattle prod, only instead of pain, my body is convulsing with mind-numbing pleasure.

"Oh, God," I pant as he swirls his tongue. "Orion."

"That's right." He uses his thumbs to spread me open and licks a long line down my slit before pushing it inside of me and then licking his way back up. "Taste like heaven."

My legs shake as he continues his ministrations, licking and sucking and teasing my overly sensitive clit. "Please."

"What?" he asks, "what do you need?"

"More. You. I need more of you." I sound crazed. Desperate and delirious with want.

He stands and presses his lips to mine, forcing me to

taste my own arousal. Surprisingly, it's not awful. Tangy and slightly sweet.

Unfortunately, the kiss is over far too soon, with Orion stepping just out of my reach. He shucks off his boxers, revealing his cock to me. It stands tall and proud, with a small bead of liquid poised perfectly at the tip.

"Take off your shirt, Frankie. Show me your pretty tits."

"You've seen them," I counter, tugging my shirt over my head.

"I've seen them covered with pasties." He moves around me and climbs onto the bed, positioning himself against the headboard like a king. "I want to see them bare. Want to play with 'em and suck on your nipples."

Reaching behind me, I unclasp my bra and let it fall to the floor.

"Goddamn, you're beautiful." He fists his erection with one hand, pumping himself slowly while beckoning me forward with the other.

I press one knee into the mattress and then the other, crawling toward him.

"Right here." He taps his sternum twice.

Somehow, I manage to swing one leg over him, planting my knees on either side of his rib cage. "Now what?" I whisper, wondering if he can feel how wet I am for him against his chest.

He leans forward and presses a kiss just above my belly button . "Now, I need you to turn around so that your back's to me."

Orion helps me into the position he wants me in, with my ass just below his shoulders. He skims his fingertips gently over the swell of my hips, up my spine, and back down, over and over until my entire body is tingling with desire.

I roll my hips, rubbing my clit against his chest, desperate for relief.

Orion lets me play, testing different angles until I find the magic spot, with my back arched and my hands pressing into his muscular thighs.

"Oh," I whimper, and he grips my hips, pressing me harder into him, "my God!"

"Fuck, Bluebird." He readjusts himself ever so slightly beneath me. "I can feel how wet you are, how much you want me."

I whimper and my entire body tenses as wave after wave of pleasure crashes into me.

"So sexy when you come," he murmurs before tightening his grip and sliding me up so that I'm literally *sitting on his face*. His tongue darts out for a quick taste, and I nearly explode again. "Let's get you to make those sounds again, yeah?"

"Wha—" I start to ask, but my words morph into a garbled cry as he flicks his tongue against my clit.

Again, my hips begin to move of their own accord as I chase after the pleasure he's so openly offering.

"That's right, ride my face."

"Orion!" I reach forward and wrap my hand around his shaft, stroking his cock like I saw him do earlier.

He groans, and the sound spurs me on. Taking the head of his dick into my mouth, I swirl my tongue around the tip like he's my favorite ice cream flavor.

"Mmm. Relax your throat and try to take me a little deeper."

I do as he says, and he bucks beneath me. "Just like that, Frankie, suck me deep and slow. Savor me, like I am you."

Bobbing my head up and down his length, I do my best to focus on making him lose control. But his pace never breaks; he just keeps on eating my pussy like it's his last meal... *his favorite meal.*

But I don't mind. How can I when it feels this good?

On a whim, I snake a hand between his legs and fondle his balls. Orion groans long and low, his entire body tensing. "Oh—Frankie. God damn."

I moan around his cock and he cracks his palm down across my ass cheek. It stings, but in the best way.

"Need you to come, Bluebird. Come all over my face so I can fuck that pretty pussy."

His filthy words are the match, and once again, I find myself teetering on the edge of release.

I release his cock with an audible pop, my body too keyed up to focus on anything other than my own climax.

"Ride my face, Frankie. Take what you want." He sucks hard on my clit. "Take what you need."

Once again gripping his thighs, I rock my hips against him, loving the friction his stubble creates while his tongue works my clit.

"Fuck!" My thighs clench around his face as I topple over into the abyss, damn near drowning in pleasure.

Orion gently eases me off of him, somehow rearranging me so that I'm on my back with my head propped on a fluffy pillow. I'm too blissed out to pay too much attention, but as long as this ends with him deep inside of me, I'm game.

He presses my legs apart, fitting his hips between mine, leaning into my space until we're chest-to-chest. "Gonna fuck you now, Frankie." He drags the head of his cock through my dripping folds, *up and down, up and down,* teasing me until I can't take it.

"Do it." I worry for a split second that it'll hurt, but I know he's worth it. "I'm clean, and on birth control," I add when he still doesn't make a move.

"I'm clean, too."

"God, please, fill me up."

"So bossy," he murmurs, pushing himself inside of me, and shockingly, there's no pain. An uncomfortable stretch, sure. But no pain.

Except Orion's as still as a statue. "What's wrong?" I ask, trailing my hands over his pecs and shoulders.

An almost pained expression crosses his face. "*So tight.*"

I wrap my legs around his waist, digging my heels into his ass. "Is that a bad thing?"

"Feels like you're strangling my dick." He flexes his hips forward ever so slightly, and I arch my back. "I need a second or I'm going to come before you do."

"I've already came twice, Orion, please just... *move.*"

He grits his teeth and pushes himself up higher onto his knees, causing my legs to release him. "Let me make you feel good." He presses his thumb to my clit, rubbing the sensitive bundle in small, controlled circles.

I moan and palm my breasts, rolling my nipples between my fingers. "More, I need more."

Orion presses harder, faster, his thighs flexing beneath me as he restrains himself from rutting into me. "I know what you need, Bluebird." He pulls back until just the tip is inside of me. "I know just what you need."

A strangled moan falls from my lips as he surges forward, plunging himself deep inside of me, his thumb still circling my clit.

I'm panting and begging and making all sorts of noises that I'm sure I'll be embarrassed by later, but here and now, the only thing I care about is the way his thick cock feels pumping inside of me.

He dips his head and sucks my right nipple into his

mouth, sucking and licking and nipping at it in perfect harmony with his thumb on my clit.

It's sensory overload as he alternates between the two.

My skin is sticky and sweat- slicked, and my legs feel like rubber. I'm floating and falling and flying all at the same time, completely and totally lost to his touch.

My walls flutter, letting me know I'm close. "Gonna... come..."

"All over my dick, Frankie. I wanna feel it dripping down my thighs." He pinches my clit and I swear to God, it's game over.

"Orion!" I claw at his back as I shout his name, unable to think past the mind-bending pleasure coursing through me.

He tenses over me, finally breaking his relentless pace. "Fuck, God, Bluebird!" He thrusts into me once... twice more, filling me with his hot release before collapsing on top of me.

"I love you," I murmur as tears—the happy kind—burn my eyes.

He swipes his thumbs under my eyes and presses the softest kiss ever to my neck before sliding out of me and rolling to his side. "I love you, too, Frankie. So, fucking much."

I loll my head to face him, a big dopey grin eating up my face. He darts forward and kisses the tip of my nose. "Told you we'd be good."

"That was more than good. That was..." I trail off, because there are no words to describe what just happened between us.

"Perfect. It was perfect."

WAKING up with Frankie wrapped up in my arms is better than my birthday and Christmas all rolled into one.

Seriously, I'm pretty sure nothing on earth can top this, you know other than falling asleep beside her after spending the night alternating between fucking like animals and talking, sharing our hopes and dreams, and all of that other mushy shit.

But right as the thought enters my mind, a vision of her wearing white shoves it to the side.

This time last year, the thought of settling down would have sent me running for the hills. But with Frankie, it's the exact opposite. I'm pretty sure I'd chain her ass to me if given the chance.

She shifts in her sleep and the curve of her pert ass brushes my rock-hard dick, making me groan.

Who knew imagining matrimonial bliss was such a turn-on?

Or maybe it's knowing she's buck-ass naked that has me hard enough to pound nails? Either way, I know exactly how to wake my sleeping beauty.

As carefully as possible, I shift away from her. Without my body there to support hers, Frankie rolls onto her back, making it all too easy for me to situate myself between her legs.

I press a gentle kiss to her creamy thigh, but she doesn't stir, so I move higher, sliding my tongue along her slit.

"Orion," she mumbles my name, her voice weighted with sleep.

"Wake up, Bluebird." I flatten my tongue and lick at her clit. "Wake up and sing for me."

She moans, opening her legs wider for me as she spears her fingers into my hair. "Talk about a way to wake up."

"I'm definitely a fan," I murmur against her heated flesh, sliding my hand higher up her thigh.

"Less talking, more licking." She tugs on the ends of my hair.

Who am I to argue with my bossy Bluebird?

I lick and suck and nibble, feasting on her pussy until she's writhing beneath me, begging for release.

"Please, Orion." She bucks her hips. "Please."

With a soft touch, I slide my index finger into her tight channel, stroking it in and out in time with my tongue.

"Yes," she pants, "more."

I add another finger, curling them on every downstroke.

The sounds falling from her lips coupled with her intoxicating taste has my hips shifting against the mattress. But this isn't about me getting mine. No, this is all about Frankie getting hers.

When her legs start to tremble, I know she's close. "That's right, baby, come for me." I stroke her g-spot and suck her clit into my mouth, sending her hurtling into oblivion.

"Yes, Orion, fuck!" She clamps her thighs around my

head, pressing her soaking wet pussy flush with my face while she rides out wave after wave of pleasure.

"So pretty when you come," I murmur once she relaxes, her legs falling open and freeing me. I press soft kisses to her lips and thighs, making sure to lap up every drop of her release.

"That was better than coffee." She tosses an arm over her eyes and laughs. "My God."

"Nah, just me, baby."

"Speaking of." She sits up and stares pointedly at my erection. "What about you?"

"Nah. We have forever for that."

"Do we?" she asks, a hint of vulnerability creeping into her voice.

"Absolutely." I nod emphatically. "Unless you plan on leaving me."

She sniffles and my spine straightens. "Frankie? What's wrong?"

"Nothing. It's... nothing."

I gather her into my arms, hauling her against my chest. "It's not nothing. Talk to me."

She crinkles her nose. "Can we maybe shower and put some clothes on first?"

"Of course." I stand from the bed. "Let me start the shower."

We make quick work of getting clean, and then we both dress in comfy clothes before heading downstairs in search of sustenance. A night of marathon fucking definitely works up an appetite.

"Talk to me," I urge her, switching on the coffee maker. "Did I do something wrong?"

She takes her time replying, focusing instead on cracking eggs into a bowl. "It's just... I love you!"

"Is that a bad thing?" I ask carefully.

"I don't know. No." She whisks the eggs together. "What if you leave?"

"Frankie." I step into her space and move the bowl out of her reach. "I. Love. You. You're it for me. For the rest of my life, you're it for me. I'm not going anywhere, baby."

"Everyone leaves." Her voice cracks, and my heart does, too.

"Not me," I vow, meaning it with every fiber of my being.

"You don't always get a choice." She looks up at me with tear-filled eyes. "Tyson didn't."

Oh, fuck. "Frankie." I lower us both to the floor, cradling her in my lap. "Baby."

"What if you get in an accident? What if you—"

It's hard to swallow past the lump in my throat. *This amazing, beautiful woman carries so much pain inside of her.*

"We can't see the future," I tell her, gently raking my fingers through her damp hair. "There's no crystal ball to tell us how things will end. But, Bluebird, I love you. I love Maverick. I love the family and the memories we're making and I'm looking damn forward to what's to come."

"But what if—"

I tip her face up to mine and press my lips to hers in a chaste kiss. "Life is full of *what-ifs*, but not all of them are bad. What if we get married? Crazy as it sounds, the first thing I thought about this morning was you wearing white. What if we have another kid or two? What if we grow old together and spend the summers here with our grandkids?"

"You really want that with me?" she asks, her cheeks damp with tears.

"All of that and more. I love you, Frankie."

"I'm still scared. But..." She sniffles and then smiles. "I love you, too, and I'm going to try. To try to conquer my fear, because all of those things you just said? I want them, too. I want them so much."

"Even the kids?" I ask, shocking myself. *If only Stella and Samson could hear me now.*

"Especially the kids. I always wanted a big family, but after, well you know, I figured it would never happen."

"How big is big?" I lift a brow.

"Three or four. I don't know."

Until Frankie and Maverick, I never—and I mean *never*—wanted kids. But now... "Four sounds good to me. Mav will be the best big brother."

"You think so?" she asks, playing with the hair at my nape.

"Hell yeah. The kid has such a big heart. He'll be a natural."

She smiles. "I guess he is, huh?"

"Thanks to you." I boop my finger against the tip of her nose. "You're such a good mother to him. You amaze me, Frankie, and I can't fucking wait to see what our future holds."

"And me working at ATF really doesn't bother you?"

I tense ever so slightly, but I don't think she notices. "Like I said, I won't ever stand between you and what you need to do to secure your future."

"I'm sensing a but."

"What's your major again?" I ask, feeling like a total ass for not asking sooner.

"General business."

As soon as she says the words, an idea takes shape. "Got any plans on what you want to do after school?"

"Honestly?" she asks, and I nod. "I have no clue. I picked business simply for the security it offered."

"You know I co-own a construction company, right?"

"Yeah." She nods. "I'm not sure a hard hat's my style though."

"Funny girl." I chuck her under her chin. "Ben and I have been talking about bringing in an office manager. The job's yours if you want it."

"Really?" She narrows her eyes.

"Swear to God. We planned on posting a job listing next month."

"Nepotism's not really my thing, but I'll gladly *interview* for the position."

"Stubborn," I murmur, but I see where she's coming from, too. Especially from the bits and pieces she's told me about her parents. "But valid. I'll get with Ben and find a date for you to interview. Sound good? I'll make sure to sit out so that it's as impartial as possible."

"Thank you. That sounds... wonderful."

"You say that now, but when you see the mountain of paperwork waiting for you—"

"*If* I get the job."

"*When* you get the job, because he'd be a fool not to hire you, you might run for the hills. Our office is kind of a trainwreck."

"You're in luck." She smiles up at me. "Trainwrecks are my specialty."

I believe it, too, because she damn sure put my life on the right track.

"AS AMAZING AS THIS WEEKEND WAS," Frankie says, stretching her seat belt across her chest and clicking the buckle into place, "I'm excited to see Maverick. I've never been away from him this long." The corners of her eyes crinkle as she laughs and kicks her feet up onto the dash. "I've never been away from him ever."

I throw the truck into gear and steer us toward the main road. "He missed you, too."

She scoffs. "Please, your mom and dad probably kept him so busy and full of sugar that I didn't even cross his mind."

"I'm sure you're right," I agree, tossing a quick smirk her way before returning my focus to the road. "You know, other than multiple texts and calls from him each day."

"If you say so." She rolls her head across the back of the seat to look out the window.

"Bluebird, you're his best friend. His whole world, really."

She crosses her arms over her chest. "He basically thinks you hung the moon."

I chuckle at her grumpiness, while also making a note to include Mav in our next getaway. My girl definitely has separation anxiety, though I can't really blame her. I miss the kid, too.

"That may be so, but you *are* his moon."

Reaching across the console, Frankie rests her hand on my thigh, curling her fingers into the threadbare denim of my jeans. "You always know the right thing to say."

"Trust me, I don't. I'm sure I'll piss you off plenty, but as long as we always make up, I'm good."

Because that's what a relationship is, right? Give and take. I know there were definitely times my mom and dad fought, but they always took the time to talk about what was bothering them. They never took cheap shots—or if they did, us kids never saw it. They instilled in me how important communication is, in all aspects of life.

I guess I never appreciated it until Frankie. But now, I'm thankful. The example my parents set and the lessons they taught me doesn't mean mine and Frankie's relationship won't have waves, it just means I'll be strong enough to keep our heads above the water while we swim to the shore.

The rest of the drive passes in relative quiet, but it's a comfortable kind of quiet, the kind that exists between two people completely at peace with one another.

By the time we make it to my parents' house, the sun is starting to set and my stomach's rumbling.

"Hungry?" Frankie asks as I park behind my sister's car.

"Starved." I cut the engine and pat my belly. "I wonder what Mom made."

"Whatever it is, you know it'll be good."

"Damn straight." I get down from the truck, walking

around to help Frankie down. "All I know is I lucked out with two women who can cook."

She swats at my chest and hops down from the cab herself. "If you think I'm making every meal we eat, you are sorely mistaken."

I sling an arm around her waist and tug her into my side. "As long as I have you, Bluebird, we could live off of takeout for all I care."

Frankie smiles up at me, with so much love shining in her eyes, I stumble and miss a step. "I love you, Orion."

"Love you, too." I swing open the door and press a hand to her lower back, guiding her over the threshold. "But let's go see our boy."

"Orion," Mom calls, undoubtedly from the kitchen, "is that y'all?"

But before I can answer, Maverick comes barreling down the hall, his arms wide open. "Mama! O! You're here!"

He slams into Frankie with the strength of a category five hurricane hitting the shore. She bends just in time to absorb his impact, allowing him to wrap his arms around her neck and his legs around her waist.

"I missed you so much, Mav."

"I missed you, too, Mama." He nuzzles his face into her neck. "But I had a lot of fun. We made a pie this morning and we're gonna eat it after dinner. And I drew a bunch of pictures for you. And Pop-Pop let me help him do yard work!"

He pauses to inhale, and his eyes catch mine. "O!" he shouts on his exhale. "O! You're here, too! Did you have fun? Did you miss me? What did you guys do?"

Frankie and I exchange knowing looks, both of us trying —and failing—to hide our smiles, because clearly, we can't tell Maverick we spent the entire weekend fucking like bunnies.

"We went to Orion's family's lake house."

"But what did you do?" He unwraps himself from around Frankie and reaches for me. I take him into my arms with zero hesitation.

"We... enjoyed nature."

"And watched the water," Frankie adds.

"Bet they even saw some birds and bees," Stella adds from the doorway to the kitchen, her tone full of mirth.

I cut my eyes toward her over Maverick's head and mouth the words *shut the fuck up,* which only makes her smile that much bigger.

"The house was quiet without y'all," she says, lowering her eyes to the floor.

"Surprised you didn't stay with Samson," I murmur, still holding Maverick close.

"I did. Well, he stayed with me. Mostly to, um, help-me-pack-my-stuff." Her words run together, but I still manage to hear them loud and clear.

"You're moving out?" I ask, and Frankie gasps.

"It's just, y'all are together now and I'm sure you want your own space, and—"

"You don't have to explain anything," Frankie cuts her off. "I just hate feeling like us being together is running you off."

"I don't feel like you're running me off." Stella joins us fully in the foyer, taking Frankie's hands in hers. "I promise. And I'm so, *so* happy y'all are together. I couldn't even begin to think of someone more perfect for my big brother. But y'all need privacy and time to really grow and connect as a family, especially with Maverick in the mix."

"Are you sure?" Frankie asks, whereas I'm internally fist pumping.

Don't get me wrong, I love my little sister, but the thought of having Frankie and Mav all to myself, like a real family, it just feels... *right.*

"A hundred percent. Plus, Samson has been after me to move in for a long time now. The timing is just right."

"I'm happy for you, Smalls," I say right as my mom steps into the foyer.

"Well, are y'all going to come eat or what?"

Maverick wriggles out of my hold and runs to my mom. "Eat! Let's eat. It smells so yummy."

He's not wrong either—Mom's roast is legendary.

"MAV, YOUR PIE WAS AMAZING," Frankie coos, licking the tines of the fork clean.

He beams proudly. "Gigi showed me how to make it."

"Well, maybe one day soon you can show me?"

"Yeah, 'cause I'm pretty much an expert now."

"Hey, Mama," he says, suddenly serious, "I have a question."

She looks at me nervously before giving him her undivided attention. "What's up, bud?"

"If Stella's moving out, does that mean I get my own room?"

Both Frankie and my mom's eyes glass over, while my dad smirks.

"Oh, um, sure." Frankie nods. "If-if that's what you want."

"Yeah! And I want red walls and a superhero bedding and a super soft rug and a desk and a lamp and—"

"Slow down, bud," Frankie says, but she's smiling now. "One step at a time."

"Okay." He takes a sip of his milk. "I have another question."

"What?"

"Is O gonna move into your room?"

This time, my dad actually laughs out loud. I'm talking big, deep, knee-slapping belly laughs.

"Why... why would you ask that?" Frankie's cheeks are atomic red.

"Well, Pop-Pop and Gigi share a room 'cause they're in love. And O said he loved you—"

"Oh my God!" Mom shouts, clutching her chest. "You love her? You really love her?" She turns to my dad. "Michael, he loves her. This calls for champagne!"

"Sit down, dear," Dad says, stopping Mom from running to the kitchen. "You're embarrassing Frankie."

Mom's eyes flit to Frankie and she bows her head before plopping back down into her seat.

"Well, are you?" Maverick asks, once everyone is calm again.

Frankie sends me a pleading look, clearly lost on how to handle this. Unfortunately, this isn't something either of us thought about, and I'm not quite sure what to say either.

So, I do what my parents did to me when I was a kid—turn it around. "How would you feel about that, bud?"

He taps his index finger against his chin, his eyes darting back and forth between his mom and me. "Could I still sleep with you sometimes? You know, like if I get scared or just miss you?"

"Of course," Frankie says.

"Okay, then. It'll make movie night easier, too!"

I can practically see Frankie's tension melt away when

her son smiles. He is the key to her happiness, and I'm damn sure going to do my best to be what he needs—what *they* need.

"Son," Dad says, pulling me from my thoughts. "You wanna help me clear the table?"

"Sure..." I murmur, wondering what he's up to.

Samson must be suspicious, too, because he quickly volunteers to help as well.

Between the three of us, we manage to get most of the dishes into the kitchen. Dad scrapes the food, and then passes them to me to rinse, and then I pass them to Samson who loads them into the dishwasher.

We go on like this for a minute or two, while my dad gathers together the words for whatever he has to say.

"So." His deep voice rings through the kitchen. "You're in love with Frankie."

I turn off the sink faucet, dry my hands, and face him. "I am."

"And you're ready to be a dad? Because it's not just her—"

"Dad, Frankie and Maverick are everything I never knew I wanted. I can't imagine my life, present or future, without them. They're it for me. I want to put a ring on her finger, and if she and Maverick are willing, I'd love to adopt him. I know it seems fast, and maybe a little crazy, but those two... they're my future."

For a long minute, nobody speaks.

But then, the biggest smile I've ever seen splits my dad's cheeks. "And to think, you said she was just *Stella's friend.* I'm proud of you, son." He chuckles and pats me on the back.

"Thanks, Dad."

"Why don't you boys finish up in here? I promised

Maverick we could put together the Legos we bought before y'all went home."

"Shit got serious fast, huh?" Samson asks, once it's just the two of us.

"Shit's been serious since the day I met her."

He arches a brow at me in question.

"She's Birdie, man." Samson freezes, staring at me in wide-eyed shock. "I told you. I knew from the second I saw her that she was it for me, and I was right. I'm going to marry her, man."

"Damn, brother." He shakes his head. "I'm really fucking happy for you. But you know you technically have to ask her first, right?"

"She'll say yes." I nudge his shoulder with mine.

"If you say so." The shit-eating grin on his face tells me he's joking.

"I know so."

"MAV, get your backpack, we don't want to be late today!" I holler, pouring myself a travel mug of coffee.

It's been three weeks since Stella moved in with Samson, Maverick into his own bedroom, and Orion into mine.

I was apprehensive at first—for nearly five years, the only place Mav has ever slept is beside me. But he absolutely loves having his own space. It certainly doesn't hurt that Orion went above and beyond, building him bookshelves, a desk, and a play table.

He spoils him... and I love it.

"I'm coming, Mama!" He flies into the kitchen. "Where's O?"

"I'm here, I'm here," he says, walking out of his old bedroom, which is now my office.

I put up a good fight, saying it made sense for him to use it, but he insisted, what with me having accepted the office manager position with his company and all.

Turns out, they really did need the help, and Ben, despite being a little clueless, is a good guy.

"You sure you don't want to take the lead on this?" Orion asks me, straightening his safety vest.

"O!" Maverick whines, and I can't help but smile.

"He's right. No one wants to hear about desk work, they want to know about tools and demo."

"As long as you're okay with it," he murmurs, sneaking a quick kiss.

"Can we go now?" Maverick tugs on my hand. "Please, Mama? Miss Jenna said to get there early!"

God love him, he's been so excited for career day ever since he brought the flier home. At first, I was worried—I hadn't left ATF yet, and God knows, I couldn't talk to a room of four year olds about the wonders of exotic dancing.

Luckily, Maverick had his sights set on Orion from the start.

We all pile into the truck, and without Maverick having to ask, Orion cues up the *Paw Patrol* soundtrack.

"I was thinking we could get lunch after?" he says, once we're on the highway. "Maybe check Mav out so we can all go?"

"Oh, um. Sure, that's fine."

He looks at me from the side of his eyes and smiles. "Good."

I narrow mine, but he doesn't give anything away.

The drive to the school is fast, but the parking lot is already full, leaving us to park at the back of the lot. Apparently, they weren't kidding about getting here early.

"C'mon!" Maverick takes off as soon as Orion helps him down from the truck, leaving us to run after him.

We follow him into the school and down the hall to his classroom.

"Good morning, Maverick," Miss Jenna greets him. "Go take your seat on the rug, okay?"

"Yes, ma'am." He shuffles past her, winding through the children already clustered on the rug, until he finds his assigned spot.

"Frankie, it's so good to see you again," she says warmly before turning to Orion. "You must be this O I've heard so much about."

His cheeks blush, and I love it. "Orion Cartwright." He offers her his hand. "It's nice to meet you."

"We're so glad y'all could join us. Feel free to grab a chair in the back of the room and we'll get started."

How are we the last ones here? School doesn't officially start for another ten minutes!

Orion takes my hand in his, stroking my knuckles with his thumb as we listen to parent after parent talk about their profession.

So far, we've had a baker, a doctor, and an engineer.

"Next up we have Maverick and his..." Jenna pauses and clears her throat. "Orion."

If anyone else catches her blunder, they don't react. *Thank God.*

"This is Orion," Maverick says once they get to the front of the classroom. "I call him O. He owns a 'struction business, and one day, he's gonna be my dad!"

I nearly fall out of my seat at my son's bold declaration, but Orion... he looks cool as a cucumber.

Seriously, how is he so calm? My heart feels like a runaway train bound for derailment. I mean, my son just announced to his entire class that he wants Orion to be his dad.

"Deep breaths," the mom next to me murmurs, rubbing my back in soothing circles. "That's right, in and out."

Guess someone did notice.

"Thanks," I whisper back, my cheeks still burning

hotter than the sun. But hey, I don't feel like I'm going to pass out anymore, so that's a win.

"...and that's what it's like to own a construction company."

I snap my focus back to Orion, just in time to hear the end of his speech. I feel bad missing it, but my brain feels like it's mashed potatoes and I'm still not sure how to process Maverick's declaration.

It's not that I don't want that for us; I mean, it's clearly the path we're on, but I also don't want him to get his hopes up.

Clearly Orion loves my son like he's his own, but I have no idea if he wants to adopt him, much less how he feels about Mav calling him dad.

I guess we have a lot to talk about at lunch...

"WAIT, so, you're really letting me come home?" Maverick asks, bouncing on his toes as he waits for Orion to unlock the truck. "Like, I for real don't have to finish school today?"

"Not today, bud." Orion ruffles his hair. I swear, the sight of the two of them together will never not make my heart squeeze in my chest.

"But why?" He drags the word out. "What are we gonna do?" Bless his heart, I can practically see his brain exploding. But, to be fair, he's never left school early before.

Orion opens the back door, bracing Maverick from behind as he climbs up into his seat. "I thought we could get lunch—"

"Can we get pizza?" Mav whips around to face Orion, his puppy dog eyes in full effect. "Please!"

"I'm fine with whatever y'all want," I say, meaning it. Mostly because I'm still obsessing over how to talk to Orion about everything Maverick said.

He's told me over and over that he's all in, and I believe him—*I do*. But stepping into an *official* dad role is a big deal. Even if he's already rocking it, *unofficially*.

Orion buckles Mav's chest clip and then steps down, his brow furrowed. "I had reservations—" he starts, but then shakes his head and says, "—you know what, pizza sounds perfect."

"Yes!" Maverick throws both hands over his head in a celebration. "This is the best day ever!"

The drive to Mr. T's is quick, and somehow, we manage to beat the lunch crowd. I defer to Orion when it comes to toppings; I'm too busy working up the courage to say what I need to say.

"Can we get ice cream after?" Maverick asks as we crowd around one of the small tables filling the space. "I want mine with sprinkles. Please, Mama?"

"Sure," I reply, because you can't get Mr. T's pizza and not get ice cream. "But I have something I want to talk to y'all about."

"Is everything okay?" Orion clears his throat.

"Yeah, it's just..." I suck in a deep breath. "Mav, what did you mean when you told your class that Orion was going to be your dad?"

God love him, my son looks at me like I'm a total idiot, before sighing and saying, "'Cause he will, Mama." He turns to Orion. "You wanna be my dad, right?"

"Actually." Orion licks his lips. "I have something I want to talk to y'all about."

A million butterflies take flight in my belly, each one

carrying a brand new, paralyzing *what-if* on its wings. "Is..." I lick my lips. "Is everything okay?"

"I hope so." He smiles, but it's different than his usual cocky grin; more subdued. "Maverick, you know how much I love you, right?"

He nods. "Yeah, a whole, super lot."

"Nailed it, bud. But you remember how I said your dad loved you, too, right?"

"You told me he was always in my heart," Maverick says proudly, patting his chest.

Speaking of hearts, mine is on some kind of fucked up fair ride right now, and can't tell up from down. It's spinning-spinning-spinning while I hold the edge of my chair with a white-knuckle grip.

I know Orion's working up to something; I just can't tell what, and it has me on edge.

No, more than on edge. It has me dangling halfway down the cliff, with only a flimsy cartoon-like sapling holding me in place.

"That's right. He loved you Mav, and I do too. So much that I would actually love to be your dad. But there's something else I have to do first."

"What's that?" Maverick asks, voicing what we're both thinking.

"Well." Orion stands from the table and drops to one knee in one fluid movement. "I have to ask your mama if she'll be my wife."

"What?" I whisper, my voice barely audible over the whooshing in my ears.

Is he asking me what I think he is? Surely not.

But then he pulls a small, velvet box from his jacket pocket, and everything and everyone around us fades away.

I stare back at him with wide eyes as my entire world tilts on its axis.

"Frankie, baby. I love you. With every ounce of my being, I love you. Both of you. Looking back, before y'all, I was merely going through the motions. But now, thanks to you, I'm truly living. You make me strive to be a better man. You and Mav, y'all are the future I want. Today, now, and forever. So, tell me, Bluebird, will you do me the immense honor of being my wife?"

He flips open the box revealing the prettiest damn ring I've ever seen. A tear-drop shaped Montana sapphire nestled into salt and pepper diamonds on a soft gold band— it's my every Pinterest dream come to life.

"Orion, it's beautiful."

"Blue," he murmurs, plucking the ring from the box, "for my Bluebird."

"I love it." I can feel fat, hot tears rolling down my face, but I can't find it in me to care. "I love it so much."

"Enough to say yes?" He smiles up at me with the most hopeful, boyish smile I've ever seen.

I glance over to Maverick who gives me two thumbs up and the most exaggerated nod ever. *It looks like he's on board.*

"Yes." I reach forward and cup his cheeks. "A million times yes. Forever, yes."

He grabs my left hand and pulls it away from his face, kissing each finger until he gets to my ring finger. "I can't wait for you to have my last name." He slides the ring onto my finger and then stands.

I launch myself at him, peppering his face with kisses. "I love you so much."

It's not until he pulls away that I realize people are clapping—and that our server is standing off to the side with our pizza, watching on with tears in her eyes.

"Oh, God! I'm so sorr—"

"Don't." She sets the pans down on the center of the table. "Don't apologize. That was the best thing I've seen all week. In fact, celebratory ice cream on the house when y'all finish. Congrats."

"Pizza, ice cream, and a dad?" Maverick exclaims, his eyes as big as the pizza tray. "This really is the best day ever!"

I smile, feeling completely at peace for the first time in a long time, because he's not wrong. Today is the best day ever, and more than that, it's the start of a lifetime of best days.

It's the start of our forever.

I READ the text for the fifth time before slipping my phone back into my pocket, willing this damn meeting to end.

What was meant to be a quick working lunch to discuss a small tweak to a build has turned into an engineering nightmare, and all I want is to get home and to see what my Bluebird has planned for me.

Note to self: no more Friday meetings; especially when Mav is staying with my parents. Kid-free nights are not to be wasted.

My phone buzzes again, and I discreetly slide it into my lap, unlocking the screen. Another text from Frankie; an image this time.

Thanks to the shitty cell reception, it takes a few minutes to load, but once it does... I'm gone. *Game-fucking-over.*

I shove the device deeper into my lap, making sure the

table completely obscures it from any prying eyes. Because Frankie like this, with red lips and her body wrapped in lace, is only for me.

"Gentleman." My chair screeches as I push back from the table and stand, not caring one bit if I'm being rude. "I'm afraid I have to head out." I smooth a hand down my chest, clearing my throat. "Urgent business. We'll have to pick this back up sometime next week."

Without waiting for a reply, I turn on my heel and stride toward the door.

I probably look like a pompous jackass, but Ben will smooth things over. He's the one who insisted on us taking this job anyway.

That photo runs on a constant loop in my mind as I make the drive to *our* home—the one we built together on the far side of my parent's property—in record time. But when I come racing through the front door, I can't help but deflate a little; my wife is nowhere to be seen.

"I'm home!" I holler, certain she'll reply, but I'm met with nothing but silence. So, I text her.

ME

I'm home.

Her reply is instant.

BLUEBIRD

Come find me...

I toss my wallet and keys onto the table in the foyer, before stalking back toward the bedroom. She's in the mood for games, and I'm definitely in the mood to play.

"Bluebird," I call for her again as I step into the darkened room, anticipation causing my pulse to drum in my throat.

She still doesn't answer, but a familiar tune drifts from the speakers... the one she danced to the first night I saw her all those years ago.

"What's going on?" I ask, wondering where my girl is hiding and what exactly she's up to.

"Have a seat," she murmurs from somewhere out of sight.

I sink into the mattress dead center at the foot of the bed, my eyes scanning the room for any hint of where she's hiding.

Adrenaline thrums through me in perfect harmony with the music as I lean forward, branding my forearms on my thighs.

"Have you missed me?" I snap my gaze toward the sound of her raspy voice, just in time to see her step into view, the light from the bathroom perfectly illuminating her silhouette.

She looks so damn fine my tongue nearly lolls out of my mouth as she slinks closer.

The music should've been a clue; Birdie is here and she wants to play.

Dressed in a red lace bralette with a plunging neckline and a barely-there black school-girl skirt, she's my every filthy fantasy come to life.

"You know I have." As soon as she's close enough to touch, I reach out, skimming my knuckles beneath the hem of her skirt, not missing her sharp intake of breath. "What about you? Have you missed me?"

She drags her teeth over her glossy red lip, coming to stand between my spread legs. "Always."

Leaning back onto the bed, I prop myself up with my arms. "Show me how much."

Frankie rocks her hips from side-to-side, her eyes locked

on mine as she trails the backs of her hands up her sides and over her belly, until she's cupping her breasts.

The erotic sight has me catching my breath.

She steps in closer, so that her knees are flush with the foot of the bed, her small fingers tugging and pinching her nipples through the lace as she writhes in time with the song.

So fucking hot.

"That's right, Bluebird. Play with those pretty tits. Pretend it's my hands." My throat goes dry. My dick impossibly hard.

"Or..." She moves to straddle my right thigh and grabs my hands, placing them on her breasts. "You can play instead."

"Fuck yeah." I tug the lace cups down and rub my thumbs over the rosy pebbled peaks before leaning forward and drawing her right nipple into my mouth, sucking hard.

"Orion!" The breathy way she says my name goes straight to my cock.

I move to her other tit, and she arches her back, pushing them farther into my face. I lick and nip and suck, damn near suffocating in her cleavage.

They almost seem... bigger, but I shake off the thought. Frankie's tits are perfect at any size.

"Touch me here, too," she says, redirecting my focus to her bare pussy.

"No panties?" I arch a brow, dragging the knuckle of my index finger up and down through her slick folds.

"Why bother when you're just going to take them off of me?"

Sliding two fingers inside of her, I give her a wicked grin and press my thumb to her clit. "Don't you know unwrapping your present is half the fun?"

She licks her lips, swiveling her hips in a figure-eight. "Then, fi-finish unwrapping m-me," she stammers, as I curl my fingers in a come-hither motion inside of her.

"I think I'd rather unravel you." Leaning forward, I shove her skirt up to her waist, dipping low enough to brush a kiss against her swollen pussy lips.

She's so turned on, her thighs glisten with her arousal.

"So fucking good," I groan as her taste fills my mouth, tart and sugary-sweet—my favorite fucking flavor.

A sultry moan topples from her lips, making my dick twitch in anticipation. I don't know how, but every time with Frankie is as good as the first time. There's no complacency between us, no going through the motions. Frankie and I, we're a fucking Molotov cocktail of passion. Explosive. Every. Single. Time.

And I love it... *I love her*.

She threads her fingers through my hair, tugging on the strands as she rides my face. "Orion—*oh!*" Her words fracture into breathy little moans as I continue my assault on her pussy.

My God, the sounds she makes—they're so illicit, so erotic, so spine-tingling sexy, and they're all for me. She's all for me. Forever mine.

The thought is so intoxicating, it's almost unbearable. To know that this goddess of a woman is mine and I'm every bit as much hers, it makes me crazy, but in the best possible way.

"Need you to come," I grunt between teasing licks, my cock painfully hard in my pants. "Need to be inside of you." I fasten my lips around her slick needy clit, devouring her with slow, pulsating sucks.

"I'm gonna—" Her orgasm barrels into her before she

can even speak the words and she melts in my mouth, and like the addict I am, I savor every single drop.

"Orion." The way she whispers my name after she comes drives me wild, and she knows it.

"Ditch the clothes, Bluebird and then get on the bed."

She immediately complies, stripping down before settling herself against the mountain of pillows she insists we need.

But as I watch her laying there like a queen, with her legs spread, fingers softly trailing over her body, I find I'm not inclined to argue.

"Why am I the only one naked?" she asks, pushing out her lower lip in a bratty little pout.

"You want me naked?"

She rolls her eyes. "You know I do. I want you naked and inside of me. I want to feel you, Orion. All of you."

I quickly strip and then join her on the bed. "You look so fucking beautiful." I drop a kiss to her temple. "So perfect." Another to the corner of her mouth. "Like a dream come true." I kiss along her jaw, down her neck, all the way to her breast.

"You're teasing me," she whines, and I grin.

"I'm loving you," I counter, my lips brushing the soft skin of her belly. "I love you and this life we've made together. So damn much."

"I love you too, Orion." She runs her fingers through my hair, making my whole-body tingle with desire.

"Let's have a baby." *Shit, that's not how I wanted to say it.* I spent weeks planning exactly how I'd bring it up—a nice dinner, some pampering, the whole nine yards, but here I am blurting it out like a jackass.

Still, the very thought of her belly swollen with my baby is... *fuck!* It's hands down the sexiest thing I've ever imagined. Which is saying something, because when it comes to Frankie Cartwright, my imagination tends to run wild.

She cradles her belly as she nibbles her lower lip. "What if I told you that we already are?"

Silence descends on us as my brain struggles to make sense of her words.

"What?" I place my hands over top of hers. "Really?"

Frankie nods, and my heart drums in my chest, a strong, pounding beat.

"You're telling me that my baby is in your belly, right now?" Warmth radiates throughout my entire body. "You're really pregnant?"

"Yeah, I'm really pregnant." She looks up at me from beneath tear-soaked lashes. "Are you happy?"

"Frankie, baby." I move back up her body until we're eye to eye. "I'm over the moon."

Her lips lift into a dazzling smile. "We should celebrate," she says suggestively, wagging her brows.

"Oh?" I move between her parted thighs, hitching her right leg over my hip. "How would you suggest we do that?"

Well..." She reaches down between us, wrapping her hand around my cock and guiding me to her slick entrance. "I'd say fucking me would be a good start."

"Not gonna fuck you right now." I inch forward, pushing into her slowly. "I'm going to love you, Frankie."

And I mean it beyond just the physical. In every way possible, for the rest of our lives, I'm going to love this woman. My best friend, my wife, my bluebird, my everything, my forever.

THE END.

LK'S OTHER TITLES

All of LK's titles can be read as standalones & are available with Kindle Unlimited. An asterisk next to the title denotes it is also available in audio.

*Sweet Little Nothing** (an enemies-to-lovers/bully romance)

*Dirty Little Secret** (an older brother's best friend/second chance romance)

*Best Laid Plans** (an older brother's best friend/secret baby romance)

*Best of Intentions** (a friends-to-lovers/little sister's best friend romance)

*Best of Me** (a second chance at love/forbidden twin romance)

Rebel Heart (an enemies-to-lovers jock/tutor rom-com)

Rebel Soul (an arranged baby/friends-to-lovers rom-com)

Rebel Desire (an unrequited soulmates/surprise single dad rom-com)

*Coming Up Roses** (a small-town/single mom romance)

*An Uphill Battle** (a frenemies-to-lovers romance)

Weather the Storm (a second chance at love romantic suspense)

Come What May (an age gap/single dad romance)

ACKNOWLEDGMENTS

ACKNOWLEDGMENTS

With each new book, the number of people deserving of my gratitude grows. Honestly, I didn't find *my* people until I found the book world, and now, my people seem to keep multiplying.

Firstly, I need to thank my PA, Renee. If not for her dealing with my many meltdowns and fits over this book, I probably wouldn't have finished it.

To my beta readers – Amy, Alyssa, and Brianna, you ladies are the best!

To my promo teams – Give Me Books and Peachy Keen Author Services, y'all are the real MVPS behind this release. Kylie & co, thank you for putting with my endless last minute *everything*. Please don't EVER leave me! Savannah and the entire PKAS crew, working with y'all has been a dream; thank you so much for all of your hard work!

Heather, bffoml, thank you for being you and for loving me.

Harloe, you're always there for me to bounce ideas and to help me out of sticky spots. Thank you, friend. Oh, and the baby pictures... keep 'em coming!

Amie, you are my person. Now, always, and forever. You get me on a level most don't. Same soul, different body. Love you!

Jen, we've been friends for so long, and every year, our

friendship just seems to grow. Keep kicking ass lady and know that I love you!

Maria, #PettyForLife my sweet friend. Petty for life.

Anna, my whoreface kitten. You're the tits and I love you!

My entire editing team—that's right, team, because I need all of the eyes—thank y'all so, so much!

Carmen, thank you so much for your stunning interior formatting! You're a dream to work with.

To my amazing husband, thank you for picking up my slack when I was in the thick of writing. Your love and endless support means the world to me.

To my NanNan, from day one, you've been my best supporter and biggest fan. I love you and I miss you more than words can say. Rest easy and fly high.

And last but certainly not least, THANK YOU! Without you, none of this would be possible. Your hunger for good reads with happily ever after is what enables us authors to write our stories, and for that, I am eternally grateful!

ABOUT THE AUTHOR

Known by Kate to most, LK Farlow is an Amazon Top 40 bestselling author of more than a dozen romances, ranging from sweet, to sexy, to rip your heart out, and everything in-between.

She has a heart built for happily-ever-afters, which is lucky since she found hers at the young age of nineteen. Now, at thirty-something, she is the wife to one hunky man and the mother to four semi-feral humans, three lizards, a chameleon, a tortoise, and a handful of stray cats.

Kate often jokes that her life is all out chaos on most days, but she wouldn't trade it for the world.

www.authorlkfarlow.com